Anthony Horowitz is one of the most popular and prolific children's writers working today. His hugely successful Alex Rider series, which includes *Stormbreaker*, *Point Blanc*, *Skeleton Key*, *Eagle Strike*, *Scorpia* and *Ark Angel*, has won numerous awards and sold over 8 million copies worldwide. In 2003 he was delighted to win the Red House Children's Book Award for *Skeleton Key* because it was voted for entirely by children. Anthony's other books include *Raven's Gate*, the first title in his new horror series, The Power of Five; the Diamond Brothers books; *Groosham Grange* and its sequel, *Return to Groosham Grange*; *The Devil and his Boy*; *The Switch*; and *Granny*. Anthony also writes extensively for TV, with credits including *Midsomer Murders*, *Poirot* and the drama series *Foyle's War*, which won the Lew Grade Audience Award in 2003. He is married to television producer Jill Green and lives in north London with his two sons, Nicholas and Cassian, and their dog, Lucky.

You can find out more about Anthony Horowitz and his books by visiting his website, at

www.anthonyhorowitz.com

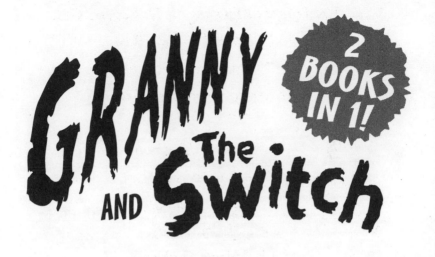

GRANNY
AND The SWITCH

2 BOOKS IN 1!

ANTHONY HOROWITZ

WALKER BOOKS
AND SUBSIDIARIES
LONDON · BOSTON · SYDNEY · AUCKLAND

First published individually as *Granny* (1994) and *The Switch* (1996) by Walker Books Ltd, 87 Vauxhall Walk, London SE11 5HJ

This edition published 2005

2 4 6 8 10 9 7 5 3 1

© 1994, 1996 Anthony Horowitz

This book has been typeset in Sabon

Printed and bound in Great Britain by
Cox & Wyman Ltd, Reading, Berkshire

British Library Cataloguing in Publication Data:
a catalogue record for this book is
available from the British Library

ISBN 1-4063-0294-5

www.walkerbooks.co.uk

ANTHONY HOROWITZ

WALKER BOOKS
AND SUBSIDIARIES
LONDON · BOSTON · SYDNEY · AUCKLAND

For my sister, Caroline

CONTENTS

PROLOGUE:
HEATHROW AIRPORT

The storm broke early in the evening and by seven o'clock it looked as if Heathrow might have to shut down. Runway One had disappeared in the rain. Runway Two was a canal. Half the planes had been delayed and the other half were circling hopelessly above the clouds, waiting their turn to land. The wind had blown an Air France DC10 all the way to Luton while, in a Jumbo Jet from Tokyo, seventy-nine Japanese passengers had all been sick at the same time. It was a night no one would forget.

The green Mercedes reached the airport at exactly half past seven, skidding round a corner and spraying water over two traffic wardens, a porter and a visitor from Norway. Swerving across the road, it missed a taxi by inches and rocketed into the car park of Terminal Three. The electric side window slid down and a hand with a signet ring and the initials GW entwined in gold reached out to pluck a parking ticket from the machine. Then the car jumped forward again, shot up three ramps with the tyres screaming and crashed into a wall. Ten thousand pounds' worth of metal and paintwork crumpled in on itself. The engine died. Steam hissed from beneath the bent and broken bonnet.

The doors of the car opened and three people got out. The driver was a short, bald man. Next to him was a woman in a fur coat. The back seat had been occupied by a twelve-year-old boy.

"You told me to park on the fourth floor!" the man screamed. "The fourth floor!"

"Yes, Gordon…" the woman muttered.

"But this car park's only got three floors!" the man moaned. He pointed at the wreck of his car. "And now look what's happened!"

"Oh, Gordon…" The woman's lips quivered. For a moment she looked terrified. Then she blinked. "Does it really matter?" she asked.

The man stared at her. "You're right!" he exclaimed. He laughed out loud. "It doesn't matter at all! We're leaving the car here! We'll never see it again…!"

The man and the woman rushed into each other's arms, kissed each other and then grabbed their luggage, which the boy had meanwhile taken out of the boot. They had only two suitcases between them and these looked as if they had been packed in a hurry. Part of a pink silk tie, a striped pyjama leg and a frilly shower cap were poking out of one side.

"Come on!" the man exclaimed. "Let's go..."

But just then there was a flash of lightning and an explosion of thunder and the three of them froze, alone in the middle of the dimly lit car park. A plane roared past overhead.

"Oh, Gordon..." the woman whimpered.

"It's all right," Gordon snapped. "She's not here. Keep your hair on. We're going to be all right. I'd keep my hair on except I packed it..."

"Come on. We've got to get the tickets," the boy said. And without waiting for his parents he began to walk towards the lifts.

Ten minutes later, the family was queuing up at the British Airways ticket desk. After the darkness of the storm, the building was unnaturally bright, like a television set with the colour turned up too much. There were people everywhere, milling around with their suitcases and carrier bags. A policeman with a machine gun patrolled the area. He was the only person smiling.

"Good evening, sir." The man at the ticket desk was in his early twenties with close-cropped hair and tired eyes. He had his name – OWEN – on a badge on his chest but in his tiredness he had pinned it on upside down. "Can I help you?"

"You certainly can, Nemo," the man said, squinting at the badge. "I want three flights…"

"Three flights, sir?" Owen coughed. He had never seen such nervous-looking passengers. They all looked as if they had just come off the worst fairground ride in the world. "Where to?" he asked.

"America," the man replied.

"Africa," the woman said at the same moment.

"Australia," the boy exclaimed.

"Anywhere!" the man said. "Just so long as it leaves soon."

"And it's got to be far away!" the woman added.

"Well, sir…" Owen swallowed. "It would help if you actually knew where you wanted to go…"

The man leaned forward, his eyes wild and staring. (They weren't staring in quite the same direction, which made him look even more wild.) His clothes were expensive – tailor-made – but the ticket salesman couldn't help noticing that he had dressed in a hurry. His tie was crooked and, more surprisingly, on the wrong side of his neck.

"I just want to go away," the man hissed, "before *she* gets here."

The woman burst into tears and tried to hide her face in her mink coat. The boy began to tremble. The ticket-seller's eyes flickered to the computer screen in front of him. The computer screen flickered back. "How about the nine o'clock flight to Perth?" he suggested.

"Scotland!" The man screamed the word so loudly that several passengers turned to look at him and the policeman dropped his machine gun.

"Australia," the ticket-seller said.

"Perthect!" the man exclaimed. He snapped a gold Visa card onto the counter. "We'll have two tickets first class and one in tourist for the boy. Ow!" The man cried out as his wife's elbow caught him on the side of his head. "All right," he said, rubbing a red mark above his eye. "We'll all go first class together."

"Certainly, sir." The ticket-seller picked up the credit card. "Mr Gordon Warden?"

"Yes. That's me."

"And the child's name?"

"Jordan Warden."

"Jordan Warden." The ticket-seller tapped the name into the computer. "And your wife...?"

"Maud N. Warden," the woman said.

"Gordon Warden. Jordan Warden. Maud N. Warden. Right..." He tapped some more buttons and waited as the machine spat out three tickets. "Check in at Desk 11. And it'll be

Gate 6 for boardin' Mr Warden."

Five hours later, British Airways Flight 777 took off for Perth in Western Australia. As the plane reached the end of the runway and lurched upwards into the swirling night and rain, Gordon Warden and his wife sank back into their first class seats. Mr Warden began to giggle. "We've done it," he said in a quivering voice. "We've beaten her..."

"How do you know she's not on the plane?" his wife asked.

Mr Warden sat bolt upright. "Stewardess!" he called. "Bring me a parachute!"

Just across the aisle, Jordan strained in the soft half-light to get a sight of the other passengers. Had they really done it? Or were they going to see that terrible, wrinkled face turning slowly to leer at them in the crowded cabin?

The plane reached thirty thousand feet and turned south on the first leg of its journey across the world.

The events that had begun nine months before were finally over.

GRANNY'S FOOTSTEPS

Nine months before, the Wardens had been a wealthy and – to all appearances – happy family living in a large house in North London. The house was called Thattlebee Hall.

It was a huge place with eleven bedrooms, five living-rooms, three staircases and about a mile of thickly-carpeted corridors. You could have played tennis in one of the bathrooms – which was something Mr and Mrs Warden occasionally did, quite naked, using the soap as a ball. It was also very easy to get lost. One man – who had come to read the gas meter – actually stayed there for three days before anyone noticed him, and that was only because he had parked his gas van in the hall.

The family occupied the main body of the house. There was a nanny, Mrs Jinks, with rooms on the top floor. The west wing was occupied by two Hungarian servants –

Wolfgang and Irma. And there was even a smaller house at the bottom of the garden where the gardener, a very old man called Mr Lampy, lived with two cats and a family of moles that he had been too kind-hearted to gas.

Gordon Warden, the head of the family, was a short and rather plump man in his early fifties. He was of course extremely wealthy. "My suits are tailor-made, my private yacht is sailor-made and I drink champagne like lemonade." This was something he often liked to say. He smoked cigars that were at least eight inches long even though he could seldom get to the last inch without being sick. His wife, Maud, also smoked – cigarettes in her case. Sometimes, at dinner, there would be so much smoke in the room that they would be unable to see each other and guests would be gasping for fresh air by the time coffee was served.

They also saw very little of their only child. They were not cruel people but the fact was that there was no room for children in their world. To Mr Warden, children meant runny noses, illnesses and noise – which is why he employed a nanny, at great expense, to handle all that for him. Even so, he always made sure he spent at least five minutes with Jordan when he got home in the evening. He nearly always remembered his birthday. And he would smile pleasantly if he happened to pass his son in the street.

Mr Warden was a businessman but he never spoke about his business. This was because it was almost certainly illegal. Nobody knew exactly what he did but some things were certain. If Mr Warden saw a policeman approaching he would dive into the bushes, and he seldom went anywhere without a luxurious false moustache. Mr Warden loved luxury. As well as the made-to-measure suits, he had a liking for silk shirts and shoes made from endangered species. He had a gold tie, a gold signet ring and three gold teeth. He was particularly proud of the teeth and as a special sign of affection had left them to his wife in his will.

Maud Warden did not work. She had never worked, not even at school, and as a consequence could not read or write. She was however a very fine bridge player. She played bridge twice a week, went out to lunch three times a week, and went riding on the days that were left. To amuse herself, she had piano lessons, tennis lessons and trapeze lessons. Sometimes to please her husband she would play a Chopin nocturne or a Beethoven sonata. But he actually much preferred it when she put on her spangly leotard and swung in the air, suspended from the ceiling by her teeth.

The Wardens had one child and weren't even certain quite how they had ended up with him. Although he had been christened Jordan

Morgan Warden, he liked to call himself Joe.

Joe did not like his parents. He didn't like the house, the garden, the cars, the huge meals, the cigarette smoke ... any of it. It was as if he had been born in a prison cell, a very comfortable one certainly, but a prison nonetheless. All day long he dreamed of escaping. One day he would be a trapeze artist in a circus, the next a flier in the Royal Air Force. He dreamed of running away to Bosnia and becoming a relief worker or hiking to the very north of Scotland and looking after sheep. He wanted to be hungry, to feel cold, to have adventures and to know danger and he was angry because he knew that so long as he was a child none of this would be his.

The strange truth is that many rich children have a much worse life and are much less happy than poor children. This was certainly the case for Joe.

To look at, he was a rather short boy with dark hair and a round face. He had brown eyes but when he was day-dreaming they would soften and turn almost blue. Joe had very few friends, and what friends he did have were unfortunately just like him, locked up in their own homes and gardens. The two people closest to him were Mrs Jinks, his nanny, and Mr Lampy, the gardener. Often he would go down to the bottom of the garden and sit in the old shed with the two cats and the family of moles and the strange smell of gin that always hovered in the air.

"Next week I'm going," he would say. "I'm really going. I'm going to join the Foreign Legion. Do you think they take twelve-year-olds?"

"I wouldn't join the Foreign Legion, Master Warden," the gardener would reply. "Too many foreigners for me."

"Don't call me 'Master Warden'! My name is Joe."

"That's right, Master Warden. That's what it is."

This, then, was life at Thattlebee Hall. But there was one other member of the family. She didn't live with the Wardens but she was somehow never far away. And the whole family, everything, would change with her coming. Even the sound of her footsteps approaching the front door would be enough to trigger it off. *Scrunch ... scrunch ... scrunch*. Suddenly the sun would seem to have gone in and the shadows would stretch out like a carpet unrolling to welcome the new arrival.

Granny.

She always came to the house by taxi and she never gave the driver a tip. She was a short woman and every year she seemed a little shorter. She had wiry silver hair which looked all right from a distance – only when you got closer could you see right through to the speckled pink surface of her skull. Her clothes, even on the hottest summer day, were thick and heavy, as were her spectacles. These were enormous with bright gold frames and two different sorts of glass. Once, just for a joke, Joe tried them on. He was still bumping into things two weeks later.

Her real name was Ivy Kettle (she was Mrs Warden's mother) but nobody had called her that since she had turned seventy. From that time on she had simply been Granny. Not Grandma. Not Grandmother. Just Granny. Somehow it suited her.

There was a time when Joe had liked his granny and had looked forward to her visits. She seemed to take a real interest in him – more so than his own parents – and she was always winking and smiling at him. Often she would give him sweets or fifty pence pieces. But as he grew older, he had begun to notice things about his granny that he had not noticed before.

First there were the physical details: the terrible caves in her wrists where the skin seemed to sag underneath the veins, the blotchy patches on her legs, the whiskers on her upper lip and the really quite enormous mole on her chin. She had no dress sense whatsoever. She had, for example, worn the same coat for *twenty-seven years* and it had probably been second-hand when she bought it. Granny was very mean to everyone. But she was meanest to herself. She never bought any new clothes. She never went to the cinema. She said she would prefer to wait and see the films on video even though she was far too mean to buy a machine to play them on. She had a pet cat which she never fed. Tiddles was so thin that one day it was attacked by a budgerigar and that was the last time it was ever seen. As for the money and sweets that she gave Joe, Mrs Warden had actually slipped them to her when she arrived. It was simply an arrangement to make Joe like Granny more.

Then there were her table manners. Although it's a sad thing to say, Granny's table manners would have made a cannibal sick. She had a large mouth framed by some of the yellowest teeth in the world. These teeth were stumpy and irregular, slanting at odd angles, and actually wobbled in her gums when she laughed. But how hard they worked! Granny would eat at a fantastic rate, shovelling food in with a fork, lubricating it with a quick slurp of water and then swallowing it with a little sucking noise and a final hiccup. Sitting at the table, she would remind you of a cement mixer at a building site and watching her eat was both fascinating and repulsive at the same time.

Another aspect of her bad table manners was her tendency to steal the silver. After lunch with Granny, Mr Warden would insist on a spoon count. Wolfgang and Irma would spend hours in the pantry checking off the pieces that remained against the pieces that had been laid and then writing down a long list of what would have to be replaced. When Granny left the house at half past four or whenever, her twenty-seven-year-old coat would be a lot bulgier than when she arrived, and as she leaned over to kiss Joe goodbye, he would hear the clinking in her pockets. On one occasion, Mrs Warden embraced her mother too enthusiastically and actually impaled herself on a fruit knife. After that, Mr Warden installed a metal detector in the front door which did at least help.

But nobody in the family ever mentioned this – either to each other or to anyone else. Mr Warden was never rude to his mother-in-law. Mrs Warden was always pleased to see her. Nobody acted as if anything was wrong.

Joe became more and more puzzled about this – and more confused about his own feelings. He supposed he loved her. Didn't all children love their grandparents? But *why* did he love her? One day he tackled Mrs Jinks on the subject.

"Do you like Granny, Mrs Jinks?" he asked.

"Of course I do," his nanny replied.

"But why? She's got wrinkled skin. Her

teeth are horrible. And she steals the knives and forks."

Mrs Jinks frowned at him. "That's not her fault," she said. "She's old..."

"Yes. But..."

"There is no but." Mrs Jinks gave him the sort of look that meant either a spoonful of cod-liver oil or a hot bath. "Always remember this, Joe," she went on. "Old people are special. You have to treat them with respect and never make fun of them. Just remember! One day you'll be old too..."

LOVE FROM GRANNY

If Joe had doubts about Granny, the Christmas of his twelfth year was when they became horrible certainties.

Christmas was always a special time at Thattlebee Hall: specially unpleasant, unfortunately. For this was when the whole family came together and Joe found himself surrounded by aunts and uncles, first cousins and second cousins – none of whom he particularly liked. And it wasn't just him. None of them liked each other either and they always spent the whole day arguing and scoring points off each other. One Christmas they had actually had a fight in the course of which Aunty Nita had broken Uncle David's nose. Since then, all the relations came prepared and as they trooped into the house, the metal detector would bleep like crazy, picking up the knives, crowbars and knuckle-dusters

24

that they had concealed in their clothes.

Joe had four cousins who were only a few years older than him but who never spoke to him. They were very fat, with ginger hair and freckles and pink legs that oozed out of tight, short trousers, like sausages out of a sausage machine. They were terribly spoiled of course, and always very rude to Joe. This was one of the reasons he didn't like them. But the main one was that Joe realized that if his parents had their way, he would end up just like them. They were reflections of him in a nightmare, distorted mirror.

But the star of Christmas Day was Granny. She was the head of the family and always came a day early, on Christmas Eve, to spend the night in the house. Joe would watch as the house was prepared for her coming.

First the central heating would be turned up. It would be turned up so high that by eleven o'clock all the plants had died and the windows were so steamed up that the outside world had disappeared. Then her favourite chair would be moved into her favourite place with three cushions – one for her back, one for her neck and one for her legs. A silver dish of chocolates would be placed on a table, carefully selected so only the soft centres remained. And a large photograph of her in a gold frame would be taken out of the cupboard under the stairs and placed in the middle of the mantelpiece.

This had been happening every year for twelve years. But this year Joe noticed other things too. And he was puzzled.

First of all, Irma and Wolfgang were both in a bad mood. At breakfast, Irma burned the toast whilst Wolfgang spent the whole morning sulking, muttering to himself in Hungarian, which is a sulky enough language at the best of times. His parents were irritable too. Mrs Warden bit her nails. Mr Warden bit Mrs Warden. By midday they had consumed an entire bottle of whisky between them, including the glass.

Joe had seen this sort of behaviour before. It was always the same when Granny came to visit. But it was only now that he began to wonder. Were they like this *because* Granny was coming? Could it be that they didn't actually want to see her at all?

It was seven o'clock on the evening of Christmas Eve when Granny finally arrived. She had told Mr Warden that she would be coming at lunch and Wolfgang had been dutifully waiting at the door since then. When the taxi did finally draw up, the unfortunate man was so covered in snow that only his head was showing and he was too cold to announce she was there. It was a bad start.

"I've been waiting out here for ten minutes," Granny muttered as Mrs Warden opened the door after just two. "Really, dear. You know this weather doesn't agree with me. I'm going to have to go to bed straight away – although goodness knows I won't sleep. This house is far too cold."

"What are you thinking of, Wolfgang?" Mrs Warden sighed, gazing at the blue nose and forehead which was just about all she could see of her faithful Hungarian servant.

Granny stepped into the house, leaving her luggage on the drive where the taxi driver had dumped it.

"A little brandy?" Mrs Warden suggested.

"A large one."

Granny stood in the hall waiting for someone to help her off with her coat and at the same time examining her surroundings with a critical eye. Mr Warden had recently bought a new Picasso of which he was very proud. It hung by the door and she noticed it now. "I don't think very much of that, dear. Too many squiggles and it doesn't go with the wallpaper."

"But Mummy, it's a Picasso!"

"A piano? Don't be ridiculous. It doesn't look anything like a piano." Granny could be deaf when she wanted to be. At other times she could hear a pin drop half a mile away. She moved towards the living-room then suddenly stopped and pointed. "But I like that very much," she said. "How original! And what a lovely colour!"

"But Mummy. That's not a painting. That's a damp patch."

Joe had watched all this from the first floor landing but hearing Mrs Jinks opening a door behind him, he realized he had to show himself. Quickly he stood up and went down the stairs.

"Hello, James!" Granny cooed. "You've put on a lot of weight!"

"My name's Joe, not James," Joe said. He was sensitive about his name. And his weight.

"No, it's not. It's Jordan," his mother said. "Really Jordan! Joe is so common!"

"Jordan? That's what I said," Granny interjected. "Haven't you grown, Jordan! What a big boy you are! What a big boy!" And with these words, Granny went into a "spread".

Joe shuddered. The spread was the word he used to describe what Granny was doing now. It was the one thing he dreaded most.

The spread was the position Granny took when she wanted to be kissed. She widened her legs and crouched down slightly with her arms open as if she wanted him to jump onto her knees and maybe even onto her shoulders. Of course, if Joe had done this, Granny would have broken into several pieces as she was over ninety years old and very frail. And with the spread came the terrible words... "Aren't you going to give your grandma a kiss, then?"

Joe swallowed hard. He was aware that his

mother was watching him and that he had to be careful what he did. But at the same time he hated what he knew he had to do.

Kissing Granny was not a pleasant experience. First there was the smell. Like many old ladies, she wore an expensive perfume that was very sweet and very musty and, if you got too close to it, made you feel a little sick. There were no labels on her perfume bottles but this one might have been called "Decomposing Sheep". Then there was her make-up. Granny wore a lot of make-up. Sometimes she put it on so thickly that you could have drawn a picture in it with your thumb-nail. Her lipstick was the worst bit. It was bright blood red and no matter how carefully Joe tried, he always came away with a glowing mirror-image of Granny's lips on his cheek. Nobody knew what make of lipstick Granny used, but Mrs Jinks could only get it off him with a Brillo pad.

But worst of all was her skin. As well as kissing her grandson, Granny insisted on his kissing her and her skin was as withery as a punctured balloon. No words could describe the feel of her skin against his lips, actually flapping slightly between the upper and the lower lip at the moment of kissing. One night Joe had woken up screaming. He had just had a nightmare in which he had kissed Granny too enthusiastically and had actually swallowed her whole.

Smack! Granny kissed Joe.

Smeruberry smack! Joe kissed Granny.

Then, with a satisfied smile, she continued into the living-room. Outside, Irma was pouring hot water over Wolfgang to thaw him so that he could carry in the cases. Mr Warden was nowhere to be seen. This was something else that had puzzled Joe – how his father was never around when Granny arrived. The year before, Joe had found him hiding inside the grand piano and he was there now. He could tell from the cigar smoke coming out of the keyboard.

Granny sat down in the chair that had been chosen for her. It was one of those old-fashioned wing chairs and she always sat in it even though her legs couldn't touch the ground, with the result that you could see straight up her dress. Not that you would look. Your eyes would stray up to her bulging knees wrapped in what looked like surgical stockings, and then beyond to the yellowing flesh of her thighs. And that would be enough. Her legs were like a set out of *Dr Who*.

Mrs Warden had poured a large brandy. Granny swallowed it in a single gulp. "Where's Gordon?" she asked, glancing suspiciously at the piano.

"I don't know..." Mrs Warden faltered.

"I can see him, Maud darling. I'm not blind you know..."

Mr Warden came out of the piano, hitting his head on the lid with an echoing thud. "I was tuning it," he explained.

"I'll have another brandy please, dear. And do you have anything other than this cooking brandy?"

"Cooking brandy?" Mr Warden exploded. "That's Remy Martin. From Harrods."

"And I'm sure the Arabs love it," Granny replied, either mishearing him or pretending to. "But it burns my throat."

Nobody slept well that night. The trouble was, Granny was a terrible snorer. At dinner she had complained of a touch of indigestion and an upset stomach after having been kept waiting in the cold and so she was only able to manage three portions of lamb stew, two portions of lemon mousse and half a bottle of wine. Finally she had tottered off to bed and ten minutes later her snores were resounding through the house. Even in the vast surroundings of Thattlebee Hall there was no escaping it. Joe went to sleep with his head buried under five pillows. Mrs Warden finally managed to drop off after squeezing a wax candle into each ear. Mr Warden didn't sleep at all. In the morning there were huge bags under his eyes – and even huger ones on the bedroom floor, which he was busily packing.

It took Mrs Warden half an hour and a fountain of tears to persuade him not to move into a hotel.

But it was Christmas Day: the snow sparkled in the garden and the church bells rang. Santa Claus had visited, the smell of turkey wafted through the house and everyone was in a good mood. Even the arrival of all the relations and the terrible crash as Uncle Michael's Volvo accidentally reversed into Uncle Kurt's Rover couldn't completely spoil the scene. The Wardens always waited for everyone to arrive before they opened their presents. Now the whole family repaired to the Christmas tree. Wolfgang, Irma and Mrs Jinks came in to join them and Mr Warden served champagne and orange juice – champagne for his wife and himself, orange juice for everyone else. It was a happy moment. Even Granny was smiling as she tottered out of the breakfast room and took her place in her favourite chair.

Joe found himself sitting between his Uncle David and one of his cousins. There were about fifteen people in the room but as he looked around, he found himself concentrating only on Granny. She was sitting in her usual place, smiling, her legs dangling a few inches above the carpet. Joe gazed at her. Was he imagining it, or was there something strange about Granny's smile? It was as if she were enjoying some secret joke. He had thought at first that she was looking out of the window but now he realized that her eyes were fixed on him. Occasionally her lips quivered and as the presents were handed out she couldn't hold back a soft and high-pitched giggle.

"This is for you, Jordan."

His father had handed him a present from under the tree. Joe flipped open the label on the top and immediately recognized the large, spidery handwriting.

TO JORDAN. LOVE FROM GRANNY.

Now although there were many presents for Joe under the tree, this was one he was particularly looking forward to and, holding it in his hands, he suddenly felt ashamed. A moment ago he had been looking at his granny as if she were ... what? Some sort of monster! But he couldn't have been more wrong. She was just a kind old lady, surrounded by her family, enjoying the day. And she loved him. The proof of it was in his hands.

Joe loved science fiction. He had seen *Star Wars* three times and had dozens of books about aliens and space travel on his bedroom shelves. But what he liked best of all was robots – and when Granny had asked him what he wanted for Christmas that was what he had said. He had actually seen one in Hamley's – about half a metre high and packed with all the latest Japanese micro-circuitry. You had to assemble it yourself – and that was the challenge – but when it was finished it would walk, talk, lift and carry ... all by radio-control.

And there it was now in front of him. Joe recognized Granny's gift-wrap at once. It was actually wedding paper – she was always economizing like that. It was a large, rectangular box, just the size it should have been. As his fingers tore through the paper he could feel the cardboard underneath. Then the paper was off. The box was open. And his heart and stomach shrank.

The robot was the sort of thing you might give to a two-year-old. It was made of brightly coloured plastic with a stupid, painted face and the name, HANK, written in large letters on its chest. Radio control? It had a key sticking out of its back. Wind it up and it would stagger a few inches across the carpet and fall over, whirring and kicking its legs uselessly. Suddenly Joe realized that everyone was looking at him: his aunts and uncles, Wolfgang, Irma, Mrs Jinks. His four cousins were nudging each other and sniggering. They were all thinking the same thing.

A baby toy! What a baby!

"Do you like it, dear?"

He heard his granny's voice and looked up. And that was when he finally knew. There was something in her face that he had never seen before and now that he had noticed it he would never be able to see her any other way again. It

34

was like one of those optical illusions you sometimes find in cereal packets. You look at a picture one way but then you suddenly notice something different and you can never see it again the same way.

He was right.

She had done it on purpose.

She knew exactly what he wanted and she had gone out and deliberately chosen this baby toy to humiliate him in front of the entire family. Of course, his mother would try to explain that Granny meant well and that she hadn't understood what he wanted. He would be made to write a thank you letter and every lying word would hurt him. But at that moment, looking at her, he knew the truth. He could see it in the wicked glimmer in her eyes, in the half-turned corner of her mouth. And it was so strong, so horrible that he shivered.

She was *evil*. For reasons that he did not yet understand, Granny hated him and wanted to hurt him in any way she could.

Joe shivered.

He knew the truth about Granny even if nobody else in the room could see it. But that wasn't what frightened him.

What frightened him was that Granny knew he knew. And she didn't care.

Maybe she knew that whatever Joe said, nobody would believe him. Or maybe it was something worse. Watching her, hunched up in the middle of the Christmas gauze and glitter, her eyes sliding slowly from left to right, he realized she was planning something. And that something included him.

TEA WITH GRANNY

A few weeks later, Granny invited Joe to tea. She always used to do this towards the end of the holidays but curiously neither Mr nor Mrs Warden were ever available. Mr Warden was at work. And Mrs Warden – who was now having lessons in Chinese cookery – was at wok. And so Mrs Jinks was the only one left to take him.

Up until now, Joe would have quite looked forward to seeing his Granny. But not any more. He knew now, and even the thought of her filled him with dread.

"I don't want to go," he told Mrs Jinks as she got into the car.

"Why ever not, Jordan? You know how your granny looks forward to seeing you."

Yes. Like a fox looks forward to seeing chickens, Joe thought. "I don't like her," he said.

"That's a cruel thing to say."

"I think *she's* cruel…"

"Now that's quite enough of that!" Mrs Jinks sniffed. "I suppose you're still thinking about that silly Christmas present. It was a misunderstanding, that's all."

Joe had set fire to the misunderstanding. He had taken the toy robot to the bottom of the garden and poured lighter fuel over it and then put a match to it. He and old Mr Lampy had watched as it melted, the plastic bubbling and blistering and the colours running into each other so that for a moment it did look like some alien creature before it shrivelled into a black and sticky puddle.

The old gardener had shaken his head. "You shouldn't ought to have done that, Master Warden."

"Why not?"

"It should've gone to a charity shop or a hospital. I'm sure there was someone somewhere who'd have wanted it."

And Joe had felt a twinge of guilt. But it was too late. The robot was gone.

Granny lived in a flat in a tall, modern block called Wisteria Lodge. This was what the estate agents would have called a purpose-built block, although they might not be able to say what its purpose actually was. Perhaps it was simply to house grannies, as hardly anyone in the building was under seventy years of age. Everything in Wisteria Lodge happened in slow motion. The lift had been specially adapted to go so slowly that you couldn't feel it moving. On one occasion it broke down and Mr and Mrs Warden stood in it for three-quarters of an hour before they realized what had happened.

Granny's flat was on the sixth floor with views over a small field and the traffic on the North Circular Road. Once she had lived in a comfortable house in a tree-lined avenue but when that had got too much for her to handle, her daughter had moved her here. It was actually a very pleasant flat with silk curtains, thick carpets, antique furniture and chandeliers but if you asked her about it Granny would shrug and sigh, "Well, I have to put up with it. I don't have any choice, do I? Oh dear, oh dear. I don't know..." And she would look so sorry for herself that you would forget that there were thousands of old people in far smaller places with no heating and no real comfort who would have given their right arm to live here.

"Hello, Jack. How lovely to see you! Come in. Make yourselves comfortable!"

Waves of pure heat shimmered in the air as Jordan stepped unwillingly into the flat, Mrs Jinks gently pushing him from behind. The central heating was on full all the time. Granny had once been given a six-inch cactus by Mr Warden after a business trip to the Sahara and obviously the intense heat suited it for it was now over eleven feet high, dominating the room with brilliant flowers and vicious spikes.

"Come in, Mrs Jinks. What an unusual hat!"

"I'm not wearing a hat, Mrs Kettle."

"Then if I were you, I'd change my hairdresser."

Granny moved forward and stooped over Jordan. "So how are you, my dear?" She reached out with a gnarled finger and prodded his cheek. "Healthy skin. Healthy colour. Full of vitamins?" She winked at Mrs Jinks.

"He gets plenty of vitamins," Mrs Jinks replied. Granny's comment about the hat had annoyed her, Joe could see.

"And how are his enzymes?" Granny asked.

"His what?" Mrs Jinks enquired.

"His enzymes! Has he got healthy enzymes? What about his cytoplasm?"

Mrs Jinks shook her head. "I'm sorry, Mrs Kettle," she said. "I don't know what you're talking about."

"Oh, come in!" Granny snarled briefly and jerked a finger into the room.

The table had already been laid for tea and Joe sat down with Mrs Jinks next to him. Briefly, he scanned the food that lay before him. There it was, the same as always. It was incredible. How could a tea possibly be so vile?

First, there were egg mayonnaise sandwiches, but the eggs had been left out so long that the yellows had taken on a greenish tint and they had so much salt in them that they made your eyes water. Then there was herring on a plate – raw and slippery and soused in some sort of particularly sharp vinegar. Granny's home-made cakes were dry and heavy, guaranteed to glue the top of your mouth to the bottom of your mouth with little taste in between. Even the biscuits were horrible: round, colourless things with neither chocolate nor cream but decorated with almond flakes and bits of dessi-cated cherry that got caught in your teeth.

But by far the worst item on the table was Granny's cream cheese special. Joe caught sight of it and felt his mouth water unpleasantly and his stomach shrivel as if trying to find some-where to hide. Granny's cream cheese special consisted of just one thing: cream cheese. That was all it was: a big bowl of cream cheese – and he knew that he would be expected to eat it all.

And he couldn't refuse it – that was the worst of it. It was part of his upbringing. Mr Warden insisted that children shouldn't be allowed to leave the table until they had finished every-thing they had been given. After all, food cost money and the money was his. As a child, Mr Warden had once remained at the table for an astonishing forty-six hours before he had finally given in and agreed to eat a plate of bread-and-butter pudding that his father had given him. The fact of the matter is that the worst thing about parents is often their parents. That's certainly where they get their most rotten ideas.

"I'll just get some serviettes…"

Granny hobbled off into the kitchen and Joe quickly turned to Mrs Jinks.

"I can't eat this," he said.

"Of course you can," Mrs Jinks replied. But she didn't sound convinced.

"No! Can't you see? She's done it on purpose. She's chosen all the things I can't stand and she's put them here because she knows you'll make me eat them. She's torturing me!"

"Joe – you're going to get a big smack if you go on like this."

"Why won't you believe me?" The whole conversation had taken place in whispers but these last words rasped in his throat. "She hates me!"

"She loves you. She's your granny!"

Then Granny returned from the kitchen carrying some faded paper serviettes. "Not started yet?" she croaked, grinning at Joe.

She put the serviettes down and picked up a green porcelain bowl, filled to the brim with thick cream cheese. Then she forked out a raw herring and laid it on the top. "That'll give it extra taste," she cackled. Finally she slid the whole thing towards him and as she did so Joe saw the trembling half-smile on her lips, the rattlesnake eyes that pinned him to his seat. Her long, knobbly fingers with their uneven, yellow nails were scratching at the tablecloth with sheer excitement. Her whole body was coiled up like a spring.

"Now, eat it all up, dear!"

Joe looked at Mrs Jinks but she turned away as if unwilling to meet his eyes. He looked at the cream cheese, slooping about in the bowl with the herring lying there like a dead slug. Suddenly his mind was made up.

He pushed the bowl away.

"No, thank you," he said. "I'm not hungry."

"What?" Granny gurgled. She had been taken off guard and jerked in her seat as if she had just sat on a drawing pin. "But..." Her mouth opened and shut. "What's the matter...? Mrs Jinks...!"

This was what Joe had been most afraid of. Whose side would Mrs Jinks take? And Mrs Jinks herself seemed unsure.

"Aren't you hungry?" she asked.

"No," Joe said.

"Can't you manage a little bit?"

"I'm not feeling well."

"Well, in that case..." Mrs Jinks turned apologetically to Granny. "If he's not well..." she began.

Granny's face shimmered. It was like looking at a reflection in the sea. One moment

43

there was a look of absolute rage and hatred, the sort of look soldiers must have seen before they were bayoneted by the enemy. But then, with a huge effort, Granny managed to wipe it away, replacing it with a look of hurtful sadness. Huge crocodile tears welled up in her eyes. Her lips drew back and puckered like a healing wound.

"But darling," she said. "I spent the whole morning getting it ready. It's your favourite."

"No, it's not," Joe said. "I don't like it."

"But you've always liked it! Have you been eating chocolate and crisps? Have you spoiled your appetite? Is that it? Mrs Jinks..."

What was happening at the table was completely unheard of. It was like that moment in *Oliver Twist* when Oliver asks for more – only in reverse as Joe was asking for less. And normally all hell would have broken loose. But Mrs Jinks had seen the look on Granny's face, the full force of her hatred. Like Joe, she had glimpsed behind the mask – and now she was taking Joe's side.

"Joe's not hungry," she said.

"Have a drink!" Granny trilled. "I've got some hot Ribena in the kitchen."

"No, thank you." Joe only liked Ribena cold. For some reason, once it was heated up it went all sweet and sticky.

"How about a nice lemon and honey milkshake?"

"No," Joe insisted.

"I could sprinkle some nutmeg on the top!"

"No, thank you."

"I think I'll take Joe home," Mrs Jinks said. She wasn't as clever as Granny at hiding her emotions. It was obvious that she wanted to get away.

Granny saw it too. Slowly the anger crept back into her cheeks. Her little eyes widened and there was a soft yellow glow in what should have been their whites. "This is your fault, Mrs Jinks," she hissed.

"Mine?" Mrs Jinks was indignant.

"You're not bringing the boy up properly. Filling him up with sweets and biscuits..."

"I did no such thing, Mrs Kettle."

"Then why won't he eat? Why won't he eat?" Granny gesticulated with a trembling fist. The edge of her wrist caught one of the bowls of cream cheese and it flew off the table, landing with a loud plop in her lap. "Now look what you've made me do!" She got up and took two steps back from the table. It was a mistake. She had forgotten the cactus. "Aaaagh!" Granny leapt three feet in the air as she came into contact with the spikes, then collapsed in a heap on the floor. Her dress was covered in cream cheese. Her face was quite purple with anger.

Joe had never seen anything like it. It was wonderful and terrifying at the same time.

What was Granny going to do? Was she going to mutter the magic words that would turn Mrs Jinks into a spotted toad? Or – more likely – was she merely going to succumb to a massive heart attack?

In the end, she did neither. She got to her feet, took a deep breath and shrivelled back into an old, defeated woman.

"All right," she muttered with a sigh. "Take him home. Leave me here on my own. I don't mind. I'll just sit by myself and maybe do some knitting."

Granny had never knitted anything in her life. Except, maybe, her brow.

And so they left. Mrs Jinks hurried Joe out of the flat and into the lift – although of course that meant the two of them had to spend another ten minutes standing in awkward silence before they reached the ground. Mrs Jinks was flushed and looked worried. And she had every reason to be.

After they had gone, Granny went to the drinks cabinet and grabbed a bottle of brandy. She pulled the cork out with her teeth (although she very nearly pulled her teeth out with the cork) and took a large swig. Then, feeling better, she went over to the telephone and dialled a number. The phone rang many times before it was answered.

"Hello?" came a thin, quavering voice from the other end.

"Is that Mrs Bucket?"

"Yes. This is Elsie Bucket."

"This is Ivy Kettle speaking."

"Yes, Ivy, dear. How very nice to hear from you." But the voice at the other end sounded faintly bored.

"Listen!" Granny spat the word into the receiver. "I've just had the boy here in my flat. My grandson…"

"Jeremy?" now the voice was a little more interested.

"His name's John! Now listen, Mrs Bucket. I've been thinking about Bideford and I've decided. I'm going to bring him along. For you…"

"How delightful of you, my dear Ivy." The voice dripped with icy charm.

"There is just one problem…" Granny went on.

"What problem, Ivy?"

"He's got a nanny. A wretched spiteful nanny. I think she may get in our way."

"Then you'll have to deal with her, my dear. Or do you need help?"

"I don't need help, thank you, Mrs Bucket!" Granny scowled and chewed air. A lump of cream cheese slithered off her dress and dripped onto her shoes. "I'll deal with Mrs Jinks," she said at last. "And then the boy will be yours…"

GRANNY *vs* NANNY

Mrs Jinks liked to say that she belonged to "the old school" which was strange because she had never actually been to school in her life. She had been Joe's nanny for five years – but the truth is that she would never have taken the job in the first place if it hadn't been for a mistake.

Before she had come to Thattlebee Hall, Mrs Jinks had earned her living by dancing. A plump, blonde-haired woman with shapely legs, she worked at a Soho club where she performed exotic dances with a snake called Anna. The owner of the club had a stutter and introducing the snake – "Anna, an anaconda" – sometimes took him three-quarters of an hour. For this reason Mrs Jinks decided to get a new job and this was when the mistake was made.

She applied to be a dancer at another club,

The Blue Balloon in Battersea, but in her haste she dialled the wrong number and got through to Mrs Warden. Now, as it happened, Mrs Warden had placed an advertisement in the newspaper that very day. Her current nanny, Miss Barking, had just handed in her notice in order to go and fight in the Gulf War and she herself was about to go on holiday. So she needed somebody fast.

Ten minutes later Mrs Warden had hired Mrs Jinks in the belief that she was a nanny and Mrs Jinks had taken the job in the belief that it was as a dancer. By the time the two of them had realized the mistake it was too late. Mr and Mrs Warden had left for a four-week safari in South Africa. And Mrs Jinks was on her own at home with Joe.

For his part, Joe was quite delighted by the error. Aged seven at the time, he had endured six and a half years of Miss Barking – a woman so tough and so muscular that he had often wondered if she was really a woman at all. There was something very attractive about Mrs Jinks. Maybe it was her round, cheerful face, her loud laugh and her generally unsuitable appearance. Maybe it was her pet snake. But she was unquestionably different.

So in the next four weeks Joe taught her everything he knew about nannying – and the fact is that at the end of the day children know more about nannying than nannies themselves.

He took her to the library and together they browsed through books such as *Childcare Made Easy* and *Tips for Top Nannies*. He took her through such activities as bathing, dressing and tidying. He even showed her how to tell him off.

The result was that when Mr and Mrs Warden returned from their safari, they found the house more organized and tidier and Joe cleaner and quieter than ever before and the two of them decided to forget how entirely unsuitable the new nanny was.

As for Mrs Jinks, she had soon decided that life as a nanny was much more pleasant than life as an exotic dancer. She smartened her appearance and became a little more severe and soon it was impossible to tell that it was not she who had taught Joe but Joe who had instructed her.

When she had been with the family for one year, Mrs Jinks took a two-week holiday in the Amazon basin where, one evening, she quietly returned her anaconda to the wild. She never spoke about the snake again. But she always kept a photograph of it in a frame beside her bed.

Joe only ever mentioned the tea with Granny once – and that was the following day.

"What's an enzyme?" he asked Mrs Jinks, remembering the word Granny had used.

"I don't know," Mrs Jinks replied, a frown on her face. She sighed. "We'd better look it up."

And so they did. They went to the library and looked up the word in a medical dictionary and this is what it said:

Enzymes. The organic substances which accelerate chemical processes occurring in living organisms. Enzyme mechanisms are the key to all biological processes.

"What does that all mean?" Joe asked.

Mrs Jinks slammed the book. "It doesn't matter," she said. "I don't think your granny knew what she was talking about. We won't mention it again."

But Mrs Jinks was never quite the same after this particular encounter with Granny. There was a worried look in her eyes. Loud noises – a slamming door or a car backfiring – jolted her. Joe got the impression that she was walking a tightrope and was afraid of falling off at any time.

And then the thefts began.

It was the second week in February and Granny had come for lunch. Joe hadn't seen her since the tea and he had been dreading it, but in fact she couldn't have been more pleasant. She gave him a smaller-than-usual kiss and a larger-than-usual present of one pound which hadn't even been given to her by her daughter in the usual way. She ate her lunch without complaining, complimented Irma (who immediately dropped all the dishes) and left all the knives and forks on the table.

It was only as she was leaving, as Wolfgang handed her her twenty-seven-year-old coat, that she let out a sudden scream.

"My cameo brooch!" she exclaimed. Tears welled in her eyes. "My beautiful cameo brooch. It's gone!"

"Are you sure you were wearing it, Mummy?" Mrs Warden asked.

"Of course I'm sure. I put it on specially. It was on the lapel of my coat."

"Well, maybe it's dropped off."

"No, no," Granny wailed. "I pinned it quite securely." She turned to Mrs Jinks. "You didn't happen to see it, did you, Mrs Jinks?" she asked with a quizzical smile.

"No, Mrs Kettle," the nanny replied. Two pin-pricks of pink had appeared in her cheeks. "Why should *I* have seen it?"

"Well…" Granny couldn't have looked more innocent. "You have often admired my cameo brooch. And I did see you looking in the hall cupboard just before lunch."

"Are you suggesting…?" Mrs Jinks didn't know what to say. Her cheeks were now dark red with anger.

"I wasn't suggesting anything," Granny interrupted. She almost sang the words and her whole body was shaking with pleasure.

Once again her lips slid away from her teeth in a yellowy smile. "I'm sure Wolfgang will find it in the garden."

But Wolfgang never did find the brooch and the next time Granny came for lunch, the whites of her eyes were quite red from weeping. In fact she was crying so much that instead of her usual tiny lace handkerchief she had brought along a tea towel.

"Never mind, Mumsy," Mrs Warden said. "I'll buy you another one. Don't be so upset. It's only a piece of jewellery."

That was the day that Mrs Warden found her diamond earrings had gone missing. She screamed the house down.

"My earrings, Gordon!" she screeched. "My lovely earrings. They matched my ears! How can they have gone? Oh no...!"

"Someone get her a tea towel," Mr Warden muttered. He was trying to read the *Financial Times*. "And put it in her mouth."

"Were they your diamond earrings, darling?" Granny asked. She was sitting in her usual chair, her face a picture of innocence.

"Yes," Mrs Warden sobbed.

"How sad. You know, Mrs Jinks was saying to me only the other day how much she liked those earrings. What a shame that they've suddenly disappeared..."

Joe was as puzzled as anyone by the thefts but already a nasty thought was forming in his mind. Two thefts. Both had taken place on days when Granny was in the house. And twice Granny had pointed the finger at Mrs Jinks...

That night, Joe got out of bed and crept downstairs. The hall was dark but he could see light spilling out underneath the door of the living-room. He pressed his ear against the wood. As he had thought, his parents were inside.

"Someone must have taken them," Mrs Warden was saying. "They can't have just walked out of the drawer."

"But who?" That was Mr Warden's voice.

"Well, Mummy was saying that Mrs Jinks..."

"Mrs Jinks would never...!"

"I don't know, Gordon. First Mummy's brooch. Now my earrings. And Mrs Jinks *was* in the cupboard."

Joe was half-crouching in the darkness, trying to hear the words through the thick wood. A floorboard creaked just behind him and he spun round as a hand reached out and touched his arm. For a horrible moment he had thought it was Granny, but in fact it was Mrs Jinks who had just come down the stairs. Joe opened his mouth to speak but she touched a finger to her lips and beckoned him back upstairs.

Mrs Jinks led him all the way to the top of the house. Only when she was back in her room with the door shut did she speak.

"Really, Joe!" she scolded him. "I'm sure I've told you something about listening at doors."

Joe sighed. "I was only…"

"I know what you were doing. And it doesn't matter. Sit down."

Joe sat down on the bed. Mrs Jinks sat beside him.

"Listen, my dear," she began. "I don't want to worry you but I think we ought to have a little talk – and I'm not sure if I'll have another opportunity."

"You're not leaving, are you, Mrs Jinks?"

"No, no, no. Not unless I have to. But I wanted to have a word with you about your granny. Just in case…"

Mrs Jinks took a deep breath.

"Did I ever tell you about my time in the Amazon basin?" she asked at last. "That time when I went to release my snake back into the wild?"

"Anna, an anaconda!" Joe exclaimed. Mrs Jinks had often spoken of her snake.

"That's right. Well, I wanted to release her as far away from civilization as I could. People are funny about snakes and I couldn't bear to think of her ending up as a handbag or a pair of shoes or something. So I went to the town of Iquitos, which is on the Amazon river, and paid a fisherman to take me by canoe into the Amazon jungle.

"We sailed for three days, Anna, me and the fisherman. I can't begin to describe that jungle to you. I've never seen anything like it before – so green and so heavy and so silent. You could feel it pressing in on you on all sides. All that vegetation! Only a river as mighty as the Amazon could have managed to find a way through.

"On the third day we turned off into a tributary. By now the town was a long way behind us. There were no huts or anything and I was certain that Anna would be safe. So I took her out of her basket, gave her a kiss, and released her—"

"But what's this got to do with Granny?" Joe asked.

"You'll find out if you don't interrupt!" Mrs Jinks paused. "Anna had gone," she went on, "and I was sitting there in the middle of a clearing feeling rather sorry for myself when suddenly..." She swallowed. "Suddenly the biggest crocodile you've ever seen burst out of the undergrowth and lurched towards me. It must have been at least five metres long. Its scales weren't green (like they are in some of your old picture books) but an ugly grey. And it had the most terrible teeth. Razor sharp and quite revolting. Obviously it had never seen a dentist in its life and if it had it had probably eaten him."

"How come it didn't eat you?" Joe asked.

"Oh, it tried to. But fortunately I was holding my umbrella and managed to force it into the creature's mouth, between its upper and its lower jaw. But that's not the point."

Mrs Jinks drew Joe closer to her.

"I have never forgotten that crocodile's eyes, the way it looked at me. And not long ago I saw another pair of eyes just like them. Exactly the same. And I'm ashamed to say, Joe, that it was your granny's eyes at that tea party of hers. I saw them and quite frankly I would have preferred to have been sitting down with the crocodile."

"So you believe me!" Joe whispered.

"I'm afraid I do."

"But what can we do?"

"There's nothing I can do," Mrs Jinks said, "except to warn you to look after yourself. And remember this, Joe. In the end, the truth will always come out, no matter how long it takes."

Joe pulled away. "You're talking as if you're not going to stay!" he cried.

Mrs Jinks looked at him tiredly. "I don't know," she said. "I really don't know. But I had to talk to you, Joe. Before it was too late…"

The next theft took place on the following Sunday. This time it was Mr Warden who was the victim. He had dozed off in his chair after lunch and when he woke up he knew at once that something was wrong. And it was. Someone had stolen two of his gold teeth.

"It'th a thcandal!" he cried out, whistling at the same time. There was a large gap at the front of his mouth. "Thith ith a matter for the polithe!"

Granny, of course, was there. As Mr Warden raged and whistled, she shook her head as if she were utterly confused. "Who would want to take two gold teeth?" she asked. "Although now I think about it, Mrs Jinks was telling me how very much she admired them..."

After that, things happened very fast.

The police arrived in two police cars and an unmarked van. This, when it was opened, revealed two of the most ferocious dogs Joe had seen in his life. They were Alsatians, long-haired with thin, angular bodies and evil black eyes. Their tongues were drooling as they began to pad around the house, sniffing suspiciously.

"There's no meat out, is there?" the dog handler asked.

"Meat? No!" Mrs Warden replied.

"Good. It's just that Sherlock and Bones here haven't eaten for five days. It keeps them keen. But I can't let them get a smell of meat."

"Please, officer," Mrs Warden gestured. "My husband is in here..."

The policemen followed her through into the living-room. Irma and Wolfgang went back to the west wing leaving Joe and Mrs Jinks in the hall. Mrs Jinks was looking rather pale.

"I think I'll go and sit outside," she said. "I need the fresh air."

As she moved away, Joe heard a door softly close. Had someone been watching them? Granny? Suddenly worried, without knowing why, he opened the door and followed the passage on the other side all the way down to the kitchen.

There was someone there. Afraid of being seen, he peered round the corner just in time to see Granny climbing down from a cupboard with something in her hand. Now she was moving rapidly towards him and Joe ducked into the larder to hide. He heard a swish of material and caught a whiff of Decomposing Sheep as she passed but then she was gone. What was she doing? What had she taken?

Joe waited until he was sure she had gone before he went back out into the hall but now there was no sign of her. In the living-room, he could hear his father talking to one of the policemen.

"Yeth, offither. They were thtolen when I wath athleep!"

He went back to the front door and looked out. Mrs Jinks was sitting on a bench at the side of the house and as he watched her, Joe heard a window open on the first floor. He wanted to call out to her but suddenly the two police dogs appeared, lumbering across the lawn, and he shrunk back.

But not before he had seen...

Something was drifting onto Mrs Jinks. At first Joe thought it was raining. But whatever it was was brown. And it was some sort of powder. Mrs Jinks hadn't noticed. She was sitting quietly, deep in thought. The powder sprinkled onto her shoulders, her lap, her hair.

And then the police dogs stopped, their bodies rigid. As Joe stared in horror, their eyes lit up and the hair on their backs began to bristle. The one called Sherlock began to growl. The other one – Bones – was panting; short, quick breaths that rasped in its throat.

Slowly, silently, the two of them closed in on Mrs Jinks.

"Hello, doggies..." Mrs Jinks had seen them. She stood up, noticing for the first time the brown powder that covered her arms and legs. She smelled it. And that must have been when she knew. The colour drained out of her face. Then she screamed, turned and ran.

"Sherlock! Bones!" The police dog handler had seen what was happening but too late. Like two bolts fired from a crossbow, the dogs took off after Mrs Jinks who had already sprinted across the lawn, through an ornamental pond, and who was now making for the bushes.

"Heel!" the police dog handler cried.

One of the police dogs bit Mrs Jinks's heel.

Mrs Jinks screamed again and disappeared into the bushes. With a terrible snarling and snapping the dogs fell on top of her.

Joe had watched all this in horror and the rest was just a whirl. He vaguely remembered the policemen racing across the lawn when it was already far too late. He heard them all shouting as they blamed each other for what had happened. Someone must have called an ambulance, for a few minutes later one arrived, but then the stretcher bearers refused to get out until the dogs had been chained and muzzled. He saw Sherlock and Bones being led back to the police van, their heads hanging in disgrace, and saw, with a wave of despair, that they looked a lot fatter than they had been when they arrived.

Later on, he heard – and somehow he wasn't surprised – that the cameo brooch, the earrings and the two gold teeth had all been found in Mrs Jinks's room. They had, however, found nothing of Mrs Jinks apart from a few blood-stained scraps of clothing.

But for Joe, the very worst memory of the day, the one that would keep him awake all of that night and most of the next was of something he had seen in the middle of all the activity. As he stood in the hall he had heard something and had turned round just in time to see Granny coming down the stairs. At that moment, with just the two of them there, the mask was off again and the crocodile smile that Mrs Jinks had described was there for him to see.

But it wasn't the smile that frightened Joe. It was what Granny was holding in her hand, what she had taken from the kitchen a few minutes before.

It was a box of Bisto gravy powder.

Without saying a word, Granny hurried past him and went into the kitchen to put it back.

GRANNY MOVES IN

Nobody felt the death of Mrs Jinks more keenly than Joe. It was as if he had lost his only friend – which, in a way, he had. And not only was she dead but she had been branded a thief and that hurt him all the more. "The truth will always come out." That was what she had said to him. But how could he go to his parents or the police and tell them that it was Granny who had taken the jewellery and the gold teeth and that it was she who had killed Mrs Jinks by pouring gravy powder over her when the police dogs were near because … because… What reason could there possibly be? They would think he was mad.

Every day when he got home from school, Joe found himself on his own. He took to walking down to the bottom of the garden where Mr Lampy would be waiting for him and the two of them would sit together next to a burning brazier with the family of moles watching them through the window of the shed.

"I'm going to run away," he would say. "I'll go to China and work in a paddy-field."

"I don't know, Master Warden," Mr Lampy would reply. "China's a long way away. And who's this Paddy you're talking about?"

Meanwhile, Mr and Mrs Warden had problems of their own. The summer holiday was about to start and that meant the departure of Wolfgang and Irma. Every year the cook and her husband went home to Hungary although, as they only owned a caravan just outside Budapest, Mr Warden would have much preferred it if the home had come to them. What it meant was that for three weeks there would be no cook and no butler. Worse still, Mrs Warden had been unable to find a new nanny to look after Joe even though she'd advertised. The fact that the last nanny had just been eaten by two dogs probably didn't help.

"We've got to find someone to look after Jordan," Mrs Warden said the night after Wolfgang and Irma had gone.

"What? What did you say?" Mr Warden was lying in bed, smoking a cigar and reading *The Economist*.

Mrs Warden pivoted round upside down. She had recently begun a course in escapology

64

and as well as being hand-cuffed, strait-jacketed and sellotaped, she was also tied by one foot to the chandelier. "I said we've got to find someone to look after Jordan."

"Oh yes. But who?"

"I was thinking about Mr Lampy."

"Mr Lampy? He's just the gardener. And he's over eighty. Completely senile…"

Mrs Warden tugged with her teeth at one of the ropes that bound her. It wouldn't give. "We could ask Mabel Butterworth. She's an angel."

"You're absolutely right," Mr Warden said. "She died two years ago."

"Did she?" Mrs Warden blinked. "No wonder she hasn't been returning my calls." She considered for a moment. "How about Barbara Finegold? She always says how much she likes kids."

"But she means goats," Mr Warden said. "She's always had a fondness for goats. She keeps two of the brutes as pets."

"Well, there must be someone."

"How about you?" Mr Warden suggested. "After all, you are the boy's mother."

"I hadn't thought of that," Mrs Warden muttered. "I suppose it is an idea… I mean, I could look after him for a few days."

Mrs Warden twisted round again, trying to release a hand from the strait-jacket without dislocating her shoulder. Nothing happened.

"This isn't working," she sighed. "I'm sorry, Gordon, but I'm afraid you're going to have to untie me. Gordon? Gordon...?"

But Mr Warden had fallen sound asleep.

The next day did not begin well. Mrs Warden had a headache (from sleeping upside down) and had no wish to be left alone with Joe. Mr Warden had left early for the office even though – as Mrs Warden realized an hour after he was gone – it was Saturday. Joe was waiting for her in the kitchen, studying a map of China.

"Good morning, Jordan," she said.

Joe looked up. He had been thinking about life in Chwannping.

"Now," Mrs Warden went on. "I'm just going to make you some breakfast. Then I'm afraid I have a hair appointment and then my bridge lesson with Dr Vitebski. This week we're learning about suspension bridges. So will you be all right on your own until lunch?"

Joe nodded.

"Good." Mrs Warden was in a hurry. She threw a spoonful of coffee granules into her mouth and sipped some boiling water from the kettle. "I'd love to have lunch with you," she went on, "but I'm meeting Jane for elevenses and as she's always late it's bound to be twelveses. The poor dear is all at sixes and sevens! Maybe I'll buy her some After Eights."

Joe had lost count trying to work this out but his mother went on anyway. "I'm going shopping this afternoon," she said. "I thought I'd go to the spring sales. The sofa in the living-room needs some new springs. Then tea at the Ritz and I should be home in time for supper."

"Do you want me to make the supper?" Joe asked.

"I don't think so, darling!" Mrs Warden giggled. "Leave that to me!"

But in fact she was so exhausted after her day's shopping that she quite forgot to cook. That evening, Mr Warden and Joe sat at the table staring gloomily at three tins of pink salmon. Mrs Warden was even gloomier. She couldn't find the tin opener.

"This house is going to the dogs!" Mr Warden muttered. "And I'm going to a hotel!"

Mrs Warden burst into tears. "It's not my fault," she wept. "I've been so busy! How can I be expected to do everything?"

"Well, is there *no* food in the house?" Mr Warden asked.

"There was a chicken and some peas."

"You could at least have cooked the peas," Mr Warden growled.

"I tried to. But the chicken ate them. And then I tried to cook the chicken but it ran away."

The days without Wolfgang and Irma crawled slowly by. Mrs Warden filled the house with ready meals. Mr Warden spent longer and longer at the office. And Joe began to teach himself Chinese. But quite rapidly things began to fall apart.

On Tuesday night the dishwasher broke down, much to the horror of Mrs Warden, who hadn't washed a dish herself since 1963 (and then she had only rinsed it). The next day she went out and bought a hundred paper plates which were fine with the main courses and puddings but caused problems with the soup. On Wednesday, Mr Warden attempted to dry his shoes by placing them in the microwave. His feet were actually glowing as he took the tube to work and he caused a bomb scare at Charing Cross. On Thursday, the toaster exploded when Mr Warden tried to light it with a match. On Friday it was the Hoover. Mrs Warden only just escaped a terrible injury when she tried to use it to blow-dry her hair.

You may think it pathetic that Mr and Mrs Warden were so incapable of looking after themselves but you'd be surprised how true this is of the very rich. They've been looked after by servants for so long that they don't know how to do anything for themselves. Ask the Queen what a Brillo pad is and she'd probably tell you it was a lovely place to live.

Anyway, as the week progressed, the house became dustier and dirtier and more broken down. Joe for the most part avoided his parents and spent most of his time with Mr Lampy.

Chinese had proved impossible to learn so he was thinking now about volunteering for the American shuttle to Mars.

And then, on Saturday, Granny came to lunch.

"You know, Maud, darling," she said, munching on a mouthful of Marks and Spencer's Instant Saturday Lunch, "you and Gordon look terribly tired."

"I am tired!" Mr Warden muttered.

"Don't you usually go to the south of France at this time of the year?"

"We can't, Mumsy," Mrs Warden sighed.

"Why ever not?" Granny had hardly glanced at Joe, sitting opposite her at the table, but he was suddenly suspicious. Granny knew perfectly well that his parents had a flat in Cannes. She also knew that the flat only had one bedroom.

"What about Jordan?" Mrs Warden said.

"I'm sure he'd love to go with you."

"There's no room," Mr Warden muttered.

"Well…" There was a pause. "I could look after him while you were away."

Joe's mouth went dry. One after another the hairs on the back of his neck stood up. Alone with Granny? He'd prefer to be alone with a sabre-toothed tiger.

"I could move in, if you wanted me to," she went on. Her whole face had gone rubbery and there was a sweetness in her voice. But

Joe could see her eyes. They were still sly. "Joe would love it. Wouldn't you, dear?"

"Aaagh!" Joe yelled. For even as Granny had spoken the words, he had felt a terrible explosion of pain. Under the table, a leather-capped shoe had just come into hard contact with his knee.

"I'm sorry, dear?" Granny gazed at him enquiringly.

"You can't!" Joe gasped.

"What?" Mr Warden was furious. "Your granny offers to look after you and that's all you can say?"

"I mean... I mean, it isn't fair on Granny." Joe was blushing now. Could he tell the truth? That was what Mrs Jinks had advised but looking at his parents now he knew it was impossible. He forced himself to think. "I'd love to be with Granny," he went on. "But wouldn't it be too much work for her? It might make her ill."

"Oh, silly me!" Granny trilled. "I've dropped my fork!" She disappeared under the table.

"Wait a minute..." Joe began.

"What is the matter with you, Jordan?" his mother asked.

A second later, Joe jerked upright in his seat as three metal prongs buried themselves in his thigh. He had been holding a glass of water but now he cried out, his hand jerked and the water sprayed over his father, putting out his cigar.

"Have you gone mad?" Mr Warden demanded.

"No, father, I…" Joe put down the glass and reached under the table. There were three holes in his trousers – not to mention in his leg.

"I'll look after him." Granny was already back in her seat. For someone so old, she had moved incredibly fast. "It would only be for a few weeks. I'm sure we'd have a lot of fun…"

Joe stared at her. Granny leaned forward and picked up the bread knife: thirteen inches of serrated steel. She looked at him and smiled. Joe shrank back into his chair. When he spoke, his voice was thin and high-pitched. "What about Mr Lampy?" he quavered.

"What about him?" his mother said.

"He's a lot younger than Granny. Couldn't he look after me? That way, you and father could have your holiday, Granny wouldn't have to bother about me and everyone would be happy."

Across the table, Granny was gripping the bread knife so tightly that her fingers had gone white and the veins were wriggling under her skin like worms. Joe held his breath, his eyes fixed on the knife.

"I did suggest Mr Lampy," Mrs Warden said.

"Maybe it's not such a bad idea," Mr Warden muttered.

"I think it's a very good idea…"

Granny put down the knife. Her lips had gone all wobbly and there were tears brimming in her eyes like rainwater in the folds of a tent. "Well, if you don't want me," she burbled. "If you don't like me…"

"Of course he likes you, Mummy," Mrs Warden said. "Jordan was just worried about you, that's all."

"I certainly was," Joe agreed.

"Well, all right." Granny forced herself to cheer up. "You two get your tickets then and have a lovely time." But then her eyes narrowed and the next words were aimed directly at Joe. "And if anything terrible happens to Mr Lampy, if he's unlucky enough to have a dreadful accident in the next few days, just you let me know."

"Now don't you worry about me, Master Warden," Mr Lampy said.

It was the morning before Mr and Mrs Warden were about to leave. Mr Lampy had just come out of the shed carrying a canister of petrol. He had been cutting back the shrubbery at the bottom of the garden and was about to light a bonfire.

"You and me … we're going to get along all right."

"That's not what I'm worried about," Joe replied. "It's Granny…"

"You and your granny!" Mr Lampy set the canister down and rubbed the small of his back. "Ooh!" he exclaimed. "I been to see the doctor today and he goes on about someone called Arthur Itis. Arthur Itis? I never heard of him."

"Please, Mr Lampy..."

Mr Lampy smiled. He was a very old man and when he smiled his face folded into a hundred creases. He had spent his whole life out of doors. In ten years in the Navy he had never once gone below deck – all the more remarkable when you consider that he served on a submarine. "I haven't seen your granny and I don't intend to see her," he went on. He leaned down and picked up the petrol canister. "I reckon she'll be leaving the two of us alone."

Joe watched as Mr Lampy walked away. He wasn't convinced but there seemed to be no point in arguing any more. The last thing he saw of Mr Lampy was the old gardener leaning over a great pile of wood-cuttings and leaves, sprinkling it with petrol from the canister. He didn't see Mr Lampy light the match.

The explosion could be heard thirty miles away and at first the police thought it was a terrorist attack. Like Mrs Jinks before him, nothing was found of Mr Lampy – which was hardly surprising. He had blown a crater five metres deep in the earth. Four trees, the rockery, the garden shed and the moles went with him, blown into so many pieces that it was quite impossible to say what belonged to what. One question puzzled everyone. How had Mr Lampy managed to sprinkle nitroglycerine on his bonfire? And how had it got into what should have been a canister of petrol?

The investigation led nowhere. One witness did come forward claiming that he had seen a figure climbing over the fence into the garden of Thattlebee Hall. But as the witness had been on his way back from the pub and as he insisted that the figure he had seen had been a woman, and one who was over ninety years old, his evidence was discounted.

A few days later, Mr and Mrs Warden left for their flat in the south of France.

The same day, Granny moved in.

GATHERING OF THE GRANNIES

Breakfast was cream cheese.

Lunch was cream cheese.

Tea was more cream cheese.

After just one day, Joe was the colour of cream cheese. The house had never felt so big and he had never felt so small. His parents were away in another country. Mrs Jinks and Mr Lampy were dead. There was just Joe and Granny and he knew with a horrible sick feeling in the pit of his stomach that he was completely in her power.

Of course, Granny was enjoying every minute of it, moving round the house, warbling to herself like a sick canary as she glued shut the windows and turned up the heating. By lunch-time Joe was sweating.

"You look ill, dear," Granny trilled.

"I'm hot."

"It must be the flu. You'd better have two

spoonfuls of cod-liver oil. Better still, I'll go to the fishmongers and buy you a whole cod's liver."

That afternoon, Mr and Mrs Warden telephoned from the south of France. Although Joe was in the room, they didn't ask to speak to him. Instead, Mrs Warden gabbled down the phone to Granny at twice her usual speed. She always did this to save money on long-distance calls.

"Are you sure everything's all right, Mumsy?" she asked.

"Don't you worry, dear. Jasper and I are having a wonderful time. He's no trouble at all!"

"There is one thing, Mummy. Could you put an advert in *The Lady* for a new nanny? We'll have to have one when we get back."

"Oh, Jack won't be needing a new nanny..."

Joe heard the words. They sent a shiver down his spine.

"Mummy...?"

Granny was holding the telephone in a claw-like hand. She smiled into it. "Lovely talking to you, dear. Must go!" The smile evaporated. Granny hung up.

Granny made a number of telephone calls after that but Joe was pretty certain that none of them were to *The Lady*. She was careful to close the door before she began but Joe did manage to hear her checking train times with British Rail and so assumed that she – and presumably he with her – was about to go away.

This was confirmed at the end of the day. Joe had eaten his supper on his own and was settling down to watch television when the door opened and Granny came in.

"Bedtime, Jane, dear!"

"I'm Joe! And it's only eight o'clock. I never go to bed before nine."

"Don't argue with Granny. Granny knows best!"

"But I'm watching *The Bill*!"

"So am I, dear." Granny flicked the television off. "The electricity bill – and that should save a bit! Now up to bed!"

But the torment didn't even stop there. Although it was a warm night, Granny had insisted on his wearing a vest as well as his pyjamas, a dressing-gown as well as a vest and two extra blankets on top of everything else.

"We don't want your flu to get any worse, do we, dear," she said when she came into his room.

"I can't sleep like this," Joe said. "I feel like a sausage roll!"

"You can't have a sausage roll now, dear," Granny replied. "But maybe I'll get you one tomorrow." And with a soft giggle, she switched off the light and went out.

Joe lay in bed for a long time. He was too

hot to sleep and also too angry. As he lay in the half-darkness, he began to think about how unfair life was. He was twelve (almost thirteen) years old. He could read, write, add up, speak French, swim, juggle and name over a thousand characters in science fiction books and films. But did he have any life of his own? No! His every movement was controlled and organized by adults with less imagination than him. His parents, the teachers at his posh prep school – they were all the same, passing him around as if he were no more than a tin of sweets. Of course, it wouldn't be so bad if the grown-ups had more sense. But nobody had to be qualified to be a parent. And his parents were not only unqualified, they had quite happily handed him to a woman who hated him and who in the last few weeks had just killed his two best friends. But who would believe him? Nobody!

If he hadn't been so hot and angry, maybe he would have slept. But he was still awake at nine o'clock when the doorbell rang. He was awake at ten past nine when it rang again. And he had given up any idea of sleeping by half past when it rang for a third time.

As the evening dragged on, Joe began to hear strange sounds coming from downstairs. The hiss of a can being opened and a peal of high-pitched laughter. A clink of glasses and the slam of a cupboard door. More laughter.

There seemed to be four or five women down-stairs. The muffled sound of arguing and then another cackle of laughter drifted up to his room. In the end he couldn't bear it any longer. He got up and went downstairs.

The hall was dark but the door to the living-room was half open which was how the sounds had escaped. Thankful for his bare feet and the thick carpets, Joe tiptoed forward and peeped in. An extraordinary sight met his eyes.

There were five grannies in the room, play-ing poker. They had assembled a green baize card table and had two decks of cards scattered over the surface, on the floor and – in at least two instances – up their sleeves. The room was thick with smoke. Two of the grannies were smoking cigarettes while a third had helped herself to one of Mr Warden's cigars. They had opened half a dozen cans of beer and a bottle of whisky. There were glasses everywhere. Granny had also provided food. There was a bowl of popcorn, some bright pink hot dogs with fried onions and American mustard, a plate of pickled cucumbers, two boxes of Fort-num and Mason chocolates, some salt beef sandwiches and several packets of chewing gum. Joe wasn't at all surprised that there wasn't an ounce of cream cheese in sight.

But what made the spectacle so bizarre as well as so revolting was the old ladies them-selves. Their combined ages must have added up to well over four hundred. Joe had once seen a few minutes of a video called *Revenge of the Killer Zombies*. It had given him nightmares for a week. Well, this was far, far worse.

Granny One was a small, shrivelled woman, no more than four feet high. Her head barely came over the edge of the table and she was blinking at the cards in her hand with small, pink eyes. She seemed to be finding it difficult to balance on her chair – perhaps because of the enormous amount of jewellery she was wearing and the bulging handbag she was clutching to her chest. This granny's hands were everywhere at once: holding her cards (and trying to stop her neighbour seeing them), guarding her bag, tilting her whisky glass towards her lips and poking her nose and ears. Look quickly, and you might think she had four arms. Her name was Granny Anne.

Granny Two was wearing what looked like a pair of curtains – but they were curtains you would draw at your peril. For this granny was immensely fat. She was so fat that she seemed to have partially melted into her chair. She was obviously a careful poker player as she was keeping her cards close to her chin – or rather, chins, for she had three of them. The third of these was crowned with a wispy beard. Granny Two was sucking a hot dog. She couldn't eat it as, for extra comfort, she had removed her false teeth and placed them in front of her on the table. Her name was Granny Smith.

The first things Joe noticed about Granny Three were her quite horrible eyes. She was wearing a heavy pair of spectacles which, over the years, had stretched her ears and sunk into her nose. In fact her entire face was lop-sided and she hadn't helped it by putting on too much lipstick – at the same time missing her lips. Her eyeballs, magnified by what looked like inch-thick glass, were a milky shade of white with one a little higher than the other. Granny Three was smoking, eating, drinking and talking all at the same time. And all the time she was watching. Her eyes, darting about in her drooping sockets, missed nothing. She answered to the name of Granny Adams.

Granny Four, shovelling enormous handfuls of popcorn into her mouth, was a vulture. She had the same long neck, bald head and cruel eyes. And she was wearing a flowing green cloak mounted with feathers which added to the illusion. This was the granny who was smoking the cigar. She was using it to point with and as Joe watched, the glowing tip caught Granny Smith on the chin. Granny Smith cried out and fell backwards, two aces tumbling out of her jacket. Granny Adams threw a glass of beer at her and screamed with laughter while Granny Anne pounded the table and chewed gum. This last granny was called Granny Lee.

Dominating the table was Granny herself, looking almost royal in a billowing dress with flouncy neck and sleeves. She was sitting with her arms and legs apart and a scowl on her face. Suddenly she threw her cards down.

"A full house. Kings high. Beat that!" She announced.

"I've got a pair of twos," Granny Anne exclaimed in a quavering voice.

Granny Smith grabbed them and tore them up. "You lose, Anne. Two twos aren't worth anything."

"Well, I've got another two in my bra," Anne exclaimed.

"Cheat! Cheat! Cheat!" Granny Adams screeched with laughter. "I haven't got anything," she added and threw her cards in a shower over her head.

"Well, I've got a royal flush," the vulture granny snapped. "Ace, king, queen, knave, ten." She spread the cards on the table.

"How did you do that?" Granny scrabbled at the cards, examining them as if they were forgeries. Her face had gone dark red. "You've been cheating as well, haven't you, Lee?"

"Of course I've been cheating," Granny Lee replied. "We've all been cheating. But I've just been cheating better than you."

"Well, how much do I owe you?" Granny

was sulking now, her lip jutting out and her shoulders slumped.

"Let me see..." Granny Lee scribbled a few figures on a sheet of paper. "That's two shillings and fourpence."

"How much is that in new money?" Granny Anne asked nervously.

"We don't have nasty new money here, Anne," Granny replied. She brought her elbow up sharply, catching the little granny in the eye. "Two shillings and fourpence is just what it says it is."

"Oh! Lovely old money!" Granny Smith sighed, her three chins rising and falling in perfect unison. "It used to be worth something once, money did. I could buy dinner for three people with two shillings and fourpence."

"Yes," Granny Lee snapped. "But the trouble was, you'd eat it all yourself!" And her whole body shook as she laughed uncontrollably.

Meanwhile Granny had gathered in the torn and crumpled cards and was once again shuffling the pack.

"So tell me, Ivy," Granny Anne asked. "What's the news about that grandson of yours?"

At the door, Joe froze.

"Yes!" Granny Adams rubbed her hands together. Her eyes rolled like two worms in walnut shells. "How are his enzymes?"

"Enzymes! Enzymes!" Granny Lee and Granny Anne chorused.

Granny held up a hand. "You'll find out soon enough," she rasped. "I'm taking him with me tomorrow."

"What?" The other grannies stared in amazement and delight.

"Can you?" Granny Smith asked. "What about his parents?"

"They're not here," Granny replied. "Anyway, they don't care a jot about him. They won't even notice."

"Do you mean…" Granny Lee twisted her neck until the bones clicked. "You've got him all to yourself?"

Granny nodded. "Yes. I've had quite a bit of fun at his expense, I can tell you." She licked her lips and began to deal. "But maybe I'm getting old. I feel I haven't quite made him miserable enough!"

Joe felt the hairs on the back of his neck prickle. If only he could have tape-recorded this conversation – his parents would have had to believe him. He'd guessed that Granny hated him. Now he had the proof of it. But all that talk of enzymes worried him. What were they planning? Where was he going to be taken?

"How I hate children!" the vulture granny moaned.

"Me too!"

"I can't stand them."

"I detest them!"

All the grannies were nodding so vigorously that Joe wouldn't have been surprised if their heads had come loose from their necks and rolled across the surface of the card table.

"You know what I hate about them?" Granny Smith said. "I hate their perfect skin. It's all pink and shiny and smooth. I hate their hair, so thick and wavy. But most of all I hate their teeth." She gazed at her own on the table in front of her. "Do you know where children keep their teeth? In their mouths! It isn't fair."

"I hate children because they're so healthy," Granny Anne went on. "They're always shouting and playing and having fun and running about. I haven't run anywhere since 1958 and that was only for a bus."

"I hate them because of everything they've got," Granny Adams muttered. "We never had computers and pop music and T-shirts and mountain bikes. But they have. I fought in two world wars but nobody ever gave me a skateboard. Oh no!"

"Children smell," Granny Lee announced. "They're too small and they make too much noise. Why can't they be more like us?"

"Yes. With arthritis!"

"And swollen knees."

"Hard of hearing!"

"What?"

"And wrinkly."

"Horrid! Horrid! Horrid! Horrid! Horrid!"
All five grannies were chorusing together now
and pounding their fists on the table at the
same time. Joe couldn't believe what he was
seeing. It seemed that the five old ladies had
gone quite mad.

At last Granny stopped them.

"But we can at least get our revenge," she
said. "There are so many ways to upset a
grandchild."

"Oh, yes!" Granny Adams giggled. Her
glasses jumped up and down on her nose.
"When I see my grandchildren, I always poke
them a lot. I do find that children hate being
poked."

"I don't just poke them," the little granny
said. "I pat them on their heads and fiddle with
their clothes. It does annoy them so, although
of course they're not allowed to complain."

"And don't forget the kiss!" Granny Smith
said. "The wet kiss on the cheek makes them
squirm like frogs in a pond!"

"What about presents?" Granny asked.
"Presents are a marvellous way of spoiling any
child's day."

"Oh, yes! A boring book token!"

"Talcum powder!"

"Something you know they've already got!"

"What I do," Granny said, "is buy them
something that's too young for them. Something that will make them feel babyish.

They feel so ashamed. It's hilarious."

(At the door, Joe remembered the toy robot and found that his face was burning once again. But this time it wasn't with embarrassment. It was anger.)

"I have a much better idea," Granny Lee said. "I buy my grandchildren hideously unsuitable clothes. I've managed to find some of the most ghastly pullovers in the world."

"I knit them myself," Granny Anne muttered.

"The children *have* to wear them," Granny Lee went on. "And you should see them! I always take them out to tea and watch their faces as they walk out in their horrible, huge, brightly-coloured jumpers..."

"I've got a much better idea," Granny Adams interjected. "My grandchildren are a little overweight. So guess what I buy them – chocolates! I get them a whole box and of course they eat them and that just makes them fatter and spottier and when they go back to school they're terribly teased and all thanks to me. You should try the chocolate wheeze! The little brats can never resist a chocolate."

"It seems to me that you should combine the two ideas," Granny said. "Give them the chocolates. And give them a jersey that's a little too small. Then, when their tummies are bulging it will really show."

The other four grannies thought about this

and then all shrieked with laughter. More glasses of whisky were poured. More beer cans were cracked open. The fat granny was laughing so much that her whole body was convulsing and her face had gone bright red.

Joe couldn't bear any more. He took three steps away from the door, shrinking into the shadows of the hall. But even as he went he heard his name once again being bounced around the card table.

"So you're going to take the boy?"

"Oh, yes. He's coming. I've had my eye on him for a long time."

"Which eye, dear? The real one or the glass one?"

"Have you spoken to ... Elsie Bucket?" This was Granny Lee's voice. She had spoken the name with awe.

"Oh, yes. I spoke to Elsie. She's delighted."

"Delighted!"

"Excited!"

"Enzymes!"

"Hee hee hee..."

The five of them were like witches. Add a cauldron and a few frogs and there would have been no difference. Joe turned and tiptoed back the way he had come. The voices followed him as he made his way back to bed.

THE GOLDEN
GRANNY AWARDS

"Pack your bags, Judas. We're going on holiday."

It was breakfast the following day and Joe had just come downstairs to find Granny tucking into a plate of eggs, bacon, sausage, tomatoes, fried bread and black pudding. She had prepared a half grapefruit topped with a small amount of cream cheese for him.

"Where are we going?" Joe asked. He knew she was always getting his name wrong on purpose and decided not to correct her.

"To Bideford in Devonshire. It's a delightful town. I spent many happy years there in the war."

"The Crimean War, Granny?"

"There's no need to be rude, dear." Granny lashed out with a curiously powerful fist. If Joe hadn't ducked at the last moment she would have broken his chin. Even so he felt the air as it punched past him. "It was the Second

World War. Ah, what happy days those were. Rationing and bombs and dried eggs for breakfast. Your grandfather got blown to smithereens in the Second World War. Such happy days!"

"I don't want to go to Bideford," Joe said, sitting on the edge of his chair in case he had to duck a second blow.

"I'm sure you don't, dear," Granny simpered. "But you're twelve and I'm ninety-four. So you don't really have any choice."

"I could ring Mum and Dad..."

"And drag them all the way back from France? I don't think they'd be very pleased. Anyway, I've already told them I'm taking you." She smiled unpleasantly.

"Why are you doing this, Granny?" Joe demanded. "What do you want?"

Granny paused with her fork inches from her mouth. Egg white dangled greasily in front of her lips. Suddenly she was innocent again. "I want to look after you," she said. "Just like any granny would."

The taxi dropped them at Paddington Station and the driver scowled as Granny counted out the fare in one, two and five-penny pieces. It took her ten minutes to pay by which time the driver was covered in coins.

"Seven pounds twenty pence?" she demanded. "There you are! That's seven pounds twenty-one. Keep the change!"

Joe grabbed the suitcases and Granny grabbed Joe and together they made their way through the station concourse. As they walked, Joe saw something rather strange. A woman had got out of the taxi just behind them – he had noticed her out of the corner of his eye because he had thought he recognized her – and now she seemed to be following them. Nervously, he glanced over his shoulder. She was still there, her face almost completely hidden by a scarf over her mouth and a pair of dark glasses over her eyes. A lock of blonde hair poked out from under a voluminous hat and she walked with a pronounced limp. Where had Joe seen her before?

But maybe he was imagining the whole thing. For when he looked around again a few moments later, the mysterious woman had gone.

Granny checked her ticket and pointed at a train. There was a guard standing beside it, leaning against it with one hand splayed out on the metal surface and the other hand in his pocket. The guard hadn't shaved that morning. There was a cigarette behind his ear.

"Excuse me..." Granny said.

The guard looked at her with a syrupy smile and almost at once Joe recognized the sort of man he was. He was just like his Uncle David, the sort of man who believes that all old people are like children, that they don't understand anything except simple words spoken loudly. Joe had always hated that sort of behaviour but now his interest was aroused. How would Granny react?

"Yes, my love. How *are* you today?" The guard shouted out the words. He was leaning over Granny, nodding his head at her.

Granny's lips tightened. "Is this the train for Bideford?" she snapped.

"No, dear!" The guard was still shouting and he shook his head vigorously for good measure. "There's no *station* at Bideford, darling. There hasn't been for twenty years! You have to go to *Barnstaple* and get a bus!"

"Is this the train for Barnstaple?" Granny demanded.

"Yes!" Now he nodded like a thirsty duck. He was showing all his teeth (and several fillings) in a wide smile. "Can you get on all right, dear? Got a *ticket*, have you?"

"Of course I've got a ticket!"

"Good! Good! Now you change at *Exeter*, all right. Do you think you can remember that?"

"Yes."

"That your grandson, is he? *He'll* look after you! Don't you worry, love. You'll be all right."

The guard hadn't noticed but Granny's cheeks had gone a dark red and her lips were so tight they could have been sewn together. She didn't say anything more but got on the train with Joe and found her seat. Then she looked at her watch.

"We've got ten minutes," she muttered, as much to herself as him. "You wait here. I'll be right back..."

As soon as Granny had gone, Joe slipped out of his seat and went over to the open door. He was curious. What was she going to do? He saw her scuttling across the concourse to the newsagent and a minute later she came out clutching something in her hand. Now she was hovering, waiting for something. Joe followed her eyes and saw the guard, still leaning against the train with his palm flat on the surface. Suddenly making up her mind, Granny moved towards him. She was going to do something, Joe was sure of it. But then a crowd of tourists appeared and for a minute, Joe's vision was blocked.

When he looked again, Granny was past the guard and walking back towards the train. The guard had been distracted by something but now he took his cigarette out, lit it and once again leaned against the train. Joe hurried back to his seat. He was sitting back with his eyes half-closed when Granny joined him.

Three minutes later, the train left.

Granny had brought a magazine with her

but she didn't read it. She was smiling to herself with that odd, dangerous light in her eyes.

Joe glanced at her handbag, which lay half-open on the seat beside her. There was a torn carton inside. What was it she had bought in the newsagent? Joe read one single word and shuddered.

SUPERGLUE.

They were delayed for one hour at Reading while they prised the guard off the train. He had run the whole way from Paddington, one hand glued to the side of the carriage. He was taken to hospital by ambulance to be treated for exhaustion, multiple blisters and shock. Granny watched through the window as the ambulance left.

"I hate being patronized," she said.

"Yes, Granny."

For the rest of the journey, Joe kept his mouth firmly shut.

Bideford was pretty enough, stretched out along a harbour with a few fishing boats moored on the other side of the parking meters. The taxi had brought Joe and Granny all the way from Barnstaple and as it cruised along the High Street he noticed two things. The first was that every single shop in the town sold Devonshire clotted cream. And the second was that there seemed to be an unusually large number of elderly ladies in the street – all of them with knitted hats and shopping trolleys.

"No wonder it's called Bideford," Joe thought to himself. "The place is full of old biddies."

The taxi turned right and followed a narrow, twisting road up a steep hill. At the top it stopped and Joe saw the hotel where they were staying.

It was a tall, double-fronted house, four floors high but with extra rooms built into the roof. The house was old but the owners had tried to modernize it with a revolving door (which looked ridiculous) and a white marble forecourt. The hotel advertised forty-five rooms "all with hot and cold running water" except that someone had crossed out the "and" and replaced it with "or". Apparently they had plumbing problems. It was called The Stilton International.

Granny paid the driver and she and Joe went in. The reception area was surprisingly large – the whole hotel seemed bigger inside than out.

While Granny checked in for both of them, Joe wandered between the artificial leather sofas and the wilting pot plants – the hotel was as hot as Granny's flat – and went over to a large sign on the opposite wall. It was made up of plastic letters, although some of the alphabet was evidently missing, and it read:

THE STILTON INTERNATIONAL
welcoMes grannies
TonigHt at 10.00pm in the
Elsie Bucket Conference Room
THe GOLDeN GRANNY AWARDS

"The Golden Granny Awards..." Joe muttered the words to himself and, looking
around him, he suddenly realized – with a
lurch in his stomach – that the hotel was occupied entirely by grannies. There were half a
dozen of them sitting in the reception area
reading magazines or nodding off to sleep. The
lift arrived and three more grannies got out,
whispering among themselves. Two grannies
met on the forecourt and Joe heard them greet
each other.

"Gladys!"

"Evelyn! I haven't seen you since ... 1942!"

"Fifty-two years ago, Gladys! You haven't
changed..."

"Haven't I, Evelyn, dear?"

"No! You're still wearing the same dress."

A coach had drawn up and another fifteen
grannies got out and formed a queue at the
reception, chatting excitedly among themselves. They were all carrying shopping trolleys
and old, heavy suitcases. But now Joe noticed
something else. It was very strange, but they
had brought what looked like scientific equipment along with them too.

One granny had a large test tube. Another had a Bunsen burner. A third granny had a series of twisting glass pipes while the granny behind her had some sort of electrical apparatus complete with copper wires, magnetic switches and complicated micro-circuitry. The last granny in the line was completely bowed down by something that could have come straight out of one of his science fiction books: it was like a glass and steel tuba with a whole series of levers and buttons and flashing lights. One of the other grannies was admiring it.

"You got an electro-static de-energizer!" she exclaimed. "How lovely! Where did you find it?"

"My grandson's a nuclear physicist," the other granny explained. "He made it for me."

"Did you tell him what it was for?"

"No. And fortunately he didn't ask."

Not one single granny had looked at Joe. He was aware that he was the only person in the building under seventy (even the receptionist was white-haired). Normally he would have expected the grannies to tussle his hair or tug at his clothes. But it was as if they were actually avoiding him. He felt their eyes settle momentarily on him but then dart away. Nobody spoke to him. They seemed almost afraid of him.

Something poked Joe in the ribs and he spun round to find Granny dangling a key in front of him. "Here you are, Jasper," she said. "You've got room 45. Go and unpack and I'll see you at dinner. And you be a good boy, now!"

Joe took the key and as his hand came into contact with the cold metal a shiver ran down his whole body. Granny's eyes had locked into his and for a moment he could see the hunger in them. He felt her eyes sucking him dry and at the same time the words "electro-static de-energizer" echoed in his mind. What did it do? What was it for?

And why was he so sure that it had something to do with him?

Room 45 was at the very top of the hotel, built into the roof with slanting walls and a small, low window. Joe quickly unpacked then set out to explore the Stilton International. He had never been anywhere quite like it in his life.

In the basement there was a swimming-pool, but the water was so hot that the entire room was filled with steam and he could hardly see anything. But there were grannies there. He couldn't see them but he could hear them, cackling eerily in the steam and pattering across the tiled surface like ghosts.

Near the swimming-pool there was a beauty parlour and Joe stared through the open door as one of the grannies lay back in what looked like a dentist's chair. The beauty specialist was a small, foreign-looking man with a wig and a moustache that didn't quite match. The granny he was working on already had two cucumber slices on her eyes, two straws up her nose and a thick white cream on her lips.

"Oh yes, Mrs Grimstone," he was saying. "To bring out the beauty of the skin, to give it back its youth, it requires the natural products only." He produced a bucket and scooped out a handful of something brown and steaming. "That is why I use only the finest quality buffalo dung. Rich in minerals and vitamins. High in protein. It will draw out the natural colour."

Joe moved away as the beauty specialist slapped the first handful of the stuff on Mrs Grimstone's cheek.

There was a fashion shop on the ground floor where Joe watched grannies trying on all sorts of brilliantly coloured clothes. One granny was standing in front of a mirror having squeezed herself – with great difficulty – into an impossibly tight leopard-skin leotard with a black top and brilliant red head-band which now matched her brilliant red face.

"Gorgeous, Mrs Hodgson," the shop assistant was crooning. "Quite gorgeous! You don't look a day over eighty-five!"

Next to the fashion shop was a health food shop. The window was filled with pills and bottles, strange roots and powders ... all of which were designed to make whoever swallowed them feel young again.

"I particularly recommend raw garlic and seaweed cocktail," the owner was saying. "Just two mouthfuls and I guarantee you'll find yourself running..."

"...running for the loo," Joe thought to himself and went on his way.

In the next twenty minutes, he covered the entire hotel and came to two inescapable conclusions.

The Stilton International had been built by grannies, for grannies and was run by grannies.

And everyone who came there wanted to be young again. They were obsessed with it.

So where, he wondered, did that leave him?

The thought was still on his mind as he joined Granny for dinner. This was served in a large room with ten round tables, each seating eight or nine grannies. Joe was joined by the four grannies he recognized from the card game at Thattlebee Hall – Granny Anne, Granny Smith, Granny Adams and Granny Lee – as well as two other grannies he didn't know. None of them spoke to him although Granny Adams spent several minutes examining him through her inch-thick spectacles until the first course was served.

The first course was quail's eggs. The grannies fell on them like wolves.

Joe remembered an old phrase he had once heard. "You can't teach Grandma to suck eggs." He could certainly see it was true now as the ninety grannies in the room grabbed the miniature eggs, smashed the shells against their plates, the tables or indeed each other and then sucked out the contents. Soon the whole room was filled with the sound of slurping as the balls of glistening white were vacuumed. Granny Smith – the fat granny – was enjoying hers so much that she wasn't even bothering to remove the shells. Joe wondered if there might be a prize for the granny who sucked the most eggs, and that made him think of the Golden Granny Awards he had seen advertised.

He turned to Granny. "What are the Golden Granny Awards?" he asked.

Granny looked at him suspiciously. "Never you mind," she snapped. "They've got nothing to do with you."

"Past your bedtime," Granny Smith added, picking a piece of eggshell out of her teeth.

"When is his bedtime?" Granny Lee asked.

Granny looked at her watch. "Now!"

"But…" Joe began. He glanced at the kitchen door, which had just opened. A waiter was carrying in a vast silver dish of poached eels with mashed potato. Joe blinked. "Maybe you're right," he said. "I am a bit tired."

Joe got up and left the room. As he went he

felt himself being followed by a hundred and eighty eyes (three of them glass). He saw one granny nudge another and point, heard a soft chuckle as his name was whispered. "Jordan ... that's the boy ... Ivy Kettle's boy..."

The first eels were being served as he left. Netted, boiled and stretched out on a plate... Joe knew exactly how they felt.

Of course, he didn't go to sleep.

At ten o'clock exactly he crept back downstairs, avoiding the lift in case the noise gave him away. The hotel was in half-darkness, the front doors locked, the reception area empty. The receptionist was still behind the desk, but she had fallen asleep.

10.00 p.m. The Elsie Bucket Conference Room...

Although Joe hadn't been inside the room on his tour of the hotel, he found it easily enough, following the sign out of the reception area and past the health food shop. As he padded along the thickly carpeted corridor towards a pair of heavy wooden doors, he heard a woman's voice, amplified by a microphone system but still muffled by the wall.

"And welcome, ladies and ladies, to the annual Golden Granny Awards..."

There was a round of applause.

Taking his courage – and the handles – in

both hands, Joe opened the doors and quickly stepped inside. He would never forget the sight that met his eyes.

The Elsie Bucket Conference Room was enormous. It was a long, low-ceilinged room with a wooden floor and a stage at the far end. It had seats for about two hundred and fifty people and every one was taken. Joe realized that as well as the grannies in the hotel other grannies must have travelled from all over the country to be here. There were grannies in every seat – two to a seat in places. There were more grannies standing at the sides and yet more grannies hunched up on the floor in front of the stage.

The stage itself was decorated with a rippling wall of gold in front of which hung a sign: THE GOLDEN GRANNY AWARDS. The awards themselves – little statuettes of golden tortoises – were arranged on a nearby table. There was a granny sitting at a piano whilst an elderly man addressed the audience. Joe thought he recognized him as someone who had once done magic tricks or something on television – but that had been about five years ago. His name was Dan Parnell and he was wearing a red dinner jacket and a silver bow tie.

Joe had entered the room at the very back. He slid behind a row of spotlights and watched with bated breath.

"As you know," Dan Parnell said, "every year we give out these awards to the grannies who have most distinguished themselves in certain fields."

"I've never been in a field!" someone shouted from the back and all the other grannies screeched with laughter.

"The tortoise lives for many, many years," the man went on. "And this is why our awards take the form of a tortoise. Do you know, ladies, that the combined ages of everyone in this room add up to twenty-two thousand, five hundred!"

This news was greeted by a huge round of applause, cat-calls and stamping feet. Joe watched nervously as the spotlights trembled and shook. Dan Parnell held up a hand for silence.

"Nobody wants to be old," he went on. "Let's face it! Being old is beastly. And it's not just the wrinkles and the false teeth." He pulled open his mouth to show his own which glinted in the light. "It's not just the aches and the nasal hair. What hurts is having to stand by and watch young people take over. That's what I hate. That's what we all hate."

There was another explosion of applause which went on a full ten minutes.

"But we can have our revenge!" Dan Parnell continued at last. "We can get in their way. We can upset them. We can do all sorts of things if we set our minds to it – and we can have a lot of fun. That's what these awards are about and without any more ado, let's get on with the presentation."

Joe peered out as Dan Parnell went over to the row of tortoises. The granny at the piano played a few dramatic chords. The grannies in the audience clapped and punched at the air with clenched fists.

"The first award is for the longest time getting on a bus. This award has been won this year by Rita Sponge who managed to take a staggering three-quarters of an hour getting on a 19 bus at Piccadilly Circus!" There was a burst of applause, but Dan held up a hand for silence. "And – wait for it – she then managed to spend another twenty-three minutes looking for her bus pass! An amazing one hour eight minutes in total!"

This time the applause was loud and sustained as Granny Sponge – a tall, drooping woman with wet, red eyes – came onto the stage to collect her award.

"The second award is for the longest queue in a post office. Again, another record, ladies and ladies. Forty-five people kept waiting for over half an hour in the Bath post office. And the man behind her actually had a nervous breakdown! Step forward Doreen Beavis!"

Granny Beavis was small and lively. She was so excited by her award that, having snatched it, she actually fell off the stage. But this only delighted the other grannies all the more.

"And now we come to the Elsie Bucket Difficult Shopper award. A very close result this year. Congratulations to Enid Crabb who spent the whole day in Harrods and had every single video recorder demonstrated to her three times without actually buying one. Also congratulations to Betty Brush for buying half an ounce of every single meat on display at her local supermarket, a performance that took three hours and kept sixty-one people waiting. But I'm afraid you were both pipped to the post by this year's winner, Nora Strapp, who spent so long complaining about a Biro she had bought at Woolworth's that the manager eventually committed suicide. Well done, Nora!"

Everyone applauded (apart from Enid Crabb and Betty Brush). Nora Strapp picked up her award and pranced off the stage.

Joe watched, unbelieving, as the other awards were presented. There was an award for the most unnecessary visits to a doctor and an award for the most absurd reason for telephoning the police. One granny picked up an award for causing the worst scene at a wedding whilst another was unable to pick up her award for causing the most violent argument in a family as she was still in hospital.

Joe's granny didn't win anything but

Granny Smith got an honourable mention for the most damage caused when trying to be helpful.

An hour later, the last award had been given and Dan Parnell had left the room to huge applause. Joe was just preparing to sneak back to his bedroom when another granny took the stage. She was older than anyone in the room. Looking at her, at the hundreds of wrinkles on her face, at the white hair reaching down to her shoulders and her trembling, claw-like hands, Joe would have said she was well over a hundred. There were terrible blotches on her cheeks. Her eyes were completely empty.

"And now…" she screeched – she had a terrible, sandpaper voice – "the moment we have all been waiting for! But before I go on, I must introduce our uninvited guest!"

Our uninvited guest…

Somehow Joe knew who the old woman was talking about and he went hot and cold at exactly the same time. She was gazing at him now, her eyes as welcoming as a shark's. He took one step back.

A huge net fell over his head, reaching down all the way to his feet. He looked up and realized that there was a balcony running along the back of the hall, that there were another ten grannies up there and that he had been observed from the moment he had come in. It had been they who had dropped the net. Now another four grannies ran forward and seized the corners. He tried to struggle but it was hopeless. He had been netted like a north Atlantic cod.

Joe squirmed and kicked, only entangling himself all the more. Somewhere in his mind he swore never to eat another fish-finger. But it was too late for that.

"Bring him forward!" the old woman cried.

With the cackling of the grannies all around him, Joe was dragged onto the stage.

THE GRANNYMATIC ENZYME EXTRACTOR

"You all know me," the oldest granny exclaimed.

Joe was on the stage beside her, struggling and straining. The grannies had not only tied him up – that would have been bad enough. They had also fastened him into a strait-jacket which they had evidently knitted themselves as it was made out of pink wool.

"My name is Elsie Bucket," the woman went on, "and I am the oldest granny in Great Britain. One hundred and six years old today!"

There was loud applause from the audience but Elsie Bucket did not smile. She held up a grey, skeletal hand for silence.

"Yes," she said. "I have received seven telegrams from the Queen. Seven telegrams! But have I so much as received one single present? Not on your nelly!" She sniffed. "So much for the Queen!"

She walked slowly to the front of the stage.

"I am old and like you, fellow grannies, I do not wish to be old. All my life I have thought about this. I was so afraid of being old that I never actually enjoyed being young. Fortunately, however, I was a brilliant scientist. It was I, for example, who invented the telephone. I can't tell you how angry I was when my sister rang me to tell me it had already been invented. Even so, I managed to invent the telephone bill. From there I went on to invent the electricity meter, the television licence and, later, the wheel-clamp.

"However, my greatest invention has taken me sixty years. It is here tonight. You, dear grannies, have all brought with you one component – as I asked you to in this very room last year. What a wonderful achievement! From a simple light bulb to an electro-static de-energizer, from a long-life battery to a teaspoon of nuclear fuel, you have all brought exactly what I asked of you. But here I must say a special 'thank you' to Ivy Kettle." Joe stopped struggling and glowered at his granny who was sitting in the third row with a smug look on her face. Elsie Bucket gestured at her. "It was Ivy who provided us with the single most important – and potentially the most difficult – component of all. He may be small and rather unhygienic. But he's real. He's alive (for the time being). And he's here. She brought us a boy!"

"A boy! Oh joy! A boy!"

The grannies had all gone into ecstasies like very religious people at a prayer meeting. Joe felt the blood rush into his face as they all gazed at him, screeching and clapping, pointing and grinning. One granny had become so excited that she had gone red in the face and keeled over in her chair – but everyone ignored her in the general chaos. Joe was certain that at any moment he would wake up in bed. It was all a nightmare. It had to be. To be tied up in a pink strait-jacket in a Devonshire hotel with over five hundred grannies hooting at you – that sort of thing just couldn't possibly happen in the real world.

Except that it had. This was no dream.

"And so, fellow grannies, no more talk! No more waiting! Let us do what we have so looked forward to doing. And let me show you my invention. Grannies – I give you … the Grannymatic Enzyme Extractor!"

There was a hush in the room as the gold curtain slid back and even Joe gasped when he saw what had been constructed there at the back of the stage.

At first he thought it was an electric chair. An ordinary wooden chair was indeed part of it with coils and wires twisting round the legs and vanishing under the seat. But there was much more to it than that. A maze of glass pipes and tubes zigzagged and spiralled away into a line of bottles, some of them empty, some of them filled with a dark green liquid. A circular gauge reading "EMPTY" in blue and "FULL" in red hung from a tangle of wires with a golden arrow waiting to travel the distance between the two. The object that looked like a glass and steel tuba – Joe had seen it briefly in the reception area – was now suspended above the machine. Joe realized it could be lowered onto the head of whoever sat there. It in turn was connected to a complicated metal structure surrounding the chair and – Joe swallowed hard when he saw this – there were no fewer than thirteen large hypodermic syringes pointing inwards, attached to it at different levels. Joe imagined himself sitting in the chair (somehow it wasn't very hard to do) and saw that there would be two needles pointing at his ankles, two at his knees, two at his thighs, one at his stomach, one at the small of his back, two at his elbows, two at his neck and one – the highest – at the centre of his forehead. The syringes, big enough to inject a horse, were built into gold, magnetic coils. All of them were wired up to work automatically.

The whole ghastly contraption was connected to a control desk a few feet away. This was made up of the usual array of dials and gauges, flashing lights and buttons that he had seen on every episode of *Star Trek*. The only difference was that it had also been decorated with a small lace cloth and a flower in a pot. There was a comfy armchair behind it for the operator to sit on.

"Take him!" Elsie Bucket commanded.

Joe lashed out as the four grannies who had captured him fell on him again, giggling and wheezing. But he was helpless. As old and as weak as they were there were four of them and he was pinioned by the strait-jacket. They pulled him, dragging his heels across the stage, and tied him into the chair. Two leather straps went over his legs, two more across his chest, one on each arm and a final one around his throat. There was nothing he could do.

He sat, facing the audience, half-blinded by the spotlights that were trained on him. He could just make out the small round heads staring at him like so many coconuts behind the glare but he was aware only of the thirteen needles pointing towards him. His hand grappled for a wire or a circuit he could pull ... anything to sabotage the machine. But he had been tied too tightly and the chair had been too well designed. Gritting his teeth, he slumped back. Now he could only wait.

"The Grannymatic Enzyme Extractor!" Elsie Bucket announced, moving into the light. "Last year, you will recall, we tested my elixir of life, the secret potion that would make me

113

and all my dear granny friends young again. Over one hundred ingredients had gone into my elixir of life! Avocado oil, ginseng, yoghurt, royal jelly, raw oysters, ox blood, iron oxide, zinc, milk of magnesia, yak's milk, cactus juice, the yolk of an ostrich egg and much, much more. But it didn't work. And why didn't it work? Because there was one missing ingredient.

"Enzymes are the stuff of life. Without enzymes there can be no life. And this boy's enzymes, added to my wonderful elixir, will turn back the clock and instantly return us to our glorious, wonderful youth! And what about this glorious, wonderful youth?" Elsie Bucket pointed at Joe. "Sadly, the operation will kill the child. But I am sure even he won't mind when he knows how happy he will be making all of us."

"I do mind!" Joe shouted.

Elsie Bucket ignored him. "In a minute I shall flick the switch," she said. "The machine will do the rest. His enzymes will be sucked out of him. They will travel down these pipes here…" She pointed them out. "They will be thoroughly disinfected and then added to my elixir here." She tapped on one of the jars of green liquid. "From just one boy I estimate we can make five hundred doses, enough for everyone here! By the time the process is over," she added almost as an afterthought, "the boy will be as shrivelled as an overcooked cocktail sausage. If you find this disturbing, I suggest you don't look."

"I find it disturbing!" Joe cried out. But Elsie Bucket was already leaning over him, lowering the tuba-contraption onto his head. "A little electro-massage," she whispered to him. "Very painful, but it helps the enzymes flow."

"You're mad!" Joe spat out the words.

"How dare you talk to an old lady like that!" Elsie Bucket smiled, her face close to his, and Joe saw her grey tongue loll out of her mouth like a dying slug, then curl back to lick her ancient, discoloured teeth and suddenly he was more sick than afraid.

"Now!" Elsie Bucket sang out the word.

"Now!" the grannies chorused.

"No!" Joe strained with every muscle but the straps that held him were too thick.

Elsie Bucket capered over to the control desk and sat down in the armchair. She raised her hands and flexed her fingers as if she were a concert pianist. Joe heard the bones clicking against each other.

Then she stabbed down.

The machine hummed and whirred into life. The green liquid bubbled. The light bulbs blinked and flickered. The leather straps around him seemed to tighten but perhaps that was his own body tensing up as it all began. Electricity buzzed through the tuba-helmet

115

which began to grow hot against his head. Joe clawed at the arms of the chair as slowly, one after another, the hypodermic needles shivered and then began to move forward. The arrow on the EMPTY and FULL gauge trembled excitedly. The whole thing was rattling and shaking, as indeed were all the watching grannies.

The hypodermic syringes slid forward.

Elsie Bucket yanked at a lever, her eyes bulging, her whole face twitching with delight.

The green liquid in the bottles surged and boiled. Electricity flickered. The needles moved again.

Joe opened his mouth to scream.

And then all the lights went out and everything stopped.

For a long moment nobody did anything. Then Joe heard Elsie Bucket's voice calling out of the darkness. "Don't panic, grannies! It's only a fuse. We'll have it mended in a moment!"

But even as she spoke, Joe was aware of someone close by him. He felt warm breath on his cheek. A pair of hands reached out to undo first the strap around his throat, then the ones on his arms. And at the same time a voice spoke to him. It was a voice he recognized, a woman's. But he still couldn't see.

"Run for it, Joe," the voice whispered. "Get out of here and get back to London. You can do it!"

The remaining straps fell away. The knitted strait-jacket was cut through with a single stroke. There was a pause and Joe realized that his mysterious rescuer had gone and that he was once more on his own. He stood up.

The lights came back on. The Grannymatic Enzyme Extractor shuddered back into life.

Elsie Bucket stood inches away, staring at him, her face twisted with fury. "Stop him!" she screamed in a voice that could have broken glass. "He's getting away!" At the same time she reached out to grab Joe herself.

Joe did the only thing he could. He twisted to one side and pushed Elsie Bucket away. Elsie gave a small, despairing gurgle and fell backwards into the seat of the Extractor just as the thirteen needles jerked forward like angry snakes. Joe didn't see what happened next. He was already running towards the edge of the stage, searching for a way out. But he heard Elsie Bucket's final scream as she was thoroughly punctured. He heard the great wail from the grannies in the audience. And he heard the sucking and bubbling as the Granny-matic Enzyme Extractor did what it had been built for.

Elsie Bucket had received her last royal telegram. The machine had attempted to extract her enzymes but having failed to find any had extracted everything else. There was nothing left of the granny apart from her clothes, punctured in thirteen places. These were now draped over the wooden seat with a few wisps of black smoke curling upwards into the light. At the same time a horrible grey ooze travelled along the tangle of pipes and spat itself out into the waiting bottles.

In the audience, the grannies moaned, yelled and bit each other, uncertain what to do next. The machine had finished with Elsie Bucket and was now vibrating dangerously, trying to tear free of the stage. A few yards away, Joe found a fire exit and, taking a deep breath, reached for the handle. He felt the cold steel under his hand and pushed. Mercifully, the door was unlocked. He felt the handle give and the door open and then he was out, tumbling into the night air.

And at that precise moment, the Granny-matic Enzyme Extractor exploded. Joe felt a fist of hot air punch him in the back. He was thrown forward, somersaulting twice and landing in a bed of flowers. He tried to stand up, then winced and covered his head as bricks, tiles, windows, wigs and false teeth showered down all around him. It seemed to go on for ever but at last everything was silent again and slowly, painfully, he got up.

The Stilton International had been partially destroyed. There was nothing left of the Elsie Bucket Conference Room. Nor could he make out a single surviving granny. It was like pictures he had seen of the Second World War – jagged broken walls, thick smoke, fires burning in the wreckage. Already the fire brigade and ambulance service had been alerted. He could hear their sirens in the far distance.

And then somebody moved, limping painfully through the smoke, coughing and spluttering. Joe tried to run but he had sprained his ankle and he could only wait there as the figure approached.

It was Granny.

Somehow Joe wasn't surprised that she had survived. But the explosion had not left her unharmed. She had lost a large clump of her hair and all her remaining teeth. Her arms and legs were covered in cuts and bruises and her twenty-seven-year-old coat hung off her in ribbons.

The two of them stood gazing at each other in the debris. At last Granny spoke.

"Are you all right, Jamie, my dear?"

"My name is Joe – and I'm not your dear!"

"Oh, yes you are." Granny's eyes flickered over to what had been the Elsie Bucket Suite. "We're very lucky," she said. "We seem to be the only survivors of an unfortunate accident…"

"An accident?"

"Oh, yes. It must have been the gas. Of course, that's what it was. Somebody must have left the oven on."

"I'm going to tell the truth!" Joe snarled.

Granny just smiled. "You could try telling your version of the truth, but do you really think anyone would believe you? A twelve-year-old boy? They'd think you were mad, Jeffrey. They'd lock you up."

Joe glanced at the wreckage of the hotel and realized that she was right. There would be nothing left of the Grannymatic Enzyme Extractor – and even if they managed to find a few tubes and valves, what expert would be able to work out what they were really for? Even as he watched, the flames leaped up, finding a way through the bricks and rubble.

Granny took a step nearer. Joe stood his ground. "Maybe you're right," he said. "But you can't hurt me any more. *I* know about you. And one day…"

"One day what?" Joe had been too kind, even now, to say what he was thinking. But now Granny said it for him. "One day I'll be dead? Is that what you're thinking?" She smiled toothlessly in the moonlight. Smoke from the ruined building curled around her legs. "Oh, yes. Even I won't live for ever. But don't you see, Joe, you'll never be rid of me. Because, you see, when I die, I'll come back. I'll come back and haunt you and there's nothing you'll be able to do."

"You're lying," Joe whispered. The fire engines were getting nearer. He could hear the

120

engines now, racing up the hill.

"Oh, no! The grave won't keep me lying down for long. I'll come back, you'll see. Just when you least expect it..." Her eyes blinked, black in the white light of the moon. "And then ... oh yes, what fun we'll have."

Half a minute later the firemen arrived with the police right behind them. They found one old lady waiting for them in the garden. She was standing next to a twelve-year-old boy lying flat out on the grass.

"You'd better look after my grandson," she said in a feeble, tearful voice as they wrapped a blanket round her and led her away. "He seems to have fainted. I suppose it must have been the shock."

GOODBYE, GRANNY

Mr and Mrs Warden returned from the south of France a few days later. They had not had a good holiday. Mr Warden had fallen asleep in the sun and was horribly burned. The top of his bald head was a glowing red and three layers of skin had peeled off his nose. He couldn't sit down without crying. Mrs Warden had been bitten by three hundred mosquitoes. Attracted by her body spray, they had invaded her bed and bitten every inch from her ankles to her ears. Her face in particular was dreadfully swollen. When Mr Warden had woken up beside her the following morning, he had actually screamed.

Wolfgang and Irma returned from Hungary the day after. They had enjoyed their holiday so much that in the four weeks they had been away they had forgotten how to speak English. They had brought everyone souvenirs of Hungary: a beetroot for Mr Warden, a book of Hungarian poetry for Mrs Warden and furry hats for Joe and Granny.

As for Granny herself, Joe had seen little of her after the events in Bideford. They had been released from hospital after one night's surveillance and had travelled back to London on the first train. The police had asked them a lot of questions but both of them had pretended they were asleep when the hotel exploded. Joe had hated doing it but he knew he had no choice. He was only twelve. Nobody would have believed him.

Even so, he got grim amusement from reading the newspapers the following day. He had always suspected you couldn't believe half the things you read in the papers but now he knew it was all a pack of lies.

300 GRANNIES PERISH IN HOTEL HORROR
FAULTY FUSE BLAMED FOR BIDEFORD BANG
BRITAIN GRIEVES FOR GRANNIES –
QUEEN MUM SENDS MESSAGE

He had stayed with Granny at Thattlebee Hall for five days but in that time he had barely seen her. When his parents got home, she had left without saying goodbye.

However, she had managed to play one last mean trick on him.

On Sunday, a new nanny arrived. Apparently Granny had interviewed and selected her personally before she had gone. The new nanny was a short, plain woman wearing no make-up and a dress that seemed to have been fashioned out of a potato sack. Her hair was grey, as indeed was the rest of her. Her name, she said, was Ms Whipsnade.

"Miss Whipsnade," Wolfgang announced as he opened the door to her.

"I said Ms," the new nanny exclaimed, dropping her suitcase on Wolfgang's foot.

It turned out that Ms Whipsnade had worked for sixteen years as a social worker before going into politics. She was a communist and had stood for Parliament seven times. At the last election she had got four votes against the winner's twenty-six thousand, five hundred and eighty. Even so, she had demanded a recount. Ms Whipsnade was also a strict vegetarian and actually wept when she saw Joe's leather shoes. Neither Mr Warden nor his wife were entirely sure about the new arrival but as Granny had already offered her the job, there wasn't much they could do. And so Ms Whipsnade was shown to her room – which she promptly declared a nuclear-free zone. She also tore off all the wallpaper in the mistaken belief that it had been printed in South Africa.

On the following Monday, much to his

relief, Joe went back to school. He had hardly slept at all since that night in Bideford and there were dark rings around his eyes. It wasn't just the horror of the Grannymatic Enzyme Extractor. That had almost faded in his mind. Much, much worse was his last encounter with Granny, outside in the wreckage. Her words seemed to hang like cobwebs in the darkness and her beady eyes and twisted mouth were somehow always there – just out of sight. He realized now that he was more afraid of Granny dead than he was of her alive.

And that of course was exactly what she had intended. Alone in his room, Joe counted the hours until daylight and the days until he would be back at school. There at least he would be surrounded by young, happy, normal people. He felt safer with other children. Other children were all right. Anybody old – the headmaster, the dinner lady, the caretaker, the lollipop lady – now belonged to another, twilight world. Joe looked at them and he was afraid.

Time passed and for a while everything was all right.

Then Granny fell ill.

Joe first heard the news one afternoon at school. After lunch he was called into the headmaster's study. The headmaster, a white-haired man of about sixty, was called Mr Ellis. He had been a teacher for forty-four years even though he was allergic to children. He was sitting in a large leather chair when Joe came in. "Do sit down, Warden," he said. "Sit down."

That was when Joe knew it had to be bad news.

Mr Ellis sneezed. "I'm afraid I have some bad news for you, Warden. It's your grandmother..."

"She's not dead, is she?" Joe exclaimed.

"No! No!" The headmaster was surprised by the boy's alarm. He sneezed twice more and tried to shrink into his chair. "No. But it is quite serious. Pneumonia."

"She can't die!" Joe whispered. "She can't!"

Mr Ellis blinked. "I have to say, it's rare to find a boy so fond of his granny," he muttered. He pulled out a handkerchief and dabbed at his eye. "It does you credit, Warden. I'm sure she'll be all right. But in the meantime, perhaps it would be better if you went home."

Joe returned home that afternoon. The new nanny was in his room, painting pink triangles on his walls to show her support for the gay movement. She had also donated his bed and all his books to the Cuban miners.

"How's Granny?" Joe asked.

Ms Whipsnade blinked. "Her name is Ms Kettle," she snapped. "As a term, 'granny' is both sexist and, worse, ageist."

"How is she?"

126

"I haven't heard. For some reason your parents refuse to speak to me."

For the next few days there were a lot of comings and goings at Thattlebee Hall. Car doors slammed at all times of the day and night and Mr and Mrs Warden seemed to speak permanently in whispers. Nobody told Joe anything and the first inkling he had that things were really serious was when he saw his Uncles David and Kurt arrive at the front door. The relations never came to the house unless it was for Christmas or a funeral and Christmas had been over long ago. Listening at the door, Joe learned that Granny's pneumonia had got worse and that her doctors had more or less given up hope. His uncles were already arguing about her will.

And then on Friday morning came the news. Granny had died in her sleep.

At breakfast, Wolfgang and Irma were both tearful. Meanwhile, Ms Whipsnade – imitating the burial customs of the Taramuhara Indians – danced in the garden and set fire to the summer house. Later that morning, as soon as the fire brigade had gone, Mrs Warden went to Harrods and bought herself a black Yves St Laurent dress with a crêpe tunic, silk veil and diamante trim. Mr Warden spent most of the time on the telephone. He then drank an entire bottle of champagne. Irma assumed he was drowning his sorrows but Joe wasn't so sure. Certainly his father was singing merrily enough when he was carried to bed.

The funeral took place on the Sunday. It was a terrible day. The weather had turned and the various relatives – the Wardens and the Kettles – had to battle their way into the cemetery against the howling wind and rain. It seemed that the entire family had turned out: Michael, David, Kurt and Nita were there along with Joe's four cousins (all in black shorts – the rainwater streaming in rivulets down their legs). But there were other relatives too: tiny Aunt Cissie, fat cousin Sidney and twitching Uncle Geoff. Then there was Uncle Fred who had flown all the way from Texas to be there and several other relatives whom Joe didn't recognize.

Wisely, the vicar kept the sermon short. The weather was just too horrible. After two minutes, Aunt Cissie was actually blown into the open grave by a particularly vicious gust of wind. The rain lashed down and all the colour ran out of Uncle Fred's suit – soon he was standing in a puddle of blue ink. About halfway through the service there was a great flash of lightning and Uncle David had an epileptic fit. The four cousins left early with chilblains. Even the vicar looked alarmed and managed to get most of the words wrong. All in all it was a dreadful affair.

But worse, in some ways, were the days that

followed. Joe had been left out of everything – as if he were too young to understand funerals, deaths and the rest of it. As for Ms Whipsnade, she had been fired after she had told Mrs Warden that her mother had not died so much as been recycled. A great silence had descended on Thattlebee Hall. It wasn't that the house was in mourning. That would have been perfectly understandable. No. It was something altogether different and more difficult to explain.

For his part, Joe was terrified.

"I'll come back…"

What could he do? He couldn't sleep. He couldn't even relax. He had lost so much weight that he had to look twice to find himself in the mirror. At any time he expected to see Granny return. How would it happen? Would she dig her way out of the grave and return, dripping mud and slime, to the house? Or would she come in the night, materializing suddenly above his bed and floating around the room? Not for a minute did he doubt that Granny would return. She had promised it and he had seen the certainty in her eyes.

Inevitably, Joe himself fell ill. His temperature shot up to one hundred and three and the sweat poured off him as he tossed and turned in his bed. He hadn't eaten anything for a week and his ribs were so pronounced that Wolfgang – much to everyone's amazement –

was able to use them to demonstrate his skill as a xylophone player. Doctors were called in and, after listening to Joe's feverish cries, announced that he had been traumatized by his granny's death. It seemed more than likely that he was about to join her.

Joe did have moments when he was cool and rational. It was at these times that he tried to work out what to do. He knew he was afraid – that he was actually being scared to death by the memory of what Granny had said. And he also knew he had to tell someone about it. That was the only way to bring the nightmare to an end. Tell someone and they'd be able to face it together. But at the same time he knew there was no one. He couldn't go to his parents. Mrs Jinks and Mr Lampy were both gone. He was on his own.

And then the postcard came.

It was addressed to him, written in neat, block capitals. On the front was a picture of Bideford. On the back was a simple message:

THE TRUTH WILL ALWAYS COME OUT.

That was all. The card was unsigned.

Joe thought long and hard. He knew he had heard the words before but he couldn't remember where. The only clue seemed to be the picture of Bideford. He had often wondered who it was who had freed him from the Enzyme Extractor while the lights were out, and had played the voice in his mind over and over again. He had always assumed that it must have been one of the grannies who had taken pity on him and who had perished in the blast. But now, looking at the card, he wasn't so sure. "The truth will always come out." Who had said that to him and when?

From that time on, Joe began to recover. It wasn't just the fact that he knew that, after all, he did have a friend. It was also his belief in what the postcard said. The truth was important. The truth mattered. It mattered more than the fact that he was only twelve and that his story was completely preposterous. People like Granny, all bullies in fact, only managed to survive because they lived behind the truth. Once people knew them for what they were, they would be powerless.

One evening, a week after the funeral, Joe got out of bed and went downstairs. His parents were in the sitting-room, watching television. It was *The Money Programme,* his father's favourite, but even so he pressed ahead.

Joe told them.

He turned off the television and told them everything that had happened since Christmas and the toy robot. He told them about the cream cheese tea, the death of Mrs Jinks and his suspicions about the death of Mr Lampy. Then he told them what had really happened in Bideford, what had caused the explosion and how he had escaped.

131

Mr and Mrs Warden listened to all this in complete silence but when he had at last finished, Mrs Warden stood up.

"Is that all?" she asked.

"Yes," Joe said. He cast his eyes down. The room was suddenly like a refrigerator. He could feel his mother's anger, chilling him.

"You do realize that's my mother you're talking about?"

"Yes."

Mrs Warden let out a single sob. "We'll discuss this in the morning," she said and walked out of the room with her nose in the air.

"Look where you're going!" Mr Warden shouted.

There was a loud clunk as Mrs Warden hit the corner of the door. Then she was gone.

"Now look what you've done," Mr Warden snapped. He did the same to his cigar even though it was only half-smoked. "Lost your marbles, have you?" he asked.

"Father..."

"I've heard some pretty daft stories in my time," he said. "But that one takes the biscuit. And on the subject of biscuits it's time for my hot milk. I'll talk to you in the morning, young man!"

Joe watched his father leave. For the first time in more years than he could remember he felt hot tears brimming on his eyelids. "I hate this house," he muttered. "I hate them all." He was still holding the mysterious postcard. Now he tore it into pieces. He didn't care who had sent it any more. Nobody would ever believe him. Nobody cared about him. He was nobody.

That was the truth.

Later that evening, Mr and Mrs Warden lay in bed. Mr Warden had decided against the hot milk and was sipping a glass of brandy instead. Mrs Warden was half-concealed under an ice-pack which was pressed against her face where the door had hit her.

"That story," Mr Warden muttered. "It was ridiculous."

"Ludicrous," Mrs Warden agreed.

"Outrageous."

"Monstrous."

"Your mother ... she would never have behaved like that!"

"Of course not!"

"No."

There was a long silence.

"She was rather horrible to me once or twice, though," Mr Warden murmured. "Of course, I adored her. She was your mother. But she could be ... difficult."

"I suppose so," Mrs Warden agreed.

"I mean, she never liked me," Mr Warden went on. "When I asked if I could marry you, she poured tea over me. And her wedding present to us. Twelve fish-fingers. That wasn't very generous."

"She could be worse," Mrs Warden murmured. "When I was a little girl, she made me share my room with two lodgers, one of whom – Mr Baster – had very unsavoury habits. And do you know, she never took me out once. Not in my whole life!"

"Really?" Mr Warden was genuinely surprised.

"Not even shopping. She never had any time for me. She once told me she didn't want children. She'd even tried to abandon me. She left me in a basket on the steps of a police station."

"Good lord! How distressing."

"It was very embarrassing. I was sixteen years old!"

Mr Warden reflected. "Your father adored her, though," he said.

"Yes. He did adore her. Only he forgot their anniversary once and she never spoke to him again."

"She was a hard woman."

"Oh, yes."

Both of them sat in silence again. Then Mr Warden scooped a cube out of his wife's ice-pack and added it to his brandy. "I suppose Jordan's story could be true, then," he muttered.

"Yes. I suppose so."

"I mean, she was a hard woman."

134

"Very hard."

On the mantelpiece, the clock struck ten although in fact it was half past nine. The clock had never worked properly since Granny, in a moment of anger, had stamped on it.

"Of course," he went on, "it's very sad, your mother passing away like that."

"It's devastating," Mrs Warden agreed.

"Tragic."

"Terrible."

"Too, too awful! I'll miss her..." Mr Warden took a large gulp of brandy.

"Will you?" Mrs Warden asked.

"Well, I will a bit." Mr Warden swallowed. "But to tell you the truth, my love, I wasn't a hundred per cent fond of her."

"Not a hundred per cent?"

"No."

"Fifty perhaps?"

"Well ... not even fifty." Mr Warden frowned. "I know it's a horrible thing to say, my angel. But no. If you really want the truth, I wasn't very fond of her at all."

Mrs Warden slid the ice-pack off her head. Most of it had melted now anyway. "Nor was I," she whispered.

"What?"

"Oh, Gordon! It's dreadful of me. She was my mother. But I have to admit it. It's true. I really didn't love her."

"I never looked forward to her visits," Mr Warden said.

"I dreaded them."

"I hated them!"

"I loathed them!"

Mr and Mrs Warden looked at each other. And in that moment – perhaps the first true moment they had shared together in twenty years of marriage – they understood many things.

The first was that they had lied to each other. The second was that they had lied to themselves. That was what was so odd and uncomfortable about this period of mourning. They weren't really mourning at all. They weren't glad that old Mrs Kettle was dead. They would never have thought that about anyone. But they couldn't honestly say that they would miss her – which was what they had been saying. That was all a lie.

Their marriage was full of lies too. They could see that now, sitting in bed with Mrs Warden's ice-pack dripping onto the electric blanket. And without saying anything they knew they had come to a crossroads. Mrs Warden was beginning to wonder if perhaps, just possibly, she hadn't treated her only child just a little bit like her mother had always treated her. And Mr Warden too was asking himself what sort of father he had really been. For that matter, what sort of husband had he been? What sort of man was he? Everything had been poisoned by lies.

And then both Mr and Mrs Warden had the same thought at the same time.

"That business about her ... coming back," Mr Warden said.

"She won't," Mrs Warden muttered. "I mean, let's be adult about this, Gordon, dearest. It's not possible."

"It's absurd."

"Nonsensical."

"Out of the question."

Mr and Mrs Warden edged closer to each other in bed. Mr Warden put his arms around Mrs Warden. Mrs Warden put her arms around Mr Warden. There was a sudden fizz, a flash and all the lights in the house went out as the electric blanket short-circuited. The two parents were plunged into blackness.

"She won't come back," Mr Warden's voice quavered in the dark. "She can't..."

But they were still clinging onto each other when dawn finally broke and the first fingers of light announced the next day.

GRANNY COMES BACK

Curiously, Granny wasn't actually dead. This is what had happened.

She had indeed been taken ill with a bad cold and, before she had even sneezed twice, she had telephoned for an ambulance to take her to hospital. By the time the ambulance men had arrived, she had decided she was too ill even to walk and had insisted on being carried to the waiting vehicle. It was then that something very unfortunate had taken place.

As the ambulance men carried her out of the block of flats a neighbour had chanced to walk past and asked them if they knew the time. Both ambulance men had lifted their wrists to look at their watches. In doing so, they unwittingly tilted the stretcher. This was a bad mistake. Granny gave a little scream and rolled off the stretcher, falling straight into a large puddle. The result was that by the time she arrived at the hospital, Granny's cold really had developed into a mild form of pneumonia and she had to be given a bed.

Even so, her illness was not life-threatening. The doctors were sure she would be able to go home in a day or two and left her quite happily sitting up in bed with a furry knitted jacket and the latest copy of *Hello!* magazine.

Now, Granny had been placed in an ordinary public ward – in the geriatric wing. There were eight beds there and each one was occupied ... indeed one bed actually had two elderly people in it, lying head-to-foot and foot-to-head – as ever, the National Health Service was finding it hard to cope. But despite the crowding, the nurses and doctors were as cheerful as possible, working long hours into the night, and nobody complained.

Nobody, that is, except for the woman in the bed next to Granny.

Her name was Marjory Henslow and she was a retired headmistress. Having spent her whole working life telling people what to do, she hadn't allowed retirement to stop her. She treated the nurses, the cleaners and her fellow patients like children, her face frozen in a permanent sneer of disapproval. She was a woman with opinions about everything and expressed them at all times of the day and night.

"Mrs Thatcher? A wonderful woman! She showed them in the Gulf War. That's what the train drivers need. A few Exocet missiles would soon show them what's what! I'd blow them all up. And the miners! I say we should close all the pits down. What's wrong with nuclear energy? Let's drop nuclear bombs on the miners and the teachers and the train drivers. Bing! Bang! Boom! When I was a headmistress I used to flog everyone. It never did them any harm. I even used to flog the other members of staff. And I flogged dead horses! Why not? A bit more flogging would put the Great back in Britain..."

This went on twenty-four hours a day (Mrs Henslow even talked in her sleep). It was hardly surprising that she alone in the ward had no flowers or grapes. Nobody visited her. Nobody liked her.

One evening she got talking to Granny.

"This is a horrible place," she said. "I wouldn't come here if I wasn't ill. These nurses! Some of them are coloured, you know. Not that I'm a racist. But, well, the Nazis did have *some* good ideas..."

"I suppose so," Granny agreed.

"This ward is so drab and uncomfortable." Mrs Henslow leant towards Granny. "Well, tomorrow I'm moving to a different hospital."

"Are you?" Granny quavered.

"Oh, yes. You see, I have private medical insurance. Well, there was some sort of mix-up and it's taken them a few days to sort it out.

140

But tomorrow I'm off to a private hospital out-side London. And I won't miss this place, I can tell you!"

"Lucky you," Granny scowled. It had to be said that the ward wasn't the most comfort-able of places.

"I am lucky. Tomorrow I'll have my own private room with a colour television and a nice view. The food there is absolutely deli-cious, I'm told. Brought in fresh from Harrods' Food Hall. You actually get a menu – not like here."

Granny thought back to her lunch that day. It had been battered fish. It had been served underneath a battered tin dish. It hadn't been very hot. And it hadn't been very nice.

"I've heard this hospital is so nice," Mrs Henslow went on, "that people actually make themselves ill to get in there. My neighbour's wife cut off her hand to be admitted and she said it was worth every finger!" Mrs Henslow smiled. "Of course I'm sure you'll get better *eventually* here. The NHS is wonderful really. If you're too poor to afford better."

By now Granny was dark red with anger – and when the doctor came round later, it was discovered that her temperature had gone up to one hundred and five. Everyone assumed of course that it was her pneumonia that had caused the rise. The doctor doubted she would even live to see the next day and this is what he had reported to Mr and Mrs Warden who in turn had called in all the relatives.

But as it turned out, it was Mrs Henslow who suddenly took a turn for the worse during the night and quite unexpectedly died. Granny was lying awake – she was too angry to sleep – and actually heard the other lady breathe her last.

And that was what gave her the idea.

Granny had been perfectly content in the public ward until Mrs Henslow had described the hospital she was being transferred to. Food from Harrods? Colour TV and a view? Why couldn't she go there? Why *couldn't* she? Granny gazed at the still and silent figure in the next bed. By chance, Mrs Henslow was wearing a very similar nightie to her own. She was about the same age. And it was true, was it not, that one very old lady in bed with the sheets drawn up to her chin looks very much like the next. Mrs Henslow had no relatives or visitors to give the game away. The nurses and doctors had for the most part avoided her. Nobody had examined her that closely.

So why not?

Why not indeed?

And so it was that Granny swapped beds with Mrs Henslow and the following morning it was Mrs Henslow's death that was reported to Mr and Mrs Warden while Granny, her eyes peeping out over the sheet, was carried into a waiting ambulance and transferred to the private hospital.

And for the next few days – while Mrs Henslow was buried in the raging storm – it was Granny who reclined on duck down pillows watching her own 22-inch colour television whilst popping grapes, lychees and other exotic fruits between her lips. It didn't even matter when she forgot to answer to the name of Mrs Henslow. She was old. She was ill. She was bound to be confused.

Nobody noticed. It had all gone exactly according to plan.

There was an awkward silence at breakfast the next day. Mr and Mrs Warden hadn't slept a wink and it showed. Mr Warden had eaten his muesli dry and then poured half a pint of milk over his toast and marmalade. Mrs Warden had cleaned her teeth with her husband's shaving foam and was quite literally frothing at the mouth. For his part, Joe hadn't intended to come down to breakfast. But he was fed up being ill and wanted to get back to school – which meant he had to start eating.

"Jordan..." Mr Warden said.

Irma, who happened to be passing at that moment, dropped her tray and gasped. In all the years she had been with the Wardens, she had never heard Mr Warden address his son at the breakfast table.

"It seems we have matters to discuss," Mr Warden went on. "I suggest we meet this evening."

"This morning!" Mrs Warden interrupted.

"I shall return early from work and we shall meet this afternoon," Mr Warden decided. "Half past four in the living-room. Irma will bake a cake. We shall have tea. As a family."

"As a family!" Irma exclaimed. "Are you feeling ill, Mr Warden, sir?"

"Yes. I am feeeling extremely ill as a matter of fact," Mr Warden replied. "But that is what we shall do."

After breakfast, Mr Warden went to work. Mrs Warden went shopping. And Joe stayed at home. His thoughts were buzzing. He had seen the change in his parents. It was incredible. It was astounding. Could it be that...? Somehow, had they decided to believe him? Joe got dressed and went out feeling more alive than he had in weeks.

But neither Joe nor his parents had a particularly nice day.

"I'll come back..."

Mr Warden tried to concentrate on his work in his office but Granny's words echoed over and over in his head. Where would she pop up? Under his desk? In his filing cabinet? Outside the window ... even if it was twenty-seven floors up? He reached for a cigar and rolled it against his cheek, taking in the aroma of the

144

tobacco. "You're being ridiculous," he muttered to himself.

Somebody touched him lightly on the shoulder. Mr Warden screamed and jumped three feet into the air. The cigar slipped and disappeared into his left ear. Then he saw who it was. It was his secretary. She was looking at him in dismay.

"Lock the doors," Mr Warden whimpered. "Lock the filing cabinets. Lock everything! I want to be on my own..."

"I'll come back..."

Mrs Warden was at the Brent Cross shopping centre. There wasn't anything she particularly needed but she often found that buying things cheered her up. Once, when she was particularly depressed she had bought three lampshades, a deck chair, an umbrella and two pairs of gloves without actually wanting any of them. She was in that sort of mood. She was thinking of buying a Swiss Army knife. It might come in useful if she ever decided to join the Swiss Army.

She was standing on the escalator, travelling up past the central fountain, when she saw the figure standing at the top, waiting for her. She blinked. The yellow cheeks, the crooked smile, the gleaming eyes ... it couldn't be! Mrs Warden stared. The escalator carried her ever nearer. It was!

"No!" she screamed. "Go away, Mummy!"

Turning round, Mrs Warden clambered down the up escalator, pushing the other shoppers out of the way. People were shouting at her, trying to stop her, but she ignored them. She just had to get back down. She could feel the metal beneath her feet carrying her the other way. It was like her worst nightmare come true. "No!" she wailed again, shouldering her way past a pair of newly-weds and scattering parcels and packages everywhere. Then somehow her foot got tangled in the escalator, she dived forward, turned a somersault and landed spread-eagled on the marble floor.

"Is she all right?"

"I think she's had a fit."

"She went mad!"

Security men were running towards her from every direction. With a soft moan, Mrs Warden looked back up the escalator. And there it was. What had frightened her wasn't Granny at all. It was a full-size cardboard cut-out of a dinosaur. It stood outside a video store with a sign reading "FANTASIA – BUY IT HERE". How could she possibly have made that mistake? Was she going mad?

The first security guard had reached her. Everyone was looking at her. Mrs Warden slowly began to laugh.

"I'll come back..."

Joe saw Granny everywhere. During the

course of the day she had popped out of the fridge, out of the toaster, out of the dustbin and out of the fireplace. She had risen, dripping water, out of the pond and clawed her way up through the lawn. The clouds had twisted themselves into Granny's shape. The birds in the trees had winked at him with her eyes. Twice, Irma had become Granny and even Wolfgang had momentarily borrowed her shadow.

It was all imagination, of course. The real horror was still to come.

That afternoon at four o'clock, Mr and Mrs Warden sat in the living-room with Joe and the tea that Irma had prepared. The Hungarian cook had decided that it was such an important occasion that she had gone quite mad. There were huge piles of sandwiches, home-made scones, sausage rolls, tea cakes, crumpets, cakes, biscuits and even a jelly. But no one was eating. Mrs Warden was a nervous wreck. Her hair was all over the place ... and not only on her head. Mr Warden had bitten all his nails and was now starting on his wife's. Even Joe was trembling.

"I have called this meeting," Mr Warden began, "because I have something important to say."

"Yes, that's right," Mrs Warden agreed.

Then the telephone rang.

Mrs Warden sighed. "I'll get it," she said.

She stood up and walked across the room. The telephone was standing on a little antique table. She picked up the receiver. "Hello? Maud N. Warden..." she said.

There was a moment's silence.

Then Mrs Warden let out a great scream and dropped the receiver as if it were a scorpion she had accidentally grasped. Everyone stared at her. Joe had never seen his mother like it. Her hair, already in disarray, was actually standing up on end, like in a cartoon. Her eyes were bulging. All the colour had drained out of her lips – including even the colour of her lipstick.

"It's her!" she screamed – but the sound came out as a hoarse, strangled whisper.

"That's nonsense!" Mr Warden muttered. "I mean. Really, Maud. It's not possible."

But Mrs Warden could only point at the telephone with a wobbling finger. "It's her!" she groaned again.

"What did she say?" Mr Warden burbled.

"She said ... she was coming back!"

"It's not possible." Mr Warden strode forward and snatched up the receiver. "Who is this?" he demanded.

Another pause. Joe waited silently. He hadn't breathed since the telephone rang.

Mr Warden's mouth fell open. Now he was holding the receiver away from him, as if it could suck him in down the wire. "No!" he

148

shouted at it. "Go away! We don't want you!" And with that he hung up – so hard that he actually broke the telephone into several pieces.

"It was her!" Mrs Warden whimpered.

"It was her," Mr Warden agreed. "I'd know that voice anywhere."

"What did she say?" Joe asked.

"She said she was much better now and she'd be here in half an hour."

"Much better?" Joe shuddered. "How can you be much better when you're dead?" Somewhere in the back of his mind he knew that the whole thing was ridiculous. Ghosts didn't announce their arrival by telephone. But seeing his parents as terrified as they were he decided to go along with them. It was better than being left on his own.

"Half an hour…" Mrs Warden whispered. And that was when the full horror of it hit her. "Half an hour!" she screamed.

"Pack!" Mr Warden yelled.

Exactly twenty-nine minutes later, the front door of Thattlebee Hall burst open and the Wardens tumbled out grasping two hastily packed suitcases. Mrs Warden had thrown on her favourite fur coat. Mr Warden was clutching his wallet, the family passports and his eighteen favourite credit cards. His car – a green Mercedes – was waiting for them at the front.

"In!" Mr Warden yelled, wrenching open the door and catching his wife with it on the head.

"Aaagh!" Mrs Warden cried.

"And me!" Joe shouted, piling into the back. He was actually enjoying all this.

"Quickly!" Mr Warden stabbed forward with the ignition key, missed and tried again. This time it went in. He twisted and the Mercedes coughed into life.

At the same time, a taxi appeared, rumbling up the drive.

"There!"

"No!"

"Aaagh!"

"Mummy!"

"Help!"

Granny – the ghost of Granny – was in the back seat. There could be no mistaking her, sitting there, gazing out of the window – back from the dead! And this wasn't a dream. The entire family was seeing her at the same time.

Mr Warden wrenched the gear-stick and slammed his foot down on the accelerator. The car leapt forward.

Granny, sitting in the back of the taxi, frowned and pursed her lips. She had been released, fully recovered, from the hospital just half an hour before. She had of course telephoned to say she was coming and had been quite unable to understand the hysterical reactions of her daughter and son-in-law. And where were they going now? One moment the Mercedes was tearing down the drive, heading straight for the taxi. Then it had swerved to one side, ploughed across the lawn and then burst through a hedge onto the main road.

The taxi stopped and she got out.

"That'll be eighteen quid, love," the taxi driver said.

With a snarl Granny slammed the car door behind her, breaking both the window and the taxi driver's nose. She strode across the lawn, her hands on her hips, and gazed at the hole in the hedge. They had gone. Left her. How could they?

Granny fell to her knees, lifted her hands to the sky and howled.

The storm broke a few minutes later.

EPILOGUE:
ANTHONY LAGOON

Anthony Lagoon was a cattle station in the middle of the Northern Territory of Australia. It consisted of a long, low wooden house with glass windows and a verandah which was the manager's house and four shacks for the workers. There was a water tower, a flaking metal cattle run and an airstrip. The nearest town, Mount Isa, was a two hour flight away. Nobody knew who Anthony was. But then the outback is full of people who prefer not to be remembered.

Mr Warden had bought Anthony Lagoon as soon as he had landed in Perth. He had seen it advertised for sale in the *Perth Exchange* and had made an instant decision.

"We'll be safe there," he said. "No roads. No telephones. No letters. She'll never find us."

And six days later, after driving all the way

across Australia to Townsville, around the one-way system and then west again, they arrived.

There were four jackeroos working on Anthony Lagoon – all of them men on the run. Rolf had poisoned his wife. Barry and Bruce were wanted for armed robbery. And Les had been hiding for so long that he'd forgotten what it was he'd actually done although, as he frequently told the others, it must have been something brutal. These were tough, brutal men. Rolf had only one leg. He'd lost the other in a car accident and hadn't even noticed for a month. Bruce chewed live bullets and Barry scoured saucepans with his beard. Les could rip a cow in half with his bare hands. They were four of the ugliest, most violent men you could hope to meet. They only had one string vest between them and played poker to decide who would wear it.

You'd think Rolf, Barry, Bruce and Les would have made mincemeat out of the new owners of Anthony Lagoon but the surprising fact is that they quickly warmed to them. But then the Wardens had changed beyond all recognition.

Mr Warden had taken off his business suit and put on a pair of jeans, a brightly coloured shirt and a ten-gallon hat that came down to his nose. After only a week he had acquired an Australian accent. Having been stuck in an office all his life, he now found he loved the fresh air. Although there were over one hundred thousand head of cattle on the station, he had decided to get to know each and every one of them by name.

After all her riding lessons, Mrs Warden quickly impressed the jackeroos with her excellent horse riding. They decided they liked her as soon as she had galloped twice round the paddock blindfold and backwards. Then she set to work rebuilding the compound, repairing the fences, planting a garden, putting pretty lace curtains into Bruce and Barry's bedrooms and generally making the place more like home.

Mrs Warden also taught Joe how to ride (she never called him Jordan now). Following her example, the four jackeroos decided to lend a hand with Joe's education and soon Joe knew everything there was to know about managing cattle and, for that matter, robbing banks.

Joe loved his life on the cattle station. He had so often dreamed of running away – to a circus, to the Foreign Legion, to wherever – that it took him a long time to realize that this was what he had actually done ... even if his parents had rather surprised him by coming along too. But now every day was an adventure as he galloped across the paddocks under the hot Australian sun, dodging down to avoid the tree-spiders and surging, waist-deep, through the lagoons.

It was hard work. The day started at five when Joe rode out alone to get the horses in. Joe had never seen the dawn before and he marvelled at the thousand shades of red that shimmered over the horizon as the sun climbed up into the sky. He loved the smell of the air and the great silence of the plains and rapidly forgot Latin, Greek, Algebra, Geography and just about everything else he had been learning at school. Joe worked all day until sunset. There was no television on the station but he didn't miss it. He actually went to bed tired, not because he had to. And every ache, every pain, every cut and every blister was precious to him because it was part of the adventure.

Naturally, Joe lost weight. He grew tall and muscular with broad, suntanned shoulders. Once a month, Rolf, Barry, Bruce and Les took him with them to Mount Isa and he would stay up late into the night, drinking and gambling. That was the best thing. He was an equal. Nobody treated him like a child any more.

News has a strange way of travelling in Australia, crossing huge distances without the help of a stamp or a telephone line. And the happiness of the Wardens was completed one day by the arrival of someone who had heard they were there and had decided to join them. As soon as he saw who it was, Joe understood everything: the strange figure he had seen at Paddington Station, the last-minute rescue at the hotel and the anonymous postcard.

The new arrival was Mrs Jinks.

"I thought I was doomed when the police dogs came after me," she explained, "and indeed I was bitten quite badly. But I was very lucky. Just as I burst through the bushes, a large rabbit appeared. The dogs decided they preferred the taste of rabbit to me and attacked that instead. I managed to climb a tree and waited there until everyone had gone."

"But you kept your eye on me after that, didn't you, Mrs Jinks," Joe said.

"Well, yes. I couldn't reveal myself, unfortunately – I was still wanted for theft, after all. But I was frightened to leave you on your own and when your granny came to look after you I knew something was going on. I followed you to Bideford in disguise and I was there at the Stilton International when they tied you to that horrible device."

"And it was you in the dark." Joe shivered. "It was lucky the lights fused."

"That wasn't luck at all. That was me. I turned the power off at the main fuse box and then crept onto the stage to untie you."

"I got your card," Joe said.

"Yes. I thought it was time your parents knew the truth. Of course, I couldn't tell them myself. So I hoped a little nudge would do the trick."

Mr and Mrs Warden were delighted to see Mrs Jinks. They knew now that they had been deceived and couldn't apologize enough. They immediately invited her to stay with them at the cattle station and Joe was delighted when she agreed.

And so time passed at Anthony Lagoon which was a very pretty place now with a duck pond, a village green, two English sheepdogs, a willow tree and a beautiful croquet lawn. Often, when the day's work was done, Mrs Jinks would stroll out with Joe and they would talk about what had happened.

"Do you think she'll ever find us?" Joe asked one evening.

"Who, dearest?"

"Granny. The ghost of Granny."

Mrs Jinks looked past the verandah where Mr Warden was pushing Mrs Warden on a swing and beyond over the outback to the deep red glow where the setting sun marked the end of the world. "No," she said. "I don't think so."

"I hated her." Joe shuddered. "Old people are horrible."

"No," Mrs Jinks corrected him. "There's nothing wrong with being old. Don't forget –

you'll be old one day. Nobody can avoid it."

"Well, I won't be like Granny," Joe said.

"Of course you won't," Mrs Jinks agreed. "If you're kind and cheerful when you're young, you'll be kind and cheerful when you're old ... only more so. Old age is like a magnifying glass. It takes the best and the worst of you and magnifies them. Granny was selfish and cruel all her life. But you can't blame her for being old."

"She could still find us here." Joe's eyes – older and more knowing – scanned the horizon. He shivered in the cool evening breeze.

"It doesn't matter any more," Mrs Jinks replied. "Even if she did find you ... you're ready for her now."

In fact Granny died two years later – this time for real. After the Wardens had left she had found there was nobody to look after her and had rapidly gone into a decline. This was her tragedy. All the spitefulness of her life had caught up with her and suddenly she was alone.

Her hair had never grown again after the accident and although she had been given new false teeth, they didn't fit, with the result that she couldn't talk or eat solids. She was moved to an Old People's Home next to a cement factory and spent the next two years on her own, sipping porridge through a straw. In an attempt to cheer her up, the matron of the home gave her a parrot. The parrot bit her. The wound went septic. And that was what finally finished her off.

That was a year ago.

But Granny is not forgotten. Deep in the heart of the Australian outback, the aborigines gather around a huge camp fire. Their black bodies are painted and they sit quite naked apart from a twist of cloth around their loins. Then the music of the didgeridoo throbs and wails through the darkness and if the magic is working a figure appears, wrapped in a thick coat against the desert chill. The aborigines see her scowling in the light of the fire, her eyes glowing, her mouth opening and closing as she chews on her invisible feast. They call her "old-woman-walk-by-night".

It is Granny. Looking for Joe.

But she hasn't found him yet.

ANTHONY HOROWITZ

WALKER BOOKS
AND SUBSIDIARIES
LONDON • BOSTON • SYDNEY • AUCKLAND

For Jill, with love

CONTENTS

BEAUTIFUL WORLD

The white Rolls Royce made no sound as it sped along the twisting country road. It was the middle of summer and the grass was high, speckled with wild poppies and daisies. Sunlight danced in the air. But the single passenger in the back of the car saw none of it. His head was buried in a book: *My 100 Favourite Equations*. As he flicked a page, he popped another cherry marzipan chocolate into his mouth, the fourteenth he had eaten since Ipswich. The automatic window slid open and yet another chocolate wrapper was whipped away by the wind. It twisted briefly in the air, then fell. By the time it hit the ground, the Rolls was already out of sight. And Thomas Arnold David Spencer was a little nearer home.

Thomas Arnold David – Tad for short – was thirteen years old, dressed in grey trousers that were a little too tight for him, a striped tie and blue blazer. He had short black hair, rather too neatly combed, and deep brown eyes. He was returning home from Beton College on this, the first day of the summer holidays. It was typical of Tad that he should have started his homework already. Tad loved homework. He was only sorry he hadn't been given more.

The Rolls Royce paused in front of a set of wrought-iron gates. There was a click and the gates began to open automatically. At the same time, a video camera set on a high brick wall swivelled round to watch the new arrival with a blank, hostile eye. Beyond the gates, a long drive stretched out for almost half a mile between lawns that had been rolled perfectly flat. Two swans circled on a glistening pond, watching the Rolls as it continued forward. It passed a rose garden, a vegetable garden, a croquet lawn, a tennis court and a heated swimming pool. At last it stopped in front of the fantastic pile that was Snatchmore Hall, home of the Spencer family. Tad had arrived.

The chauffeur, a large, ugly man with hooded eyes, crumpled cheeks and a small, snub nose, got out of the car and held the door open for Tad. "Glad to be home, Master Spencer?"

"Yes, thank you, Spurling." Tad's voice was flat, almost emotionless. "Rather."

"I'll take your cases to your room, Master Spencer."

"Thank you, Spurling. Just leave them on the bed."

Tad went over to the swimming pool, where a bored-looking woman was lying on a sun-lounger, gazing at herself intently in a small mirror. This was his mother, Lady Geranium Spencer.

"Good afternoon, Mother," Tad said. He knew not to kiss her. It would have ruined her make-up.

"Oh hello, dear." His mother sighed. "Is it the holidays already?"

"Yes."

"Oh. I thought it was next week. What do you think of the nose?"

"It's jolly good, Mother. They've moved it a little, haven't they?"

"Yes. Just a teensy-weensy bit to the left." Lady Spencer had visited no fewer than six plastic surgeons that summer and each one of them had operated on her nose, trying to give her the exact look she required. Now she was sure she had at last got it right. The only trouble was that she wasn't allowed to sneeze until Christmas. "How was school, darling?" she asked, putting the mirror away.

"It was fine, thank you, Mother. I came first in French, English, Chemistry, Maths and Latin. Second in Ancient Greek and Geography. Third in..."

"Ah! Here's Mitzy with the tea!" his mother

167

interrupted, stifling a yawn. "Just what I fancied. A teensy-weensy tea."

The front door of the house had opened and a trolley, piled high with cakes and sandwiches, had appeared, seemingly moving by itself. As it drew closer, however, a tiny woman could be seen behind it, wearing a black dress with a white apron. This was Mitzy, the family's servant for the past forty years.

"Hello, Master Tad!" she gurgled breathlessly as she heaved the trolley to a halt. It was so heavy it had left deep tyre-tracks across the lawn.

"Hello, Mitzy." Tad smiled at her. "How are you?"

"I can't complain, Master Tad."

"And Bitzy?" This was Mitzy's husband. His real name was Ernest but he had been given his nickname after he'd been blown to pieces by a faulty gas main.

"He's still in hospital." Mitzy sighed. "I'm seeing him on Sunday."

"Well, do give him my regards," Tad said cheerfully, helping himself to a smoked salmon roll.

Mitzy limped back to the house while Tad ate. Lady Spencer cast a critical eye at her son. "Have you put on weight?" she asked.

"Just a little, Mumsy. I'm afraid you're going to have to buy me a completely new uniform for next term. This one's much too tight."

"What a bore! That's the third this year."

"I know. The elastic on my underpants snappped during the headmaster's speech. It was rather embarrassing..."

Just then there was a loud bark and a dog bounded across the lawn towards Tad and his mother. It was a Dalmatian – you could easily tell that from its black and white coat – but it was like no Dalmatian you had ever seen.

For a start it was huge. Its teeth were incredibly sharp and its mouth, instead of grinning in the friendly way ordinary Dalmatians do, was twisted in an ugly frown. The reason for all this was that the Spencers had taken the unfortunate dog to a vet who had turned it into a killing machine, filing down both its teeth and its claws until they were needle-sharp. The last burglar who had tried to break in had needed 107 stitches when Vicious had finished with him. In the end the police surgeon had run out of thread and had been forced to use glue.

But Vicious recognized Tad. Panting and whimpering, the dog sat down and raised a paw, its eyes fixed on the tea trolley.

"Hello, Vicious. How are you?" Tad reached out with an éclair. The dog leapt up and half of Tad's arm disappeared down its throat as Vicious sucked the éclair free.

"You spoil that dog," his mother remarked.

After tea, Tad went up to his room, taking the elevator to the third floor. Spurling had carried his cases up and Mrs O'Blimey, the Irish housekeeper, had already unpacked them. Tad sat down on his four-poster bed and looked around him contentedly. Everything was where it should be. There were his two computers and fourteen shelves of computer games. There was his portable television plugged into his own video recorder and satellite system. His favourite books (Dickens and Shakespeare) bound in leather and gold, stretched out in a long line over his butterfly collection, his stereo and interactive CD system and his tank of rare tropical fish. Then there were nine wardrobes containing his clothes and next to them a door leading into his private bathroom, sauna and Jacuzzi.

Tad stretched out his arms and smiled. He had the whole summer holiday to look forward to. As well as the country house in Suffolk, there was the villa in the South of France, the penthouse in New York and the mews house in Knightsbridge, just round the corner from Harrods. He unbuttoned his jacket and took it off, letting it fall to the floor. Mrs O'Blimey could pick it up later. It was time for dinner. And soon his father would be home.

In fact Sir Hubert Spencer didn't get in until after nine o'clock. He was a large, imposing man with wavy silver hair and purple blotches in his cheeks, nose and hands. He was dressed, as always, in a plain black suit cut from the very finest material. As he strode into the room and sat down he pulled out an antique pocket watch and glanced at the face.

"Good evening, Tad," he said. "Good to see you. Now. I can give you nine and a half minutes..."

"Gosh! Thank you, Father."

Tad was delighted. He knew that his Father was a busy man. In fact, business ruled his life.

Ten years ago, Sir Hubert Spencer had set up a chain of shops that now stretched across England, Europe and America. The shops were called simply "Beautiful World" and sold soaps, shampoos, body lotions, sun creams, vitamins, minerals, herbs and spices ... everything to make you feel beautiful inside and out. What made these shops special, however, was that the ingredients for many of the products came from the Third World – yak's milk from the mountain villages of Tibet, for example, or crushed orchids from the tropical rain forests of Sumatra. And all the shops carried a notice in large letters in the window:

> **NONE OF OUR
> PRODUCTS
> ARE TESTED ON
> ANIMALS**

Sir Hubert had realized that people not only wanted to look good, they wanted to feel good too. And the better they felt, the more they would spend and the richer he would become.

Sir Hubert never stopped. He was always developing new products, finding new ingredients, dreaming up new advertising ideas, selling more products. It was said that while he was being knighted by the queen, two years before, he had managed to sell her ten gallons of face-cream and a lifetime's supply of Japanese seaweed shampoo. He had appeared on the front page of all the newspapers after that. Because, despite his great wealth, Sir Hubert was very popular. "Good old Sir Hubert!" people would shout out if they saw him in the street. "He may be stinking rich, but he's all right."

The reason for this popularity – and also for his knighthood – was his charity work. At about the same time that he had set up Beautiful World he had started a charity called ACID. This stood for The Association for Children in Distress and was based in London. ACID aimed to help all the young people who had run away or been abandoned in the city, giving them shelter and providing them with food or clothes. Tad himself had donated two pairs of socks and a Mars bar to the charity. He was very proud of his father and dreamed of the day when, maybe, he would be knighted too.

"Sorry I'm late," Sir Hubert announced now as he sat himself down in his favourite armchair beside the fire with Vicious curled up at his feet. "We've got problems with our new Peruvian cocoa-leaf bubble bath. Not enough bubbles. We may have to do more tests..." He turned to Spurling, who was standing beside him. "Have you poured me a brandy, Spurling?"

"Yes, Sir Hubert."

"Have you warmed it for me?"

"Yes, Sir Hubert."

"Well, you can drink it for me too. I haven't got time."

"Certainly, Sir Hubert." Taking the glass, the chauffeur bowed and left the room.

Sir Hubert turned to Tad, who was playing Scrabble with Lady Spencer. Tad was a little annoyed. He had a seven-letter word but unfortunately it was in Ancient Greek. "So, Tad," he exclaimed. "How was school?"

"Jolly good, Father. I came first in French, English, Chemistry, Maths and Latin. Second in..."

"That's the spirit!" Sir Hubert interrupted. "Now. What have you got planned for the summer holiday?"

"Well, I was thinking about going on safari in Africa, Father."

"Didn't you do that last holidays?"

"Yes. But it was rather fun. One of the guides got eaten by a tiger. I got some great photos."

"I thought you wanted to go to the Red Sea."

"We could do that afterwards, Father."

"Oh – all right." Sir Hubert turned to his wife. "You'd better take the boy to Harrods and get him some tropical clothes," he said. "Oh – and some scuba-diving lessons."

"And there is one other thing, Father."

"What's that, Tad?" There was a jangling sound from Sir Hubert's top pocket and he pulled out one of his mobile phones. "Could you hold the line, please," he said. "I'll be with you in ninety-three seconds."

Tad took a deep breath. "Rupert said he'd come up this week. You know – he's my best friend. And we thought we might go to Maple Towers together."

"Maple Towers?"

"It's that new theme park that's just opened. It's got an amazing new ride – the Monster. Apparently it's almost impossible to go on it without being sick…"

"A theme park?" Sir Hubert considered, then shook his head. "No. I don't think so."

"What?" Tad stared at his father. Perhaps unsurprisingly "no" was his least favourite word.

"No, Tad. These theme parks seem very vulgar to me. Why don't you go horse–racing at Ascot?"

"I'll do that too, Father."

"What about flying lessons? You've hardly touched that two-seater plane I bought you..."

"I will, Father, but..."

"No. I don't want you going on those rides. They're dangerous and they're noisy. And all those people! You're a sensitive boy, Tad. I'm sure they're not good for you."

"But, Father! Mother...!"

"I have to agree with your father," Lady Spencer said. She looked at her Scrabble letters which she had been studying for the past ten minutes. "Is Zimpy a word?" she asked.

Tad was in a bad mood when he went to bed. Dressed in his brand new silk pyjamas, he flicked off the light and slid himself between the crisply laundered Irish linen sheets. The trouble was that he was a boy who had everything. And he was used to having everything. He expected it.

"It's not fair," he muttered. His head sank back into his goose-feather pillow. Moonlight slid across the wall and onto his pale, scowling face. "Why can't I go to the theme park? Why can't I do what I want to do?"

Suddenly Snatchmore Hall seemed like a prison to him. His parents, his great wealth, his school and his surroundings were just the shackles that bound him and he wanted none of it.

"I wish I was somebody else," he muttered to himself.

And 127 million light years away, a star that had been burning white suddenly glowed green, just for a few seconds, before burning white again.

But Thomas Arnold David Spencer hadn't seen it. He was already asleep.

THE CARAVAN

Tad knew something was wrong before he'd even opened his eyes.

First there was the sound, a metallic pattering that seemed to be all around him: frozen peas falling on a tin plate. That was what had woken him up. At the same time he became aware of the smell. It was a horrible smell – damp and dirty – and the worst thing was that it seemed to be coming from him. He moved slightly and that was when he knew that something had happened to the bed too. The sheets were wrinkled and rubbed against his skin like old newspaper. And the pillow…?

Tad opened his eyes. His face was half buried in a pillow so utterly disgusting that he was almost sick. It was completely shapeless, stuffed with what felt like old rags. It had no cover and, though it might once have been white, it was now stained with dried-up puddles of sweat and saliva, various shades of yellow and brown. Tad pushed it off his face, gasping for air.

He looked up, staring through the grey light. But what he saw made no sense. His brain couldn't take it in. He lay there, unable to move.

Instead of the chandelier that should be hanging over his bed, there was a neon tube with a tangle of naked wires twisting out of a broken plastic fitting. The sound of the frozen peas, he now realized, was rain hitting the walls and the ceiling. He was lying in a small bed in the corner of a small room in … it had to be a caravan. He could tell from the shape of the walls. There was a window with no curtains but he couldn't see out because the glass was the frosted sort that you sometimes get in bathrooms or toilets. The room was very cold. Tad drew his legs up and the bed creaked and groaned.

The room was only a little larger than the bed itself, divided from the rest of the caravan by a plastic-covered wall with a door. Somebody had left some clothes crumpled in a heap on the floor. A pair of torn and soiled jeans poked out from a tangle of T-shirts, socks and underwear. There were also some comics, a battered ghetto-blaster and a few toys, broken, missing their batteries.

How had he got here? Tad tried to think,

tried to remember. He had gone to bed like he always did. Nothing had happened. So how...? There could only be one answer. He had been kidnapped. That had to be it. Someone had broken into Snatchmore Hall getting past the wall, the moat, the security system and the dog, had drugged him while he was asleep and kidnapped him. He had read about this sort of thing happening. His father would have to pay some money – a ransom – but that was no problem because Sir Hubert had lots of money. And then he would be allowed to go home.

The more Tad thought about it, the more relieved he became. In fact, it was almost exciting. He'd be on the television and in all the newspapers: MILLIONAIRE'S SON IN RANSOM DEMAND, BOY HERO RETURNS HOME SAFE. That would certainly be something to tell them when he got back to school! And when the kidnappers were finally caught (as of course they would be), he would have to go to court. He would be the star witness!

Tad glanced at his watch, wondering what time it was. The watch was gone. That didn't surprise him. It was a Rolex, solid gold, with built-in calendar, calculator and colour TV. His mother had given it to him a year ago to thank him for tidying his room when Mrs O'Blimey was off sick. The wretched kidnappers must have taken it. (They also seemed to have taken his silk pyjamas – he was wearing only pants and a black T-shirt that was several sizes too big.) Tad lowered his hand – then raised it again. Was he going mad ... or was his wrist thinner than it had been? With an uneasy feeling in his stomach, he closed his third finger and his thumb in a circle around where his watch had once been. They met.

Tad began to tremble. How long had he been in the caravan? Could it have been weeks – even months? How had he managed to lose so much weight?

Cautiously, he swung himself out of the bed. His bare feet came to rest on a carpet so old and dirty that it was impossible to tell what colour it had once been. The smell of stale cigarette smoke hung in the air. Tip-toeing, one step at a time, he crossed the room, making for the door.

His hand – the hand was thinner too, just like his wrist – closed round the doorknob and slowly he turned it. The door was unlocked. Tad opened it and stepped into a second room, larger than the first and shrouded in darkness.

This room was dominated by a large, fold-down bed – he could just make out its shape as his eyes got used to the gloom – and now he realized there were two people inside it, buried beneath a blanket that rose and fell as they breathed. One of the figures was snoring loudly. Tad was sure it was a woman. Her

180

breath was rattling at the back of her throat like a cat-flap in the wind. The man next to her muttered something in his sleep and turned over, dragging the cover with him. The woman, still asleep, groaned and pulled it back again. Tad stepped forward, his foot just missing an empty whisky bottle on the floor. The wall on the other side of the room was nothing more than a ragged curtain, hanging on a rail. He had to get to it before the two people – his kidnappers – woke up.

He forced himself to take it slowly, making no sound. He was helped at least by the rain. It was coming down more heavily now, striking the metal skin of the caravan and echoing throughout, the noise masking the sound of his own footsteps as he edged round the bed. At last he reached the curtain. He padded at the material until he found a gap and, with a surge of relief, passed through.

He found himself now in the third and last section of the caravan. It was without doubt the most disgusting part of all.

It was a kitchen, shower and toilet combined, with all the different articles of those rooms jumbled up together. There were dirty pots and pans stacked up in the shower and used, soggy towels next to the sink. A roll of toilet paper had unspooled itself over the oven and there were two grimy bars of soap, a razor and a toothbrush on the hob. Unwashed plates, thick with food from supper the night before, lay waiting on a shelf over the toilet while the oven door hung open to reveal two flannels, a sponge shaped like a duck and a hairbrush that was matted with curling black hair. All the walls and the ceiling were coated with grease and there were pools of water and more hair on the floor. Tad was amazed that anyone could live like this. But it wasn't his problem. He just wanted to get out.

And there was the front door! He was amazed that it was as easy as this. All he had to do was get out the door and run. He would make it to the nearest telephone and call the police. Tad took one step forward. And that was when he saw the other boy.

The boy was thin and pale and about a year younger than Tad. He had long fair hair that hung in greasy strands over a rather sickly looking face dotted with acne. His right ear was pierced twice with a silver ring and a stud shaped like a crescent moon. The boy could have been handsome. He had bright blue eyes, full lips and a long, slender neck. But he looked hungry and dirty and there was something about his expression that was pinched and mean. Right now he was standing outside the caravan, staring at Tad through a small window.

Tad opened his mouth to cry out. The boy did the same.

And that was when Tad knew, with a sense of terror, that he wasn't looking at a window. He was looking at a *mirror*. And it wasn't a boy standing outside the caravan. It was his reflection!

It was him!

Tad stared at himself in the mirror, watched his mouth open to scream. And he did scream – a scream that wasn't even his voice. His hands grabbed hold of his T-shirt and pulled it away from him as if he could somehow separate himself from the body that was beneath it.

His body.

Him.

Impossible!

"Whass all this racket, then? Whass going on?"

Tad spun round and saw that the curtain had been pulled back. Before him stood a man, wearing a pair of stained pyjama trousers but no top. His naked stomach was dangling over the waistband, a nasty rash showing round the belly button. The man's face was pale and bony and covered with a gingery stubble that matched what was left of his hair. His eyes were half-closed. One of them had a sty bulging red and swollen under the lid. There was a cigarette dangling from his lips and Tad realized with a shiver of disgust that he must have slept with it there all night.

"Who are you?" Tad gasped.

"Whaddya mean who am I? What the devil are you talking about?"

"Please. I want to go home..."

The man stared at Tad as if trying to work him out. Then suddenly he seemed to understand. A slow, nasty smile spread across his face, making the cigarette twitch. "You been at the glue again," he muttered.

"What?" Tad's legs were giving away beneath him. He had to lean against the wall.

Then a voice called out from the other side of the curtain. "Eric? What is it?" It was a woman's voice, loud and shrill.

"It's Bob. 'e's been sniffing the glue again. I reckon 'e's 'ad an 'ole tube full. And now 'e doesn't know 'oo 'e is or where 'e is."

"Well, slap some sense into 'im and throw 'im in the shower," the voice cried out. "I want my breakfast."

"I'm not Bob," Tad whimpered. "There's been a mistake."

But before he could go on, the man had grabbed hold of him, one hand closing around his throat. "There was a mistake all right!" the man snarled. "And what was it? Bostik? Araldite? Well, you'd better get your head in order, you little worm. 'cos it's your turn to wash up and make the breakfast!" And with that, the man threw Tad roughly into the corner, spat out the cigarette and went back into the bedroom, drawing the curtain behind him.

Tad stayed where he was for a long time. His heart was racing so fast that he could hardly breathe. He looked at his hands again, his stomach, his legs. With trembling fingers, he touched his cheeks, his eyebrows, his hair, tugged at the two pins in his right ear. He let his hands fall and gazed at his palms. He knew, even without understanding why, that he had never seen those hands before. They weren't his hands.

Somehow, something horrible had happened. He had gone to sleep as Tad. *But he had woken up as Bob.*

A few minutes later the curtain was drawn back and a woman came out.

She was one of the ugliest women Tad had ever seen. For a start, she was so fat that the caravan rocked when she moved. Her legs, swathed in black stockings, were thin at the ankles but thicker than tree-trunks by the time they disappeared into her massive, exploding bottom. She had arms like hams in a butcher's shop and as for her face, it was so fat that it seemed to have swallowed itself. Her squat nose, narrow eyes and bright red lips had sunk into flabby folds of flesh. Her hair was black and tightly permed. She wore heavy plastic earrings, a wooden necklace and a variety of metal bangles, brooches and rings.

She took one look at Tad and shook her head. The earrings rattled. "Gawd's truth!" she muttered to herself. Then suddenly she lashed out with her foot. Tad cried aloud as her shoe caught him on the hip. "All right, you," the woman exclaimed. "If you're not going to 'elp, you can clear out. Go out and be sick or something. That'll sort you out."

"Please…" Tad began, getting to his feet.

"I told you that glue was no good for you. But would you listen? No! You get yourself dressed…" The woman snatched a handful of clothes from the top of the fridge and threw them at Tad. "Now get out, Bob. I don't wanna see you again until you got yourself sorted."

"No. You don't understand…"

But the woman had clenched her fist and Tad realized she didn't want to know. Clutching the clothes, he scrabbled for the door, found the handle and turned it. Behind the woman, the man had appeared, now wearing a knitted shirt and jeans and smoking a fresh cigarette. He saw what was happening and laughed. "You show 'im, Doll!" he called out.

"Shut up!" his wife replied.

Tad fell through the door and into his new world.

THE FUNFAIR

Tad was standing in the middle of a fair that had been set up on a patch of lumpy ground near a main road. There were about a dozen rides and the usual shooting galleries and sideshows. But everything was so old and broken down, with flaking paint and broken lightbulbs, that it didn't look fun at all. The fair was completely encircled by a cluster of caravans and trucks, some with electric generators. Thick cables snaked across the ground, joining everything to everything in a complicated tangle. There was nobody in sight.

Although the rain had eased off, it was still drizzling and this, along with the grey light of early morning, only made the scene more wretched. Tad felt the water dripping down his arms and legs and remembered that he was almost naked. Hastily he sorted out the clothes the woman had thrown him; a pair of jeans, faded and torn at the knees, a jersey, socks and trainers. Holding them up in front of him, Tad knew at once that they were much too small. There was no way they could possibly fit him. But when he did finally pull them on, they did!

Tad looked back at the caravan. It was one of the largest in the fair. Once it had been white but rust had eaten away most of the paintwork and dirt covered what little was left. The door was still firmly shut but there was a buzzer next to it and below that a slip of paper under a plastic cover. It read:

ERIC AND DOLL SNARBY

Doll. That was what the man had called the woman. Next to the name-plate somebody had added three letters, gouging them into the side of the caravan.

BOB

Tad ran his finger along it and swallowed hard. Bob Snarby. Was that who he was?

"I am not Bob Snarby! I'm Tad Spencer!"

But even as he spoke the words, he knew that they weren't true. Like it or not, something had happened and, for the time being anyway, he was this other boy. He was also very hungry. The smell of bacon was seeping out under the caravan door. He could almost hear it sizzling in the pan. He had no money and no idea where he was. But breakfast was cooking on the other side of the door. What choice did he really have?

Tad opened the door and went back in.

Doll Snarby was sitting, wedged behind the table with a mountain of eggs, bacon, sausages and toast in front of her. As Tad came into the room she pronged a whole fried egg on her fork and slipped it into her mouth, a trickle of grease dribbling down her chin. Eric Snarby was at the stove, a new cigarette between his lips. He had a bad cough. In fact he was spluttering as much as the bacon in the pan.

"So you come back in, 'ave you," Eric coughed. "Just like you to shove off when it's your turn to do the cooking."

"Don't be cruel to the boy," Doll Snarby shouted. She reached out and jabbed Tad hard in the ribs. "That's *my* job!"

"I suppose you want some bacon," Eric asked.

"Yes, please," Tad said.

"Oh! *Please!*" Eric sang the word in a falsetto voice. "'aven't we got airs and graces today." He coughed again, spraying the bacon with spittle. "'e'll be saying *thank you* next an' all!"

"Leave the little maggot alone," Doll said. She slid an empty plate in front of Tad.

Tad looked down. The plate was coated in

grease and dried gravy from the night before. "This is dirty," he said.

Doll scowled. "Well, there's no point washing it, is there!" she said, reasonably. "You're only going to put more food on it."

Eric Snarby slid two lumps of bacon, a fried egg and a piece of fried bread onto Tad's plate. Doll picked up two pieces of toast, emptied half a jar of marmalade between them and pressed them into a sandwich. Eric had made himself a cup of tea and sat next to his wife.

She sniffed at him. "You smell!" she exclaimed.

"So what?" he replied, the eye with the sty twitching indignantly.

"Why don't you 'ave a barf?" his wife complained.

"Because we don't 'ave a barf," Eric Snarby replied. "And I'm not going in the shower. Not 'til you take out your knickers!"

Tad tried not to listen to any of this but instead concentrated on his breakfast. He had never seen food like it. Back home at Snatchmore Hall breakfast would have been freshly squeezed orange juice and a croissant, perhaps lightly scrambled eggs on a square of wholemeal toast and three pork sausages from Fortnum & Mason. This food was disgusting. Tad was sure he would only be able to manage a few mouthfuls and he was amazed to find himself eating it all. After that he drained a whole mug of tea and only felt a little queasy when he found a cigarette end nestling in the dregs at the bottom.

"Feeling better?" Eric Snarby asked.

"A bit." Tad had almost said "thank you" but stopped himself at the last minute. Doll Snarby shifted on her seat and the next moment there was an explosion as she let loose a jet of stale air. Tad was horrified but Eric just grinned. "Cor!" he exclaimed. "That nearly put out my cigarette!"

Doll grunted with satisfaction. She wiped her mouth on the sleeve of her dress and stood up. "All right," she said. "Let's get to work."

"Work?" Tad blinked.

"Don't you start, Bob," Doll yelled, casually striking the back of Tad's head with her hand. "You pull your weight or you don't eat."

"Come on! Get off your backside." Eric slapped him again from the other direction. "Let's get stuck in."

It turned out that the Snarbies ran the Lucky Numbers stall at the fair and Tad spent the rest of the morning helping to rig it up. First there were the prizes to be set out: large stuffed gorillas hanging comically from one hand with a half-peeled banana in the other. Then the stall itself had to be washed down, the electric light bulbs hung and a few loose planks of wood hammered into place. The work was easy enough – but not for Tad. He had never done anything like this before and found it almost impossible. He got a stiff neck from carrying the toys, a handful of splinters from washing the stall and had only managed two bangs with the hammer before he had caught his thumb and gone off howling. Eric Snarby watched Tad with disgust. At midday, he shook his head, rolled another cigarette and went back into the caravan. There he found Doll, reading *The Sun* and munching a packet of chocolate digestive biscuits.

"What is it?" Doll wasn't pleased to see him.

"It's the boy. Bob." Eric lit the cigarette and sucked in smoke. "There's something about 'im. 'e's not 'imself."

Doll blew her nose noisily, then looked around for a handkerchief. "Of course he's not himself!" she exclaimed. "What do you expect with 'alf a tube of Araldite inside 'im!"

Eric Snarby nodded and bit his lip. He seemed about to go but then he stopped and looked up and suddenly there was fear in his eyes. "What 'appens if Finn wants him again?" he asked.

"Finn." Now it was Doll's turn to go pale. Even as she spoke the word, she seemed to shrink into herself, her rolls of flesh quivering.

"Suppose Finn wants the boy?" Eric persisted.

Both the Snarbies were silent now. Eric's

cigarette was so close to his lips that it was actually burning them but he didn't seem to notice. Smoke crept up the side of his face like a scar. Doll Snarby was clutching the last chocolate digestive. Suddenly it exploded in her hand, showering her husband with crumbs.

"Bob'll be all right," she said. "Finn's not due back for a couple of days. By the time he gets here, Bob'll be fine." She took a deep breath and lashed out with one hand, catching her husband by the ear. As he squealed in pain, she drew him close. "Just keep 'im away from the glue," she hissed. "The Bostik, the Araldite, the Pritt Stick, the lot! And Finn won't notice a thing!"

The fair was busy that night. The rain had stopped and the people had come out, milling round the stalls and queuing for the rides. By then, Tad had learnt two things, overhearing the conversation of the other stall owners.

First it was Friday. Less than twenty-four hours had passed since he had gone to bed at Snatchmore Hall as Thomas Arnold David Spencer. And second, the fairground had been set up in a place called Crouch End, not too far from his parents' second, London home. Tad could run away. Surely he would be able to find his way home.

But what would he do when he got there? If he knocked on the door, his parents wouldn't even open it – not to a scruffy, fair-haired kid who probably looked like he'd come to steal the silver. They might even set Vicious on him! The thought of the Dalmatian dog with its razor-sharp teeth was enough to make Tad tremble. He had nothing to prove that he was telling the truth. He didn't even have his own voice!

The more he thought about it, the more he realized he had no choice but to stay where he was – at least for the time being. Perhaps when he woke up the next day he would find he had switched back again. Perhaps Spurling would turn up in the Rolls Royce and drive him home. Perhaps...

The truth was that Tad wasn't used to making decisions for himself. He didn't know what to do and even if he had known he would have been too afraid to try.

A movement caught his eye. Tad turned. And that was when he began to think he really had gone mad.

There was a man standing on the other side of the funfair, partly hidden in the shadows. Or was it a man? He was less than four feet tall with hair reaching down to his shoulders. He had dark skin and wore a tunic that left his legs and arms bare. There were two streaks of blue paint on his cheekbones and a leather collar round his neck. He was an Indian, Tad realized. Some sort of pygmy.

The man was staring at Tad. Tad could see the lights of the funfair reflected in his dark eyes. Now he gestured with his head and walked slowly, deliberately, away. The message was clear. He wanted Tad to follow him.

Tad stepped forward, pushing through the crowd. He passed close to a hot dog stall and caught the sweet, heavy smell of frying meat. The Indian had stepped out of sight and Tad quickened his pace, stepping over the cables and leaving the brightly lit centre of the funfair. It was only now, in the darkness outside the ring of caravans, that he wondered if this was a good idea. Perhaps he was being led into some sort of trap. Perhaps the Indian had something to do with what had happened to him.

The chimes of the merry-go-rounds and the clatter of the other rides seemed suddenly very distant. The Indian had completely disappeared. Tad was about to turn round and go back when he noticed a caravan, set apart from the others. It was a proper, old-fashioned gypsy's caravan, lavishly painted with silver and gold leaf. Above the door hung a sign:

Doctor Aftexcludor —
Your Future In The Stars.

The Indian was standing in the doorway, three steps above ground level. He was lit now by a yellow glow that came from within. He nodded at Tad again, then turned and moved inside. Tad thought for a moment. Then he crossed the grass and gravel and walked up to the caravan.

The door was still open but there was nobody in sight.

"Hello…?" Tad called out.

Far away, the merry-go-round started up again. There was a snap and a clang from an air rifle aimed at a metal plate. A shout of laughter from the other side of the darkness.

Tad made his decision.

He climbed the three steps to the caravan door and went in.

DOCTOR AFTEXCLUDOR

It was like being inside some strange church or temple. Tad looked around him wondering just how much more could happen to him today.

The walls of the caravan were covered with thick material, like a tapestry. The floor was richly carpeted. Even the ceiling was hidden by folds of what looked like silk. There were no windows and hardly any furniture. Cushions were scattered on the carpet round a low wooden table on which stood a gleaming crystal ball. There were old, leather-bound books piled up in crooked towers but there were no shelves. Dozens of joss-sticks poked out of strange bronze holders, their tips glowing, filling the room with smoke. The only other light came from a row of candles, perilously close to the wall. Sneeze and the whole place will go up in flames, Tad thought.

The owner of the caravan was sitting cross-legged on one of the cushions, smoking a long pipe. He was wearing a red silk dressing gown with a heavy collar and a strange black hat, a bit like a fez. The man had brown skin, deep black eyes and a pointed nose and chin. His hair was silver. Tad would have said he was about sixty or seventy. He had the look of a statue that has been left out in the open – not just weather-beaten but somehow timeless. His was a very odd face and a rather unsettling one.

"Good evening," the man said in a slightly sing-song voice. "Would you mind closing the door?"

Tad did as he was told, instantly cutting out all the sounds of the fair. The man waved a languid hand. "Please sit down."

Tad looked for a chair, couldn't see one, so sat down on a cushion. "Who are you?" he demanded.

"They call me Dr Aftexcludor," the man said.

"Dr Aftexcludor?" Tad thought for a moment. "That's a stupid name," he said. "I don't believe it's your real name at all."

The man sighed. "What are names?" he asked. "They're labels. Things people use to make us into what they want us to be." He fell silent for a moment. "And what of your name?" he demanded. "Bob Snarby." He spoke the two words with a smile.

"That's not my name!" Tad looked more closely at the old man. "But you know that, don't you. You know who I am!"

Dr Aftexcludor nodded slowly. "Yes. I do know what has happened to you. At least, I think I can guess."

"What *has* happened to me? I insist you tell me. If you don't tell me, I'm going to the police! It's horrible and unfair and I'm fed up with it. This funfair, the Snarbies, having to work! I want my mother. I want my Rolls Royce. I want to go home!"

Dr Aftexcludor chuckled. "Well, you certainly don't sound like Bob Snarby," he muttered.

Just then a curtain parted and the Indian reappeared, holding a tray. Tad hadn't realized that the caravan had two sections but looking over the Indian's shoulder he saw what seemed to be a corridor extending some way into the distance. But that was impossible. The corridor was longer than the caravan itself. The curtain fell back and the Indian moved forward. On the tray were two steaming glasses of tea.

"I haven't introduced you," Dr Aftexcludor said. "This is Solo."

"Solo?"

"That's not his real name either. I call him that because there's only one of him left."

"What do you mean?"

"He's from Brazil. An Arambaya Indian –
but he's the last of the tribe. I met him in Rio
de Janeiro and brought him with me to
Europe..." Dr Aftexcludor turned to the
Indian and muttered a few words in a language
that sounded a little like Spanish, a little like a
dog barking. The Indian nodded and withdrew. "I won't tell you his story now," he said.
"You're not ready for it."

"What do you mean?" Tad snapped. There
was something about Dr Aftexcludor he didn't
like. Maybe it was that the old man seemed to
know so much but explained so little.

Dr Aftexcludor picked up his tea. "Perhaps
we should begin with you," he said. "Tad
Spencer. That's your real name, if I'm not mistaken."

"How do you know my name?" Tad
demanded.

"It's my job!" The old man nodded at the
table and for the first time Tad noticed the
crystal ball. He looked into it and saw the
inside of the caravan, the doctor, himself, all
twisted into a swirl of colours, trapped inside
the brilliant glass. "Your future in the stars,"
Dr Aftexcludor explained. "Two pounds fifty
and I tell people everything they want to
know. Although, of course, most people don't
know what they want to know and what they
do want to know isn't what they ought to want
to know." He shook his head as if trying to

200

make sense of this. "Anyway," he went on, "telling their name is the easy bit."

"What's happened to me?" Tad demanded. He forced himself to look away from the crystal ball.

"That's not so easy. Obviously you've switched places with Bob Snarby..."

"You mean he's in my body with my parents in my house!" The thought hadn't occurred to Tad until this moment.

"I'm afraid so. But the real question is, how has this happened?" Dr Aftexcludor smiled to himself and for just one moment Tad wondered if he knew more than he was letting on. "I would say, if you want a professional opinion, that you've been hit by a wishing star."

"A what?"

"A wishing star. They're an extremely rare phenomenon and they have to be in exactly the right position at exactly the right time. Let me see..." Dr Aftexcludor reached out and took one of the books. He opened it and Tad saw that it was an old book of astronomy, the heavy pages (handwritten, not printed) filled with diagrams of stars and planets and their possible alignments. "Yes. Here we are." He pointed to one of the pictures. "In the Andromeda Galaxy. This little star here – Janus, its name is. That's Latin, although of course I wouldn't need to tell you that. Janus moved into the right orbit for about thirty seconds last night. That would have been around about ten o'clock. And the simple fact is that if you had made a wish at exactly that moment, the wish would have come true."

Tad stared at the picture, trying to think back. Then he remembered. "I wished I was somebody else," he said, slowly.

"Well, there you are then," Dr Aftexcludor said. "That's just what you are. Somebody else. Perhaps you'd better have a sip of tea."

Tad blinked. "Wait a minute," he spluttered. "You're telling me ... I wished. And my wish came true?"

"Evidently."

"But then ... I can wish again! Why can't I wish myself back the way I was?"

"Well, of course you can," Dr Aftexcludor said. "But the one snag is that you'll have to wait for the same star, Janus, to return to the same orbit."

"When's that?" Tad was excited now. For the first time he could see a way out of this nightmare.

Dr Aftexcludor opened the book at another page and ran a long, skeletal finger down a column of figures. He flicked back a few pages, closed his eyes as he worked it all out, then slammed the book shut. "January 13th," he said.

"January 13th!" Tad almost burst into tears. "But that's seven months away!"

"Rather more, I'm afraid," Dr Aftexcludor muttered. "I'm talking about January 13th in the year 3216."

"But that's … that's…"

"One thousand, two hundred and twenty years from now. Yes. I know. You'll be one thousand, two hundred and thirty-three years old."

And then Tad did begin to cry, more than he had ever cried in his life. Dr Aftexcludor looked at him sadly. "I'm sure it's not that bad," he said.

"Of course it's bad!" Tad wailed. "It's terrible! It's the worst thing that's ever happened."

The doctor handed Tad a handkerchief and Tad blew his nose. "What am I going to do?" he asked miserably.

"I'm not sure there's anything you *can* do," Dr Aftexcludor replied. "You are Bob Snarby now – whether you like it or not." He reached out and patted Tad on the shoulder. Tad looked up and once again he wondered if the old man wasn't hiding something. It was there in his eyes. Dr Aftexcludor was doing his best to look sympathetic but Tad knew that deep down he was enjoying this. "I can give you one bit of advice though."

"What's that?"

"Well. I know it won't look that way at the moment, but perhaps you might end up actually enjoying being Bob Snarby. Or to put it another way, maybe you can do a better job of being Bob Snarby than Bob Snarby ever did."

"But I'm not Bob Snarby!"

"That's just my point."

Tad had had enough. He threw down the handkerchief and stood up. "I don't know what you're talking about," he said. "And I don't believe you anyway. I've never heard of wishing stars. I don't believe they exist. I think it's all just a lot of lies and when I wake up tomorrow I'll be back to myself and that will be that. I'm not interested in you or your stupid servant. In fact I never want to see either of you again." Tad stormed out of the caravan, slamming the door behind him. Dr Aftexcludor watched him go.

"Goodbye, Tad," he muttered. "Or should I say … hello, Bob?"

Tad spent the rest of the evening hiding and crept back into the Snarbies' caravan only when the fair had closed for the night. He had begun to feel ill and wondered if he had caught a cold when he had been sent out, half-naked, into the rain. One moment he was too hot, the next he was shivering with cold. There was a heavy thudding in his head.

Eric and Doll were not pleased to see him.

"Skived off all afternoon, 'ave we?" Eric complained. "Where've you bin then, Bob? 'aving a bit of a laugh? Breaking into cars, I'll bet. Or vandalizing old age pensioners again."

"I've been thinking," Tad said. He coughed loudly and shivered again.

"Thinking? Thinking?" Both the Snarbies burst into malicious laughter. "You never done no thinking in your life," Doll exclaimed. She had been holding a cream éclair and now she took a huge bite. Cream oozed out of her hand. "You was bottom of the class in everything at school," she went on with her mouth full. "Bottom in Maths. Bottom in History. Second to bottom in Geography – and that was only because you gave the other boy multiple stab wounds!"

"So what was you thinking about?" Eric Snarby asked. "Don't tell me!" He grinned. "It was Einstein's theory of electricity."

"It's relativity," Tad said. He found it hard to catch his breath. "Einstein invented the theory of relativity."

"Don't you contradict your father!" Doll exploded, grabbing hold of Tad's ear.

"That's right." Eric cried, grabbing hold of the other one.

"Wait a minute. Please. You don't understand..." Tad tried to get to his feet but suddenly the caravan seemed to be moving. He felt it spin round, then dive as if down a steep hill. He flailed out, trying to keep his balance. Then fell unconscious to the floor.

There was a long silence.

"Blimey!" Doll said, looking at the silent boy. "That's a bit of a shocker! Is 'e dead?"

"I don't fink so," Eric Snarby muttered. He leant down and put a hand to Tad's lips. "'e's still breathing. Just." He blinked nervously. "Wot we gonna do?" he went on. "I suppose we'd better call a doctor."

"No way! Forget it!" Doll snapped. "A doctor'll take one look at all them bruises we given the boy and then we'll have the social workers in and then the police."

Eric Snarby went over to an ash-tray and rummaged inside it. A moment later he pulled out an old cigarette end, re-lit and screwed it into his lips. "So what are we going to do?" he asked again.

Doll Snarby thought for a long moment, twisting her wooden necklace with one pudgy hand. "We'll look after 'im ourselves," she said.

"But 'e looks awful!" Eric Snarby protested. "'e could be full of glue, Doll. Maybe 'is 'eart and lungs 'ave got all stuck together and that's wot's doing it. What are we going to do if 'e dies?"

"He won't die…"

"But what if 'e does? What will we tell Finn?"

At the mention of Finn, Doll froze. "Don't talk to me about Finn," she rasped.

Eric Snarby went over to Tad, picked him

up and carried him through to the bed. But for the faintest movement of the boy's chest as it rose and fell, he could have been dead already. Doll stared at him with bulging eyes, then threw a soiled blanket over him. "Go out and get 'im two Mars bars and a bottle of Lucozade," she rasped. "And don't worry! The boy's going to be fine!"

FINN

But Tad only got worse.

Wrapped in filthy sheets in the corner of the caravan, Tad seemed to be breathing more and more slowly as if he had found the one sure way out of his new body and was determined to take it. Eric Snarby sat watching over him while, in the next room, Doll Snarby blinked back the tears and tried on different hats for the funeral. But then, three days after Tad had fallen ill, there was a knock on the door. It was Solo, the Indian from Dr Aftexcludor's caravan.

"Blimey!" Doll exclaimed, staring at the tiny figure. "It's the last of the blooming Mohicans. What do you want, dearie?"

By way of an answer, Solo held out a curious bottle. It was circular in shape, fastened with a silver stopper. It was half-filled with some pale green liquid.

"What is it?" Doll demanded.

Eric Snarby appeared at the door beside her. "Don't touch it," he muttered. "It's some sort of foreign muck." He waved at Solo. "'oppit!" he shouted. "Go on! Allez-vous! Push off!"

"Medicine." Solo muttered the single word and nodded at the bottle.

"What do you know about medicine?" Eric sneered.

Doll snatched the bottle from him. "Shut up!" she exclaimed. "That old geezer 'e works for ... Aftexcludor. 'e's a doctor, innee?"

"Medicine," Solo repeated.

"I 'eard! I 'eard!" Eric muttered, sourly. He turned to Doll. "'ow do they even know the boy's ill?" he whispered. "We didn't tell no one."

"What does it matter 'ow they knew?" Doll uncorked the bottle and smelled the contents. She wrinkled her nose. "It smells all right," she said. She nodded at Solo. "All right, you can shove off, shorty!" she said. "And tell your boss ta, all right?"

Whether Solo had understood or not he turned and walked away.

Doll turned to Eric. "Get me a glass!" she ordered. "And make sure you wipe it first with your sleeve."

Dr Aftexcludor's medicine was the first liquid that Tad had accepted since he fell ill. Even the smell of it seemed to revive him a

209

little and he emptied the glass in one swallow. After that he slept again but his breathing seemed to have steadied and a little colour crept back into his face. Then, that evening, quite suddenly he woke up. The fever had broken.

"My baby!" Doll threw her arms round Tad and burst into tears.

"Be careful!" Eric muttered. "You're so fat you'll smother 'im!"

Eric and Doll Snarby were so relieved to have their son back with them that later that evening they went out and bought fish and chips for him – although Doll Snarby ate most of the chips as she carried them home. That night Tad ate properly for the first time. And when he slept again it was a normal, healthy sleep.

With the change in Tad's health came a change in the weather. The sun shone and the crowds came out, enjoying the first weeks of the summer holidays. When she was sure he wouldn't collapse on her, Doll Snarby set Tad to work on the Lucky Numbers stall.

It wasn't difficult to run. All Tad had to do was to sit in front of the stuffed gorillas holding a big basket of tickets. And as the crowds walked past, he would shout out a patter he had quickly learnt from his new father.

"Come on! Try your luck! Three tickets for a pound. If it ends in a five you're a winner!

Lots of chances! Come on, sir! See if you can win a nice cuddly toy for the missus!"

This is what Tad did for the next four days. He felt safe in the stall, sitting on his own, and he even enjoyed the work, sitting out in the sun, watching the crowds go by. There was one thing that puzzled him to begin with. Not one single ticket that he sold actually ended in a five and soon he was surrounded by hundreds of coloured scraps of paper – torn up and thrown away by the losers. The gorillas stayed where they were. But it didn't take him long to work out the answer. There *were* no fives. No fifty-fives, no sixty-fives, no hundred-and-fives. They had never even been printed. And the punters had as much chance of winning a cuddly toy for the missus as they did of waking up on the moon.

But Tad didn't mind. He didn't feel a twinge of guilt. Eric Snarby was giving him five pence out of every pound he made and the money was quickly mounting up. Tad felt better with coins in his pocket. He felt more like his old self.

Before he knew it, he had settled into a routine. The fair closed just after midnight and Tad shut up the stall and crawled into his bed at the back of the caravan after quickly swallowing down a meal. The Snarbies bought him take-away Chinese, take-away Indian, take-away fish and chips. And the cost of each meal they took away from his earnings. Bed was the worst time for him. Lying curled up on the lumpy mattress, he would think back to his life at Snatchmore Hall. He had been away from home for less than a week but somehow home had already become a distant memory. As he shivered in the damp air, Tad would remember his electric blanket, the chocolate that Mitzy placed on his pillow last thing at night, the Jacuzzi waiting for him in the morning. Could he go back? Tad doubted it. If he turned up at Snatchmore Hall looking the way he did now, talking the way he did, smelling the way he did ... they wouldn't even let him through the gate.

"You are Bob Snarby now – whether you like it or not."

That was what Dr Aftexcludor had told him and Tad believed him. He *was* Bob Snarby. He had no choice.

Another week passed and the fairground prepared to close. Eric and Doll Snarby were planning to travel north to join another, larger fair in Great Yarmouth. Tad had almost laughed when he heard that. Great Yarmouth was only forty miles from Snatchmore Hall. He was actually moving closer to home! But at the same time he knew that it might just as well have been four hundred miles for all the difference it would make.

He sold almost two hundred tickets on the last day. It was a Saturday afternoon and he had been left on his own. Eric and Doll had opened a bottle of wine at lunch-time and had gone back to the caravan to sleep it off. He had watched the caravan shaking on its wheels and had heard their screams of laughter as they chased each other round the bedroom but now it was silent and he imagined they were asleep. Tad picked up the bucket of tickets and shook them.

"Come on! Try your luck..." he began. Then stopped.

A man had limped up to the stall and was standing in front of him, looking at him strangely. Tad's first impression was of a shark in human form; the man had the same black eyes and pale, lifeless flesh. Although he wasn't physically huge, there was a presence about him, something cold and ugly that seemed to reach out and draw Tad helplessly towards him. The man had grey hair, cropped short to match the grey stubble on his chin. He wore a shabby suit and a pair of perfectly round wire-frame spectacles.

And then he turned his head and Tad gasped. His face was normal on one side but the other was completely covered by a tattoo. Somebody had cut an immense spider's web into the man's white flesh. It stretched from his ear to his forehead to his nose, to the side of

213

his mouth and down to his neck. The tattoo was livid black and – most horrible of all – it seemed to be eating its way into the man's flesh. Somehow it was almost more alive than the face on which it hung.

"Try your luck…?" Tad muttered but the rest of the words refused to come.

"Hello, Bobby-boy!" The man smiled wickedly, revealing a line of teeth riddled with silver fillings. He had more fillings in his mouth than teeth. "I hope you're well."

"I'm OK." Tad looked at the stranger warily.

"I asked if you was well," he said. "Are you one hundred percent? 'OK' is not good enough!"

"I'm fine," Tad answered, mystified.

"That's good. Because I hear – I'm reliably informed – that you been ill," the man said.

"What about it?" Tad had learnt that the ruder he was, the more people would accept that he was Bob.

The man smiled again. He had been leaning on a black, silver-capped walking stick but now he leant it against the stall. "Glue was what I heard," he murmured.

"What about it?"

The man shook his head slowly. "You modern kids," he said. "When I was your age, you wouldn't have found me touching stuff like that. No. Gin was good enough for me. A half bottle of gin in my schoolbag, that's what got me through the day." He took out a cigarette and lit it. "Mind you," he went on, "gin could be a treacherous friend too. It's gin I got to thank for this…" He tapped the tattoo on the side of his face.

"What happened?" Tad asked, feeling queasy.

"I was drunk. Drunk as a lord. And some mates of mine took me down the tattooist for a laugh. When I woke up, this was what he'd done to me. The web and the spider." Tad glanced at the tatoo. The man laughed. "One day I'll tell you where he put the spider," he said. He blew out smoke. His eyes behind the round lenses were suddenly distant. "Anyway, I had the last laugh, so to speak. I went back to the tattooist and gave 'im what you might call a piece of my mind."

"You told him what you thought of him…" Tad said.

"I *wrote* him what I thought of him. That's what I did. I tied him to a chair and wrote it all over his body. Used his own needles. Oh yes. I turned that man into a walking dictionary – and not the sort of words you'd want your mother to hear. He went mad in the end, I understand. He's in an institute now. An institute for the insane. The other inmates never talk to him. But sometimes they … *read* him." The man broke off and laughed quietly to himself.

There was a commotion as the caravan door opened and Eric and Doll Snarby appeared, hurrying across the fairground towards them. Eric was half-dressed, his shirt out of his trousers and the sty under his eye throbbing in time with his breath. Doll was also a mess, her lipstick smeared and one earring missing. Tad had never seen them like this. They were, he realized, terrified.

"Finn!" Doll exploded. "What a pleasure to see you! What a joy!"

"We wasn't expecting you 'til later," Eric added. "Or naturally we would 'ave bin 'ere to welcome you."

"Please, my dear Snarbies!" The man called Finn positively beamed at them. "No need to get your underwear in a twist. I've had all the welcome I need, thank you." He nodded at Tad, and in that moment it was as if a conjuror had waved a silk over the man's face. Suddenly the smile was gone and in its place was a leer of such force and ugliness that Tad shivered. "The boy's not 'imself," he snapped. "What have you done to 'im?"

"We looked after him!" Doll wheezed. "You know how precious he is to us, Finn. He was ill…"

"…'e made 'imself ill!" Eric interjected.

"What are children coming to?" Doll Snarby trilled. "You beat them senseless and it doesn't do any good at all! I don't know…"

"He got at the glue?" Each word was a bullet, fired at the Snarbies.

"It wasn't our fault, Finn!" Eric had gone chalk white.

"Oh Gawd! Please, Finn…!" Doll tried to slide herself behind her husband but he pushed her away.

Finn thought for a moment. Then he relaxed and his face rippled back to what it had been before. "I'm taking him with me this evening," he explained in a gentler voice. "A little business engagement. A business enterprise. I need my partner."

His partner? Tad heard the word and swallowed.

"Is he ready?" Finn asked.

"Of course he's ready, Finn," Doll croaked. "We wouldn't let you down!"

"That's settled then," Finn said. "I'll be back for him at nine o'clock."

He picked up his stick and used it to unhook one of the gorillas. The gorilla slid down the length of the stick and into his hand. Finn smiled. "My lucky day!" he exclaimed. "It looks like I won!"

Holding the gorilla, he turned and limped away.

NIGHTINGALE
SQUARE

There was a full moon that night. As Finn and Tad crossed the empty square, their shadows raced ahead of them as if searching for somewhere to hide. It was a few minutes after midnight. Tad had heard the church bells toll the hour. They had seemed far away, almost in another world. Here, everything was pale and grey, the buildings like paper cut-outs against the black night sky.

Nightingale Square was in Mayfair, one of the smartest areas of London. Tad had been here before and now recognized the square. Sir Hubert Spencer had friends here and had once brought Tad here for tea. Tad scanned the handsome Georgian houses with growing discomfort. He already had a nasty idea just what sort of "business" Finn had in mind. But what would he do if the chosen house was the very one where he had once been a guest?

Finn leant against a metal railing in the middle of the square and raised his stick. "That's the one," he whispered. "Number twenty-nine. That's my lucky number, Bobby-boy. It's the number of times what I been arrested."

Tad glanced at the house. It was tall and narrow with classical white pillars and wide marble steps leading up to the front door. It was on the corner of the square with an alley-way next to it leading, presumably, to a garden at the back. Thick ivy grew up one side of the house. Tad followed it with his eye. The ivy twisted past three windows and a balcony, stopping just short of the roof. At the very top there was a brightly coloured box with a name and a telephone number. A burglar alarm.

"It's the London home of a real milord," Finn explained. "A member of the harry stocracy. 'is name is Lord Roven."

At least it wasn't one of his father's friends. But Tad still couldn't relax. He listened with dread as Finn went on.

"I seen 'im in the papers, Bobby-boy. Lord Roven and his lovely wife, the two of them dripping with diamonds and gold and mink." Finn's eyes had gone dark now. A bead of sweat trickled down the side of his head. "It's not fair, is it?" he hissed. "Them so rich and us so poor. I never had no education, Bobby-boy. OK. It's true. I did burn down the school.

And maybe it was wrong of me to lock all the teachers inside it first. But I never 'ad a chance. Never! And that's why it's all right, you see. To break into 'is 'ouse and steal 'is things. Because he's got everything and we got nothing and stealing is the only way to make things change."

Breaking in. Stealing. Tad's worst fears had been realized. His mouth had gone dry and it took him a few moments to find his voice. "How do you know Lord Roven won't be in?" he asked.

"'e always goes out tonight," Finn replied. "Tonight is 'is bridge night. It'll be four in the morning before 'e gets home."

"And Lady Roven?"

"In the country."

Finn licked his lips, then pointed again with the stick. "There's the window, Bobby-boy. Up there by the alarm. You can get in there."

Now Tad understood why he had been chosen. A man wouldn't have been able to climb up. The ivy wouldn't hold him. He needed a boy. "How do you know the window will be open, Finn?" he asked. His mind was desperately searching for a way out of this nightmare.

"I arranged it."

"But what about the alarm...?"

The stick whistled down, missing Tad's head by less than an inch. "What's the matter

220

with you?" Finn demanded.

"Nothing...!"

"Nuffing, Bobby-boy? Oh yes. There's something queer all right. Finn can smell a fish. A rotten fish." Finn rested the stick on Tad's shoulder and gazed into his eyes. "You been ill," he continued. "I can respect that. I've made lots of people ill myself. But you're acting like you never been on a job before. What's happened to you?"

"I'm all right, Finn. Nothing's changed."

"I wonder." Finn let the stick slide off Tad's shoulder. "But you better not let me down, Bobby-boy. Stuffed with nice things this 'ouse is. Nice pictures and candlesticks. Smart jewellery and antiques. And you got to get me in!"

Finn looked left and right, then hurried across the road. Feeling sick and frightened, Tad followed. The last time he had come to Nightingale Square it had been for crumpets and tea. Now he was back as a thief in the night. It was impossible. When he had woken up in the Snarbies' caravan he had thought things were as bad as they could get. But this was far, far worse.

Finn had already reached the other side of the road and was crouching down. As Tad joined him, he straightened up and now he was holding what looked like a circular section of the pavement. Looking closer, Tad saw it was the cover of a manhole. Finn grunted and set

221

it down, then pulled out a tangle of multi-coloured wires which he began to examine.

"What are you doing?" Tad asked.

"What do you think I'm doing?" Finn shook his head and sighed. "The alarm's connected to the police." He pulled out a pair of wire-cutters, selected an orange-coloured wire and snipped it in two. "At least, it was."

"You've cut it!"

"Don't disappoint me, Bobby-boy." Finn glanced upwards and suddenly it seemed to Tad that he was holding the wire-cutters like a weapon. "You've seen it all before. You know the procedure. You know what's what."

"Of course, Finn."

"Good." Finn flipped the cutters over and put them away, then slid the manhole into place and stood up. "Fifteen minutes," he said. "That's how long we got before they'll send someone round to check." He gestured at the house. "I want the door open in five."

Tad stood staring at the house. A hundred excuses formed in his mind but died before they could reach his lips. He couldn't risk asking anything. Finn was already suspicious and if Tad asked something he was supposed to know … he thought of the wire-cutters and hurried forward.

Gingerly he reached out and took hold of the ivy, testing it against his weight. He had been right about one thing. The twisting stems

222

would never have taken the weight of a man but holding on tight he was able to lift himself off the ground. The ivy bent but held firm.

"Five minutes," Finn reminded him.

Tad began to scale the wall, pulling himself up a few centimetres at a time. Finn stood below, keeping a look-out along the empty pavement. Somewhere a car door slammed and an engine started up. Tad froze. But the sound grew more distant and finally disappeared. Tad grunted and dragged himself up over the first window.

He had passed the balcony and was making his way up to the third floor when he made the mistake of looking back down. It was the worst thing he could have done. The ground seemed a very long way away and for a moment he couldn't move. This sort of thing might have been easy for Bob Snarby but Tad Spencer had always been afraid of heights. The whole house had begun to spin with him attached to it and he was certain he would have to let go. Already he could imagine the wind sailing past him, the crushing impact as he hit the concrete below. He wanted to shout out but he was too frightened even to draw breath.

There was a low whistle from the pavement. Finn. The sound snapped Tad out of his paralysis and he began to climb again. He was more afraid of Finn that he was of falling. It was as simple as that. He had to go on.

But the further up he went, the thinner the ivy became. It was bending now, pulling away from the wall. Tad heard the unmistakeable sound of a branch snapping and his left foot suddenly kicked out into space. For a ghastly moment, he hung there, feeling himself topple backwards away from the wall as the ivy came loose. Another branch broke. But then Tad lurched out and managed to grab a thicker clump. Carefully, he transferred his weight across. Then, gritting his teeth, he began to haul himself up further.

He was only half a metre from the window and was about to reach out to open it when there was a second, low whistle – this time a warning. A moment later, a car drove past, its headlights spilling out over the white front of the house. Instinctively, Tad stopped and pressed himself against the brickwork, not moving, not turning round. The car continued through the square and darkness fell like a curtain behind it. Finn whistled an "all clear". Tad began again.

He pressed his hand against the window and almost shouted with relief as it began to open inwards. It wasn't locked! At least Finn had been right about that. The strange thing was that Tad wasn't frightened any more. The truth was, he felt almost pleased with himself. At school he had never been any good at sports. He had never managed to get more than ten centimeters up a rope and the parallel bars had made him feel sick. He had been excused football and rugby – his parents thought they were too dangerous – and had even cheated at cross country running by getting a taxi to wait for him around the first corner.

And now he had climbed fifteen metres up the side of a building and he wasn't even out of breath! Tad didn't want to admit it but it was true. He was proud of himself. He was pleased.

Letting go of the ivy with one hand, he reached out for the window. This was the difficult part but he knew he had to keep moving. At least three minutes had passed since he had begun the climb. Finn had given him five. The police would be here in fifteen. Carefully, he swung his weight from the ivy onto the window sill. Then he pulled himself up and in.

It was only at the very last moment that he lost his balance. Half in the house, half out of it, he suddenly found himself flailing at the air, his centre of gravity hopelessly lost. Even then, some instinct saved him. He knew that he could topple backwards and down or throw himself forwards and in. He took the second option, twisted in mid-air and dived forwards. His shoulders passed neatly through the window. Unable to stop himself, he pitched forward, then fell to the floor with a crash. The noise seemed deafening, but nobody came. Nobody had heard. So Finn was right again. It seemed that there was nobody in the house.

The window had opened into a box room, stacked high with suitcases and tea chests. Tad could just make out a door in the half-light and crept over to it. The door led out to a corridor with, straight ahead of him, a flight of stairs going down. Tad tip-toed out.

Someone had left a light on in the hall. Tad hurried down four flights of thickly carpeted stairs past paintings by Rubens and Picasso. A huge chandelier hung over him and a gold-framed mirror reflected his image as he scuttled over to the front door. Tad was certain now that the house was empty. It had that feel. His own feet rapped out a brittle sound on the marble slabs in the hall. A grandfather clock ticked. But nothing else stirred.

He reached the front door and slid off the security chain and drew back the bolts. The door opened and there was Finn, standing in front of him, his spectacles two brilliant white discs as they caught the streetlight.

Finn lifted his walking stick and pushed Tad aside. He hurried into the house and closed the door behind him. There was a sheen of sweat on his forehead and a vein in his neck was throbbing rapidly. The spider's web was pulled taut.

"What the devil happened?" he hissed.

"What do you mean...?" Tad began.

"You made the devil of a racket at the window, Bobby-boy. An 'orrible racket. I'd have heard you three blocks away."

"I fell," Tad replied. "Anyway, what does it matter? The house is empty. You said so yourself."

Finn half-smiled. "Got a tongue in your head, have you?" he snarled. "That sounds more like my old Bob." He glanced at his watch. "Seven minutes," he said. "We'd better move."

"Where are we going?"

"We'll start with the safe. On the second floor." Leaning on his stick, Finn hurried towards the stairs and began to climb. Tad followed, saying nothing.

They had reached the first landing when the door opened.

Finn saw it first and stopped. He was on a landing about five steps below the level of the door with Tad just behind him. A man in a blue silk dressing gown and leather slippers stepped out. He was in his sixties with silver hair and a gaunt face and Tad didn't need to ask his name. It had to be Lord Roven. The owner of the house was looking down at them, clutching a heavy silver candlestick as a weapon in his hand.

"Stop there!" he said in a cultivated voice.

"I heard you come in the window and I've already called the police. You might as well wait where you are and make it easier on your-selves."

Finn looked over his shoulder at Tad and snarled at him with the cob-webbed side of his face. "You little fool!" he hissed. "You little idiot! I told you, didn't I? All that blooming noise!"

Tad took a step back. Everything was swim-ming again. He felt sick. He just wanted to dis-appear.

Finn turned back to Lord Roven. "What are you doing here?" he demanded. "Wednesdays is your bridge night."

Lord Roven frowned. He shook his head slowly. "It's Thursday…" he said.

"Thursday!" Finn almost shouted the word. A tic had appeared at one of his eyes, making the cobweb dance. "Thursday?" he whim-pered again. "Then it's not my fault, is it? It was a perfect plan. Perfect! I just got the day wrong, that's all!"

Then everything seemed to collide with itself. Tad would never be quite sure what hap-pened – or when.

The shrill sound of a siren cut through the night. Finn took a step forward. Lord Roven moved towards him, reaching out as if to grab him. Finn dropped his ebony walking stick – or part of it. When Tad looked again, he was still holding the handle but the rest of the stick had fallen away and an ugly length of steel protruded from his hand. A sword stick, Tad realized. But Lord Roven hadn't seen it. Whether Finn lifted the sword or whether his victim walked onto it, Tad couldn't say. But the next thing he knew, Finn had laughed out loud, a single cry that danced in his throat. At the same time, Lord Roven groaned and fell to the floor. Then there was a screech of tyres. A blue light flashed on and off through a downstairs window. A hand hammered at the door.

"The kitchen!" Finn hissed, snatching up the rest of his walking stick. "We can get out the back way!"

"You've killed him!" Tad whispered.

Finn swore and then grabbed Tad by the throat. For a moment their faces were pressed so close that they touched and Tad could feel the stubble of the man's beard rubbing against his own skin. "I'll kill you too if you don't move!" he snarled. "Now – come on!"

The thumping on the door continued, harder now, and a second police siren echoed across the square. Finn ran down the stairs – five steps at a time – and slid across the marble hallway. Tad followed. He could just make out a uniformed shape through the stained glass next to the front door but he ignored it, twisting round to follow the passage back past the grandfather clock. Then Finn grabbed hold of him and pulled him through an open doorway even as a booted foot crashed into the front door, splintering the wood and smashing the first of the locks.

Tad found himself in the kitchen, a long, narrow room all white and silver with French windows leading into a garden at the end. Finn was already trying the handles but they were securely locked.

"Stand back!" he ordered. As Tad obeyed, he raised his walking-stick, then brought it whistling through the air into the glass. The window shattered at exactly the same moment as the front door was kicked in. Tad heard the falling wood, the sound of voices shouting in the hall. "Move!" Finn commanded.

Tad followed Finn into the garden. The lamps on the police cars were still flashing and the bushes and trees loomed up on him, flickering blue against the night sky. The garden was surrounded by a low wall with other gardens on each side.

"Split up!" Finn hissed. "Confuse 'em. We got more chance that way. Meet back at the caravan…" Then before Tad could stop him, he hoisted himself over the wall and disappeared down the other side.

Tad swung round. Two policemen had stepped out of the kitchen and were standing in the garden. Slowly, they began to approach, and Tad realized they were afraid of him.

"All right..." one of them began.

Tad turned his back on them and ran. He felt his feet first on the grass, then in the soft earth of the flower-beds. His scrabbling hands found the garden wall and he pulled himself up, half-expecting the two policemen to grab him and pull him back. But he had been too fast for them. He twisted over the top of the wall and fell, squirming down the other side.

"There goes one of them! Round the other side!"

A heap of garden rubbish had broken his fall. Tad stood up and brushed some of it away. There were more whistles, more shouts. Lights had gone on in the adjoining houses, illuminating the gardens that ran along the back. Tad looked one way, then another, then began to run. He reached another garden wall and threw himself over it. Then another. He had forgotten all about Finn, didn't care if he had been caught or not. Tad couldn't stop. A window opened in one of the houses and somebody shouted. He came to a garden fence, kicked out at it with his foot and broke through.

He found himself in a narrow alleyway. Down one end he could see flashing lights and hear voices. The other end was dark and silent. That was the direction he chose.

Tad never knew how he got away without being arrested. But the alleyway led to a main road and suddenly he was in the clear with no policemen in sight and the chaos of Nightingale Square far behind him. He ran for an hour and only stopped when he could run no more.

He had escaped from Finn. He had escaped from the Snarbies. But now he was on his own and wanted for murder. He had little money, nowhere to go. Tad found an entrance to an office and slipped inside, burying himself in the shadows. He was still there six hours later when the first of the traffic hit the streets and the city of London woke to another day.

HOME

"Bacon sandwich and a cup of tea, please."

Tad had found his way to a run-down café in a Soho back street. He was the only customer. He paid for his breakfast using the last of his money and chose a table in the furthest corner. He had bought a late edition of the morning paper and now he opened it, thumbing through the pages.

He found the murder of Lord Roven in a single column on page four. There was a photograph of the house in Nightingale Square and a headline that read: BRUTAL MURDER IN LONDON'S MAYFAIR. The report concluded that the police had chased two intruders, a man and a boy, but both had escaped. So Finn hadn't been arrested either! Tad didn't know whether to be pleased or sorry. If Finn was free, he couldn't lead the police to Tad. On the other hand, he would

233

almost certainly be looking for Tad himself. After the disaster of the failed break-in, Tad didn't like to think what would happen if he were found.

Tad bit into his sandwich and actually found himself enjoying it. He should have been terrified or in despair but the truth was that he was neither. He felt confident ... even calm. As he sat in the café with his elbows on the table and his long hair falling over his eyes, Tad wondered if he was changing in some way that he couldn't understand.

A couple more people came into the café and ordered coffees. Neither of them even glanced in his direction. Cupping his hands round his tea, feeling the warmth, Tad tried to work out his options.

He was a thirteen-year-old, on his own in London, wanted by the police. He knew that he had been seen at Lord Roven's house and it surely wouldn't be hard to track him down. And what then? The fact was that it had been Tad who had broken into the house and let Finn in. He was as responsible for the old man's death as if he had held the sword himself. If the police caught him, he would go to prison. It was as simple as that.

He had to get out of London. He knew that. But with no money in his pocket, it wasn't going to be easy.

Briefly, he considered going back to the funfair. Whatever he thought of them, Eric and Doll Snarby would look after him. And they'd take him with them when they moved to the fair at Great Yarmouth. But if he went back to the Snarbies, he would be going back to Finn. Tad remembered the look on Finn's face as he stabbed forward with the sword. He shivered and took a sip of tea. He couldn't go back to Finn. There had to be another way.

And that was when the idea came to him.

Go home.

Not to the Snarbies but to his real parents and his own home. Sir Hubert Spencer had a house in Knightsbridge – only an hour's walk from where he was sitting now. It was his only chance. He had considered it before, when he was at the fair at Crouch End. But things had been different then. He had been too frightened to think straight, too frightened to act. Tad had come a long way since then. He was certain now that he could make his parents believe what had happened to him. After all, he knew everything about them. He could describe things that only their true son would know. All he had to do was talk to them.

He finished his breakfast and set off, up through Green Park and on towards the heart of Knightsbridge. He followed the road past Harrods Department Store and thought sadly of the times he had visited it with his mother. Lady Geranium used to take him there on his birthday and let him choose his own present. One year it had been a grand piano (although he had never played it). The next he had chosen the entire chocolate department. But now, of course, they wouldn't even have allowed him through the door.

The Spencers' London home was in a quiet street on the other side of Harrods. Number One, Wiernotta Mews was a pale blue house on three floors with a kitchen and dining-room in the basement. Tad had a bedroom on the first floor and slept there whenever the family was visiting London. He wondered if they would be there now.

It was eleven o'clock and the mews was empty. The other house owners were probably all at work. Tad crossed the cobbled surface and reached for the bell. It was only then that he had second thoughts. If the Spencers were at home and he rang the bell, Spurling would probably come to the door. And what would the chauffeur see? A dirty, dishevelled boy whom he wouldn't recognize. The door would be slammed before Tad had a chance to explain.

Tad sighed. It would be much easier to explain things once he was *inside* the house. But how was he to get in? Break in – for the second time in twenty-four hours? Then he remembered. His mother always left a spare key in one of the baskets of flowers that hung on either side of the front door. Tad quickly found it, opened the gate and followed the metal stairway down to the kitchen entrance.

As quietly as he could, he slipped the key into the lock and turned it. The house was silent. Tad stepped inside.

He stood for a few seconds in the quarry-tiled kitchen. His heart was pounding in his chest and he had to remind himself that he wasn't a thief. He wasn't breaking in. This was his house. He lived here. Even so, when he moved forward it was on tip-toe and his ears were pricked for the slightest sound.

He passed through the kitchen and crept upstairs. The first floor consisted of a single, open-plan room with leather sofas, Turkish carpets and a huge, wide-screen TV. A spiral staircase led upwards and he followed it to the second floor, where his own bedroom was located. He stopped in front of a door, tapped gently and went in.

The room was just as he had left it – evidently nobody had been there in the last few days. His bed, with its duvet patterned like a giant dollar bill, was freshly made. His London toys, books and computers were exactly where he had left them. Tad ran his hand over one of the surfaces, taking it all in. He had come home! Quickly he stripped off his clothes and went through into the adjoining bathroom. He didn't care if anyone heard

237

him now. He turned on the shower and stood for ten minutes in the hot, jetting water. It was as if the shower were washing away not just the dirt but all the memories of the past week. He dried himself in one of his own American towels. He had never appreciated how soft and warm they really were.

Outside, he heard a car draw up. A door slammed and a voice called out. He recognized it at once. It was his mother! His parents had arrived.

He felt a surge of excitement. In just a few moments he would see them again, talk to them, tell them what had happened. They would be shocked, of course. But once they understood, they could all begin again. The nightmare would finally be over.

Moving quickly, Tad pulled some clothes out of the cupboard and tried to get dressed. It was only now that he realized he had a problem. The pants he was holding were obviously several sizes too big. The trousers were the same. Reluctantly, he picked up Bob Snarby's clothes and put them back on. At least they fitted and, washed and groomed, he felt a bit more like an ordinary boy, less like a street urchin. Even so he was nervous. What if his parents refused to listen to him? What if they simply threw him back out on the street?

He could hear footsteps coming up the stairs. Tad thought for a moment, then went over to a drawer beside the bed, opened it and pulled out a cheque book. It was his own cheque book, and he was certain that he would still be able to sign Tad Spencer's signature. There was over ten thousand pounds in his current account; his pocket money for the past six months. Whatever happened, that money was now his.

He had just shoved the cheque book in his pocket when the door to the bedroom opened. Tad stared. He wasn't sure what he had been expecting but, whatever it was, it certainly wasn't this.

A short, fat, dark-haired boy in a ginger-and-brown checked suit had just walked in and was staring at Tad with the same shocked expression with which Tad was staring at him. Tad tried to speak. He felt the bed pressing against the back of his legs and he sat down. The other boy smiled.

And that was when Tad knew. He had thought at first that he was looking at himself and in a way, of course, he was. It *was* his own body that had just walked into the room but there was somebody else inside it. And the suddenly narrowed eyes – the cruel smile – told him who that somebody was.

"Bob Snarby!" he whispered.

"Tad Spencer!" the other boy replied. "I been expecting you."

FACE TO FACE

Bob Snarby closed the door and moved into the room. Tad watched him with a sense of wonderment. His first thought was how fat this boy was, how arrogant he looked with his puffed-out cheeks and slicked back hair. But then he remembered that he was actually looking at himself! Bob was wearing one of his own favourite suits. The Rolex watch that his mother had bought him was on the other boy's wrist. Tad realized that he was jealous, that he disliked Bob Snarby on sight.

But it wasn't Bob Snarby. It was him! Tad rested against a chair, thoroughly confused.

For a long minute the two boys stared at each other; Bob Snarby in Tad's body and Tad Spencer in Bob's body. At last Tad spoke.

"Do I call you Bob or Tad?" he asked.

The fat boy smiled. "I suppose you can call me Bob," he said. "You know that's who I am."

"What happened?" Tad demanded. "How did you turn yourself into me?"

"I didn't," Bob replied. "I didn't have nothing to do with it."

"You're lying!"

Bob moved further into the room. "I'll tell you what happened," he said. "But you'd better not get nasty with me. Spurling's downstairs and one shout from me and you'll be out on your ear. Know what I mean?"

Tad nodded.

"All right." Bob sat down on the bed. "I'd had an 'orrible day at the funfair. Up in Crouch End. Moving in is always the worst part and I was dog tired ... only if I was a dog they'd 'ave put me out of my misery. Mum and Dad were out at the pub. I went to bed."

"What time?"

"It must have been about half ten. Anyway, I fell asleep and woke up in your place. That's all there was to it. One minute I was in the van, the next..." Bob shook his head. "It gave me a nasty turn, I can tell you. Waking up in that bed! It was so big it took me a while just to find my way out."

"So what did you do?" Tad asked.

"I couldn't believe it at first. There I was, surrounded by all this gear – CDs and computer games and the rest of it. You know what my first thought was?"

"I can guess," Tad said.

"Bob, my boy, I thought, you've got to nick as much of this stuff as you can carry. You can ask questions later. But right now you've got to get out of here before someone comes and throws you out." Bob sighed. "That was when I caught sight of meself in the mirror." He paused. "I mean, *my*self, don't I. I've got to learn how to talk proper, haven't I! Anyway, that was when I started screaming the place down. It was like a horrible dream – only I knew I was awake."

"That's more or less what happened to me," Tad muttered.

"I bet. You must have been sick waking up with Eric and Doll! I wish I could have seen your face!"

"You've got my face!" Tad retorted, angrily.

"Let's not make it any more confused, shall we?" Bob Snarby said. "Where was I? Oh – right. I'm screaming my head off when the door flies open and this old biddy comes rushing in. I didn't know who the hell she was but then she starts calling me 'Master Tad' and tries to get me to calm down…"

"It was Mrs O'Blimey," Tad said.

"That's right. The housekeeper. Well, I got back into bed and the old lady fussed over me but I kept my mouth shut. You see, I knew something strange was going on and I didn't want to queer my own pitch, like. You know?

I could smell the money and I was thinking to myself – Bob, old mate, I don't know what's going on 'ere. It's a right mystery and no mistake. But you could do yourself quite nicely out of all this. Just take your time. Try and work it all out..."

Bob Snarby pulled a bar of chocolate out of his pocket and broke a piece off. "I never used to like this stuff," he said, half to himself. He offered the bar to Tad. "You want some?"

Tad shook his head.

"Well, I did manage to work it out in the end," Bob continued, munching the chocolate. "Somehow – Gawd knows how – I'd switched bodies with a fat, posh boy called Tad Spencer. It was like something out of a comic. Or maybe a film. I once saw a film on telly where something like that happened. I don't know. Anyway, as I lay there in that great big bed, surrounded by all that lovely stuff, I realized it had happened to me and after a bit I stopped worrying about how or why and just decided to ... go with it."

"But how could you persuade them?" Tad thought back to his own experiences with the Snarbies and with Finn. "My mother and father would never have believed you were me. You're much too common. You don't know anything. You never been to public school."

"You mean – 'You never *went* to public school' " – Bob corrected him. "It's true what you're saying, although if you don't mind me saying so, Tad, you're not exactly in a position to be snobbish." He smiled. "But all right, I admit it. There were a lot of things I didn't know that I ought to if I really was going to be you. I knew that."

"So what did you do?"

"In the end it was easy. I hadn't said much yet so they didn't know anything was wrong. The old woman – Mrs O'Blimey – thought I'd just been having a bad dream. And that afternoon, Spurling asked me if I'd like to go out riding. I said yes – I thought he was talking motorbikes or something. I didn't realize he meant on a horse! No, ta very much, I thought. But then, as I said, I had this idea. I got on the horse and the two of us trotted along for a bit. And then I fell off." Bob rubbed his backside. "I didn't have to fake that bit, I can tell you. Your mum saw me fall. She had the horse shot immediately – but this is the good part." He winked at Tad. "I told her I'd banged my head when I fell and I wasn't seeing things straight. You know ... like I had amnesia or something."

"Amnesia..." Tad almost admired Bob despite himself. The idea couldn't have been simpler.

"Right." Bob broke off another piece of chocolate. "Well, of course your mum was worried sick. She called in a whole army of doctors and I told them I wasn't sure who I was and that I'd forgotten all my Ancient Greek and Latin and all that stuff and they said that I was definitely concussed. I had to stay in bed while they did all these tests and they only let me out a couple of days ago. Now your mum – or I should say my mum – has brought me down to London to go shopping. We're going on holiday in a couple of weeks..."

"A safari in Africa," Tad said, gloomily.

"That's right! First class flights. Five star hotel. It's like winning the blooming pools!" He finished the chocolate and dropped the wrapper on the floor. "How about you?" he asked. "What have Eric and Doll had to say about the new Bob Snarby?"

"They think I've been sniffing glue," Tad said.

Bob thought about this for a moment, then threw his head back and laughed. "I bet they have!" he said. "Yeah. That'd explain everything."

Tad moved closer to the bed. "Listen to me, Bob," he pleaded. "We've got to sort this out..."

"What do you mean?"

"We've got to tell them what's happened. Your parents and my parents. If we both tell them, they'll have to believe us and maybe they'll be able to find a way to turn us back into ourselves."

245

Bob stared at Tad as though he were mad. "But why should I want to do that?" he demanded.

"What?" Tad felt something cold reach out and touch the back of his neck.

"Why should I want to change back?" Bob said.

"Because you've got to!" Tad cried. "I can't be you and you can't be me. We've got our own parents and our own lives. We've got to put things back the way they were."

"Forget it!" Bob exclaimed. "I'm better off now than I've ever been in my entire life and if you imagine I'm going to let you spoil it, you've got another think coming."

"It's all wrong...!" Tad began.

"It's perfect!" Bob shouted the words. "I never had a chance. I never had anything. Not from the day I was born. Eric and Doll, they made me what I was and I was stuck with it. And do you know what made it worse? All around me, in the newspapers, on the TV, in the shops, I saw all the things I could never, ever have. Computer games and hi-fi. Smart clothes. TVs and videos. I'd never have them – not in my whole life – just because of who I was..."

"That's not true..."

"It is true! But you wouldn't understand that. You had it all, didn't you. It was all just given to you on a plate. Yeah – well now you're finding out what it's like on the other side of the fence and I'm not surprised you want to switch back again. Only you can't. Because I won't let you."

"You must!"

"I won't!"

Something inside Tad snapped and before he knew what he was doing he had thrown himself on to Bob Snarby, his fists flailing, his face twisted with anger and hatred. He expected the other boy to defend himself but Bob just fell backwards onto the bed with Tad on top of him, not even trying to push him off. Tad hit him, again and again, but his fists seemed to make no impact, slapping against the skin and sinking into the soft folds of flesh. He only realized now that Bob was shouting, calling for help. Suddenly the door crashed open. Out of the corner of his eye Tad saw a great bulk in a blue and grey uniform descending on him. Two hands reached out and grabbed him; one round his neck, the other under his arm. He was pulled off Bob and into the air as easily as if he were nothing more than a set of empty clothes.

"Are you all right, Master Tad...?"

"Yes, Spurling. Thank you." Bob got unsteadily to his feet. His shirt was rumpled and there were tears welling up in his eyes.

"Spurling..." Tad twisted round in midair, his feet ten centimetres off the ground.

As much as he squirmed and struggled, he couldn't free himself from the chauffeur's grip.

"Who are you?" Spurling demanded. "What are you doing here?"

Tad opened his mouth to answer but, before he could speak, before he could find the right words, Bob moved forward. "He was here when I came in," he sobbed. "He was searching the room. I think he was looking for something to steal."

"Tad, darling?" The voice came from outside the room and the next moment Lady Geranium Spencer appeared. She took one look at Tad and her face paled. "How frightful!" she exclaimed. "It's a burglar!"

"Mummy...!" Bob Snarby ran into Lady Geranium's arms. "He attacked me!" he wailed.

"Spurling! Call the police immediately," Lady Geranium snapped. She pushed Bob away from her. "Do be careful, darling," she continued. "You're going to rumple Mummy's hair."

"Wait a minute!" Tad shouted. "You're not his mother! You're *my* mother!"

"I'm nothing of the sort!" Lady Geranium replied. "Oh, Spurling! Take him downstairs. I think I'm going to have one of my turns."

"Yes, ma'am."

Tad opened his mouth to speak again but Spurling shook him so hard that all the breath

248

went out of him. There was nothing he could do as he was carried out of the room, half-across the chauffeur's massive shoulders.

Spurling carried Tad back downstairs, threw him into a cupboard and locked the door. Suddenly everything was black, apart from a tiny chink of light coming through the keyhole. Tad pounded at the door, then, realizing it was useless, sank to his knees. He heard something outside. He pressed one eye against the keyhole. Spurling was on the telephone, waiting to be connected. There was a movement and Lady Geranium appeared, hand-in-hand with the boy she thought was her son.

"We're going out, Spurling," she snapped.

"Yes, ma'am."

"Come along, Tad!"

Inside the cupboard, the real Tad watched Bob Snarby turn round and gaze directly at him. Bob's lips twisted in a cruel, triumphant smile.

And then he was gone.

ACID

The office was small and square with a desk, two chairs, a filing cabinet and a low coffee table. There was no carpet. A single window looked out over a tangle of railway lines with King's Cross Station in the far distance. Tad was sitting on his own. He had been here now for twenty minutes but he still had no idea where he actually was.

After Bob Snarby had left with his mother, Spurling had unlocked the cupboard door. Of course, Tad had tried to speak, to explain who he was, but after just two words the chauffeur had cut him off.

"You don't talk to me. I don't want to know. Keep your mouth shut – or else!"

Tad had known Spurling all his life. Only two weeks before the man had been collecting him from school, carrying his suitcases for him. But it was a completely different creature

250

who had pulled him out of the cupboard and who towered over him now. Behind the smart uniform, the brightly polished buttons and the chauffeur's cap, the man was a thug. He had the same lifeless eyes as Finn. Tad didn't try to speak again. But he found himself wondering what such a man was doing working for his father.

With his arm twisted painfully behind him, Tad had been led out of the house and thrown into the back of a black Volkswagen Estate. It must have been Spurling's own car. Tad had never seen it before. They had driven in silence for about half an hour, passing King's Cross Station. Then Spurling had suddenly swerved off the road, through an archway and into an office car park. Tad hadn't had time to see what the office was. They had gone in through a side door, up two flights of stairs. Tad had glimpsed one large room, full of people talking on telephones, tapping at computers, shuffling papers amongst themselves. But the chauffeur had led him away from here, along a corridor and into the room where he found himself now. As soon as Spurling had gone, Tad had tried the door. It was locked.

He wasn't in a police station. At least, he didn't think so. There had been no police cars near the building and anyway it didn't have that sort of smell. But if it wasn't a police station, what was it? Tad looked around him, searching for clues.

The desk and the filing cabinet were locked, like the door, and told him nothing. There were two posters on the wall. One showed a syringe with the line: SAY NO TO DRUGS. The other was an advertisement for the Samaritans. Tad gazed out of the window as a train trundled past. King's Cross ... somehow that meant something to him but he couldn't remember what.

Then there was the click of a key turning in a lock. The door opened and a young woman came in, carrying a file.

"Hello," she said. "My name is Marion Thorn. Please sit down."

As Tad moved away from the window, he examined the new arrival. Marion Thorn was tall and slender with long, black hair and dark skin. She was wearing a grey jacket and trousers with a brooch, her only jewellery, pinned at the lapel. Her manner was businesslike but she had a pleasant smile with the perfect, white teeth of a film star.

Growing more puzzled by the minute, Tad sat down.

"I expect you're wondering who I am," Marion said. "The first thing is to assure you – I'm not the police."

Tad was relieved but said nothing.

"What's your name?" Marion asked.

Tad thought for a moment. "Bob Snarby," he said.

"Bob Snarby." Marion opened the file and

wrote the name down. "You do realize," she went on, "that Sir Hubert Spencer could have pressed charges. Breaking into his house, attacking his son ... these are very serious offences."

"It wasn't like that..." Tad began.

Marion held up a hand. "You're very lucky, Bob. Sir Hubert is a very unusual man. A very kind man. He's dedicated a lot of his life to helping young people like you. That's why he decided to pass you over to us."

"Us...?" But suddenly Tad knew where he was. Suddenly it all made sense.

"This office belongs to a charity," Marion explained.

"We're called ACID."

"The Association for Children in Distress," Tad muttered.

"You've read about us?" Marion asked.

Tad almost wanted to laugh. How could he tell her that he had known about ACID all his life? "I read about you in the papers," he said.

Marion Thorn nodded. "ACID was founded by Sir Hubert Spencer," she explained. "We have a terrible situation in London. Children ... out on the streets, some of them as young as eleven and twelve. They have nowhere to go. And there are terrible temptations." She nodded in the direction of the poster. "Drugs. Crime. And nobody cares about them. Nobody wants to know."

She paused and Tad was amazed to see real tears in her eyes. Marion took out a handkerchief and blew her nose. "We go out and find these children," she said. "We search the railway stations, the back streets, the amusement arcades ... and we bring them in. We help them and we want to help you, Bob. But first we have to ask you some questions. Do you mind?"

Tad shook his head. "Go ahead..."

Suddenly Marion Thorn was businesslike again. She spread the file on the desk and sat with pen poised. "How old are you?" she asked.

"Thirteen."

"How long have you been in London?"

"A couple of weeks."

"Are you homeless?"

"Yes." Tad hesitated. He didn't want to lie but there was no way he could tell the whole truth. "I ran away from home."

"Your mum and dad must be very worried about you." Marion's voice was reproachful now.

"They don't care about me," Tad replied. "I bet they haven't told anyone I'm missing."

"Can you give me their address?"

"They don't have an address. They live in a caravan. They were in Crouch End when I left but they could be anywhere now. I think they've gone north."

"So nobody knows where you are. You have no friends or relatives? No social workers? Nobody to look after you?"

"I'm all on my own," Tad said, feeling miserable.

"Good! Good!" Marion muttered.

Tad glanced at her. There was something in her voice that hadn't been there before. She sounded almost hungry. And her face seemed to have changed too. Her dark eyes were gleaming as she made a hurried note at the bottom of the file. She looked up and saw Tad staring at her. At once she relaxed. "What I mean is ... it's good that we found you," she explained. "ACID is always interested in young people with no families. That's where we do our best work."

"What exactly do you have in mind?" Tad asked.

Marion glanced at him curiously, as if there was something about him that didn't quite add up. But whatever was in her mind, she dismissed it. All we want to do is to get you off the street," she said. "That means somewhere to live, a good meal inside you and a chance to earn some money to support yourself. ACID has a centre just outside London where we run education programmes for boys like you. That's what it's called ... the Centre. I'd like to take you there now."

For some reason that he couldn't understand, Tad was uneasy. Perhaps it was the look he had seen in Marion's eyes a moment before. "What if I don't want to come?" he asked.

And there it was again. A sudden hardness behind that smiling, beautiful face. "Then we'd have no choice but to hand you over to the police, Bob. The break-in at Sir Hubert's was a very serious matter. I'm afraid it's us or it's prison."

Tad considered. Marion reached out and clasped his hand. Her fingers were long, her nails perfect. "We only want to help, Bob," she said. "Have you got anywhere else to go?"

And suddenly Tad was angry with himself. This was his parents' charity! What was there to worry about? For the first time since the switch had taken place someone was actually trying to help him, and instead of being grateful, he was almost being rude. He sighed. "I haven't got anywhere else to go," he said. "And I'm glad I was brought to you. You can take me to the Centre."

Marion smiled. She closed the file. "Good," she said. "We'll leave at once."

There was a black van waiting for Tad in the car park behind the building. As Tad walked across the tarmac towards it, he felt a sudden chill. The evening was drawing in but it was still warm and he paused, wondering what was wrong. Marion Thorn was next to him

256

and she rested a hand on his arm. "It's half an hour to the Centre," she said. "You can sit in the back."

Tad looked at the van. It had no windows at the back, not even a small panel set in the door. Nor did it have any logo on the side. Its colour made him think of a hearse.

"Is something wrong, Bob?"

Tad remembered the moment in the office, the chill in Marion's eyes. Then he dismissed it. ACID was his parents' charity. ACID was going to look after him. "No. I'm fine."

He got into the van. There was a bench along one side, metal with no cushions. A sheet of metal separated the back from the driving compartment. When Marion closed the door, Tad found himself entombed in a metal box which would have been pitch black but for a single bulb burning behind a metal grille in the ceiling. He heard Marion walk round the side. A driver must have turned up for there was a brief exchange. Two doors slammed shut and the engine started.

It was only then that Tad realized that – apart from Marion – nobody had seen him since he had left the Knightsbridge house. He had seen nobody. If anybody came searching for him now, it would be as if he had vanished off the face of the earth.

He had put himself completely in the power of ACID and its staff. As the van moved off, picking up speed, Tad wondered if he hadn't made a terrible mistake. ACID was a charity. ACID wanted to help him. Everything was going to be all right. Tad sat back and waited for them to arrive.

THE CENTRE

Tad, washed and dressed in pale blue dungarees that reminded him uncomfortably of prison uniform, followed Marion Thorn down a seemingly endless corridor, lit by a line of tiny, halogen lights. Video surveillance cameras swivelled to follow them as they walked and a hidden air-conditioning system whispered all around them. Tad glanced through a large, plate-glass window where test tubes and bottles, glass pipes and burners fought for desk-space with computers and CD Rom and machines so complicated that he could only guess at their use. A man and a woman, both in white coats, came down the corridor the other way and passed them without speaking. Somewhere an intercom called out: "Dr Eastman to Room 113, please. Dr Eastman to Room 113."

He had barely glimpsed the Centre as he had

been led out of the van and into the nearest building. From the outside it looked like an ordinary industrial estate: a cluster of dull, red-brick buildings with frosted glass windows allowing no view in or out. True, it was surrounded by a high wire fence with an electric security barrier permanently manned by a uniformed guard. But there was nothing unusual about that. People who lived nearby (and the Centre was surrounded by ordinary houses) probably thought it was a small factory. If they ever thought about it at all.

Marion Thorn had reached a door and was punching in a combination number on the electronic panel next to it. Tad stopped. "Where are we?" he demanded. "What's going on?"

There was a buzz and the door clicked open. "In here, please, Bob," she said.

The room was a surgery. If Tad had been uneasy before, he was now positively alarmed. But, following Marion's pointing hand, he sat down on a narrow bed. A second door opened and two men came in. Both were short and round with curly black hair and wide, loose mouths. Both were bearded. It took Tad a second to realize that they were identical twins. He grimaced, wondering if he were dreaming. Tweedledum and Tweedledee in white coats with stethoscopes! What next?

That question was soon answered as the two men began a medical examination that started

260

at Tad's head and went inch by inch all the way to his toes. The doctors – if that's what they were – seemed particularly interested in his hair, his teeth, his eyes and his skin.

"Excellent condition."

"Unusually good. Yes. Good dermatology..."

"Yes..."

They spoke to each other in short, clipped sentences. But never did they say a word to Tad. Lying on the bed, he felt like a piece of meat in a butcher's shop and he was relieved when it was finally over.

One of the doctors nodded at Marion. "You can take him down."

"Down where?" Tad demanded. He was angry now.

"This way, Bob." Marion opened the door.

Tad didn't speak as Marion led him back down the corridor to a wide area with a series of lifts. Various thoughts were turning over in his mind and none of them were very pleasant. If ACID really wanted to help him, they had an odd way of going about it. He wondered if his father had any idea what went on in the Centre. This place was beginning to turn his stomach – and he decided to get out the first moment he could.

The lift arrived and he and Marion got in.

"Up?" Tad asked.

"Down," Marion replied. Tad glanced at the panel beside the door. The lift didn't have any buttons. The doors closed and it began to descend as if with a mind of its own.

"Where are we going, exactly?" Tad demanded.

"You'll find out, Bob." Marion's voice was as calm as ever. "We're going to help you. But first we want you to help us…"

The lift stopped. The doors opened. Tad stepped out and stared.

He was in a huge, vaulted chamber. It could have been an underground health club, a hospital or a television studio… Tad's first impressions were of all three. First there were the showers and baths with steam rising into the air. Then there were what looked to be orderlies, doctors and scientists, dressed in white, bustling about with trolleys piled high with bottles, basins, bandages and the occasional syringe. And finally there were the television monitors flickering on steel gantries and, high overhead, the banks of brilliant arc lamps, flooding the scene with a hard, unnatural light.

And then he noticed the other children.

Marion Thorn had told him that ACID collected children off the streets of London. What she hadn't told him was what happened to them next.

One boy was dressed only in swimming trunks, standing in an elaborate shower cubicle. The floor was slowly turning and as the boy rotated he was sprayed by different-coloured jets of water. An elderly woman was watching him closely and every few minutes she took a Polaroid photograph, clipping the results to a wall-chart nearby.

Opposite him, a black youth of about eighteen was lying on a bed, completely covered in some sort of pale silver grease. The grease started at his ankles and went all the way to his neck. His eyes were hidden behind a large pair of goggles, obviously designed to protect him from the glowing neon tubes that hung only inches from his skin. Two men in white coats were watching him. Tad recognized the twins who had just examined him.

There were girls there as well. One was strapped to a high-backed chair, her feet immersed in a large bucket that buzzed and vibrated beneath her. A few metres away from her, a second had been hung upside down with wires attached to her ears and nose. Opposite her, in a partly screened-off area, another boy was being slowly spun in what looked like a giant washing machine, while next to him a girl of about twenty sat in a bath, with green foam bubbling around her neck.

Laboratory rats!

Tad felt something – a shiver or a scream – rising to his throat and had to force himself to hold it back. He had never seen anything like it in his life. He had had no idea what experiments were being conducted in this dreadful, secret place. But they were being conducted on children.

How had it happened? Somebody must have taken over ACID and twisted it to their own, evil purposes. Even as he stared at the incredible activity all around him, Tad knew that he had to get out of here. He had to let his father know what was happening. Sir Hubert Spencer had powerful friends. Once he knew the truth, he would put an end to it.

A hand clamped down on Tad's arm and he looked up to see a blank-faced man dressed as a security guard. "This way," the man said in a voice that didn't allow for argument.

"Wait a minute..." Tad began.

But then Marion Thorn was at his side. "Don't worry, Bob," she said. "We're not going to hurt you..."

"What's going on here?" Tad began to struggle. The security man's grip tightened.

"It's just tests," Marion explained. "On your hair. On your skin. Your nails and your eyes. You did say you wanted to help us, Bob."

"But I didn't mean..."

Marion nodded at the security guard. "Take him to Area Seven."

Before Tad could say another word, the guard had jerked him forward, dragging him by the shoulder. Tad was shouting now, using words that he didn't even know he knew. Even then as he was pulled further into the chamber, Tad realized that he didn't only look like Bob Snarby: he was beginning to sound like him too.

"Prepare experimental Area Seven!" This voice came from a set of hidden loudspeakers and boomed in the air. Tad tried to dig his heels in. He passed a boy, lying asleep on a bed. The boy's hair had gone a brilliant shade of pink. Two more men were seeing to a second boy, helping him out of the washing machine.

"Amazing! He's been washed twenty-six times…"

"Yes. And he's hardly wrinkled at all!"

Tad yelled and dug his heels in. The security guard dragged him towards an empty bed.

Before he could do anything about it, he found himself thrown onto his back and firmly tied down with three straps over his neck, his ankles and his chest. The security guard moved away and for a minute Tad wriggled like a fish on dry land. But it was hopeless. He couldn't break free. He sank back and twisted his head – just in time to see another boy in what looked like a telephone box disappear in an explosion of mauve steam. Tad shut his eyes. It was horrible! It was impossible!

And what were they going to do to *him*?

It was only now as he lay still that he became aware of the smell in the air. Strong air conditioning had managed to get rid of most of it but now, lying in the middle of the chamber, he felt almost suffocated by the smell of crushed strawberries. The strange thing was, the smell meant something to him. It reminded him of something. But what?

There was a movement in the corner of his eye and Tad turned back as the twin doctors approached, one holding a page of notes, the other a plastic bottle.

"What are you…?" Tad began but stopped as his ear was given a sharp twist. Obviously the two men weren't in the mood to discuss things with him. Instead they muttered to each other.

"What's the active ingredient?"

"Very rare. Some sort of berry grown by the Arambayan Indians in Brazil. Just came in. The code is B/341."

Arambayan Indians. That meant something to Tad too. But, confused and frightened as he was, he couldn't remember where he had heard the words before.

One of the doctors opened the bottle and Tad recoiled, his skin crawling. One of the doctors called out and Marion Thorn approached, now wearing a white coat over her suit.

"Are you nervous, Bob?" she asked.

"Let me go!" Tad cried.

"There's nothing to worry about! We just

want to rub something into your face. It's a special sort of cream. It's perfectly safe."

"Then why do you want to test it on me?"

Marion smiled again. "We know it's safe," she repeated. "And we know it's good for you. What we don't know, though, is *how* good it is for you. So that's why we want you to try it for us."

"Well, I don't want to." Tad pressed against the straps. "I want to go home!"

"You don't have a home, Bob," Marion replied, reasonably. "That's why we brought you here." She leaned down and brushed the hair out of his eyes. "Let's not forget that you're a crook, Bob. A house-breaker. It's either here or the police."

"I choose the police!"

"I'm sorry, Bob. It's too late now."

Marion nodded and one of the twins squeezed a bright yellow cream into his gloved hand. The cream looked a little like custard, only thicker and even at this distance it had a heavy, exotic smell. Positioning himself above Tad's head, the man rubbed some of the cream into his face and neck, being careful to avoid his eyes while the second man made notes. Soon Tad's face was completely coated. Marion Thorn walked away.

The cream was cool, not cold, and smelt of … it wasn't quite lemon and it wasn't quite pineapple but something in between. Despite himself, Tad had to admit that it was a very pleasant smell and he didn't even mind when the first man opened his dungarees and attached a wire to his chest. The cream was smooth and the smell was delicious. He could feel it invading his nostrils and seeping into his brain. Pineapples and lemons say the Bells of St Clements. Next to him a machine began to bleep softly, in time with his heart.

"Slight dilation of the eyes," one of the twins muttered in a low voice. "How's his pulse?"

"Fast."

"This is nice," Tad said, slurring the words. "This is very, very nice."

"Loosen the straps," one of the men said. Or perhaps it was both of them. Tad's vision was beginning to blur.

"There's too much active ingredient."

"Moon-fruit?"

"Yes."

"Let's leave him and see..."

"Moon. Goon. Balloon. See you soon," Tad replied and giggled. Now that the straps had been loosened he could move his hands and he tried to wipe some of the cream off. But his arms wouldn't obey him.

After that, everything seemed to stretch out of shape. Tad was hardly aware of the chamber any more. He was floating, spinning, rocking, his mind far away. He thought the twins came back a couple of times. Once they wiped some of the cream off and added some cold liquid from a bottle. Another time they took his temperature. But he didn't care. He was above it all.

Somewhere an alarm went off and the boy who had been doused in the mauve steam was carried away, his skin a mass of bright spots. A girl was led into the telephone box in his place. Tad whimpered. The cream was less cool now. He could feel it burning his skin. But he was too weak and giddy to cry out. He twisted round on his bed, looking for Marion Thorn.

And then he saw a door open and a man step out. The man was far away, high up on a gantry and Tad wasn't sure at first if he was imagining things. It had to be the cream that was doing it to him. It couldn't be true.

But then Marion Thorn approached the man. The two of them exchanged a few words and Marion laughed. The man took out a cigar and lit it. And suddenly Tad knew.

He was looking at the man behind ACID, the man who had set up the Centre and who ran it.

Sir Hubert Spencer.

He was looking at his father.

BREAK-OUT

It was as if Tad had been plunged into freezing water. The strange, dream-like state that the cream had thrown him into was suddenly shattered and he was wide awake, struggling with his thoughts, trying to make sense out of what he knew to be true.

The products in the Centre. He knew what they all were and had known from the moment he had been brought in.

The boy under the lamps was coated in grapefruit and aloe sun-tan oil. The girl with her feet in the bucket was testing coconut corn remover. The girl in the green foam was trying out a cucumber and kiwi fruit bubble bath. The boy in the shower was being sprayed with body lotion made from different types of seaweed, while the one in the telephone box was being subjected to a beetroot and banana bodyrub.

They were all products sold by Beautiful World. He had been seeing and smelling products like them all his life.

Beautiful World.

NONE OF OUR PRODUCTS
ARE TESTED ON ANIMALS

But they were tested. *On children!*

Tad was horrified. A sudden bleeping made him turn his head and he saw that the machine he was connected to had speeded up. It was a heart monitor – of course! He watched, fascinated as his heart, beating rapidly now, sent huge peaks across the screen. But at the same time he forced himself to calm down. The doctors had loosened his straps, believing him to be in a trance. If any of them looked at the machine, they would know otherwise and he would be strapped down again.

Tad lay back and closed his eyes. Gradually the heart monitor slowed and quietened. Could it be true? Beautiful World, owned by his parents, was taking kids off the street and using them as laboratory rats to test the safety of their products! And the charity that actually went out and found them – ACID – had also been set up by Sir Hubert and Lady Geranium.

But that was impossible. That would make them...

Monsters.

Tad took a deep breath, then opened his eyes again.

BLEEP. BLEEP. BLEEP.

The heart monitor had almost exploded and there was nothing he could do to stop it. Sir Hubert Spencer had climbed down a metal staircase and was heading straight for him, Marion Thorn at his side. Now it took every ounce of Tad's will-power to bring himself back under control. He had to pretend to be drugged. It was his only chance.

"He's just over here, Sir Hubert..." Marion's voice reached his ears. Not trusting himself, Tad closed his eyes once again. Suddenly he felt the presence of the man standing right next to him.

His father.

His enemy.

No...!

"So this is the boy?" A wisp of cigar smoke crossed Tad's nostrils. "A nasty-looking piece of work. What's he testing?"

"The moon-fruit, Sir Hubert. B/341."

"Any adverse effects?"

"It's much too strong, Sir Hubert. As you can see, the subject is virtually unconscious. There's also a little burning around the ears. Do you see?"

Tad felt Marion's finger drawing a line down the side of his face. How he managed to stop his heart from giving him away he would never know. As she withdrew the finger, the bleeping quickened again and he groaned, pretending to be having a bad dream.

"The little viper broke into my house, you know," Sir Hubert snarled. It was his own father, talking about him! But it was as if Tad were hearing his voice for the first time. "I don't want to see him again. Do you understand me?"

"Absolutely, Sir Hubert. We'll be testing that new microwave sauna for the first time tomorrow morning. I'd have said that Master Snarby was perfect for it. What do you think?"

Sir Hubert laughed. "Let me know what happens," he said.

The two of them walked away. Left to himself, Tad let out a great sigh and listened as the heart monitor once again resumed a steady pace. Even as Sir Hubert had been speaking, he had resisted the temptation to cry out, to try and explain who he really was. It would have been no good. He was sure of it. Sir Hubert wouldn't have listened, and it would have destroyed the one chance he had to get out of here.

The straps were loose. He was wide awake. And nobody knew it.

Cautiously, Tad looked around him. Sir Hubert and Marion Thorn were already some distance away and there was no sign of the twins. It must have been getting towards the end of the night, as the chamber was emptying. There were certainly fewer staff than when he had arrived.

Tad knew what he had to do. The very mention of a microwave sauna had been enough to conjure up the most horrible images. He had to get out of here before he ended up like a television dinner and he had perhaps only seconds in which to do it. Marion Thorn would be coming back to check on him. So would the twins. It had to be now!

Tad slipped one arm out of the straps and quickly unfastened the buckles on his chest and neck. Finally he bent double and freed his ankles. So far so good. Nobody had seen him. There was a cloth nearby and he used it to wipe off the moon-fruit cream. Marion had certainly been right about one thing. The skin on his cheeks was puffed up and sore. The cloth felt as if it were made of iron wool. Now, how did he get out of here? There was a door at the far end of the chamber – Sir Hubert and Marion had just passed through it, but the thought of running into the two of them was too horrible to contemplate. Then there were the lifts. But Tad remembered that they had no controls. He wouldn't even know how to call them and anyway they were too far away. That just left the metal staircase which Sir Hubert had taken. It had to be the right way. The chamber was underground. Tad had to go up.

Tad checked again that no one was looking, then pulled the heart monitor off his chest.

That was his only mistake.

The connections were no sooner free than the machine began to scream, sending an alarm signal that could be heard from one side of the chamber to the other. Everybody turned. The twins appeared from behind a screen and began to move towards him. At the far end of the chamber a group of security guards ran forward, looking around to see where the disturbance had come from.

Tad swung himself onto his feet and set off. The first of the twins reached him and grabbed hold of his arm. Tad twisted out of his grip and pushed as hard as he could. The twin was sent flying into a shelf of bottles that collapsed all around him, glass smashing and liquid splashing out. The twin screamed. One of the bottles must have contained acid. As Tad watched, the man's shoes began to dissolve.

Some of the other children were sitting up now, shouting encouragement. But the second twin had worked out where Tad was heading. The man, twice Tad's size, had positioned himself at the bottom of the stairs.

"All right," he began. "Don't move!"

There was a trolley loaded with bottles and test tubes and, as the second twin edged towards him, Tad grabbed it and propelled it forward. The trolley slammed into the man, glass falling and shattering all around. The twin was caught unprepared. The side of the trolley thumped into his stomach and at the same time his foot slipped. With a great shout he lost his balance and fell, crashing down onto his back. Tad leapt over him and onto the first step.

The other children were cheering him on, their cries echoing around the chamber. But the fastest of the security men had already reached the stairs, just behind Tad. Halfway up, Tad suddenly wheeled round and kicked out. His foot caught the man on the chin, knocking him over the bannister and onto a work surface below. The security guard fell with a great cry, smashing into a row of test tubes and a Bunsen burner. The burner was still on. The jetting flame came into contact with the spilled chemicals and there was a satisfying "whumph" as a sheet of flame mushroomed to the ceiling. Immediately a bell began to ring. The sprinkler system came into operation and suddenly Tad found himself climbing through a tropical storm. He was grateful for the water. It would add to the chaos. And it would wash the last of the cream from his face.

Tad reached the top of the stairs. There was a short corridor, then a door. He scrabbled for the handle, almost crying out with relief when it turned. Not daring to look back at the chaos he had left behind him, he jerked the door open and ran through, colliding with some sort of secretary who was just coming in. He didn't apologize. The woman fell in a shower of graphs and typewritten sheets. Tad leapt over her and on down a wide, softly lit gallery.

He hadn't found a way out yet. This was some sort of storage area. One side of the gallery was lined by a series of large copper vats, each labelled: FACE CREAM, FOOT LOTION, AFTERSHAVE and so on. A pipe ran out of each of them, running up the wall to join a complicated network across the ceiling. The other side of the corridor contained a row of levers. Tad walked slowly past them. In front of him there was a double door. There was still nobody behind them.

He had almost reached the doors when they swung open and he found himself face to face with Marion Thorn.

She must have taken a second lift, leaving Sir Hubert somewhere on the surface. Then, when the alarm was raised, she must have doubled back. But Tad didn't stop to consider how she had got there. He stared at the woman who had met him when he had been taken to ACID, hardly able to recognize her. Then he had thought her beautiful and kind. Now her eyes were bulging, her mouth was twisted in a grimace of hatred and her hair seemed to stand on end.

"You stay there!" she cried in a high-pitched voice and, to his amazement, Tad saw that she had produced a gun and was pointing it at him. She steadied it with both hands. "If you move, I'll shoot you in the heart."

Tad looked left and right. Behind him he could hear the commotion in the main chamber, the jangle of the alarm bells, the hiss of the sprinkler system. He wondered how long it would be before the security guards burst through the door. He knew he wouldn't get a second chance. If they caught him he had a one-way ticket to the microwave. His eyes darted left and right. In a split second he had taken in the pipes, the levers, the position of the vats.

"I'm going to enjoy experimenting on you," the charity worker continued. She was confident now, enjoying her victory. "Sir Hubert warned me you were a nasty piece of work."

Tad looked down. "Please..." he muttered.

Marion Thorn threw back her head and laughed. It was what Tad had been waiting for.

He lunged to one side even as Marion lifted the gun and fired. The bullet missed him, passing over his head and ricocheting off a metal pipe. At the same moment, his hands found two of the levers. He pulled them. Marion aimed the gun again. But she was too late. The next moment there was a rush and a gurgle as two hundred gallons of bright red vanishing cream shot out of a pipe and crashed down

278

onto the unfortunate woman.

Marion Thorn vanished.

Tad looked back. The door burst open and two more security guards appeared, both of them armed. Grateful now for the speed and agility he must have inherited from Bob Snarby, Tad twisted round and ran. There was an explosion and a bullet whistled past, smashing into a pipe close to Tad's head. A thin spray of pink ooze jetted into the air. Tad ran forward, vanishing cream licking at his ankles, and threw himself through the door.

And he was out! The cold night air embraced him and he ran into it with a sense of exhilaration. Quickly he took in the low, red-brick buildings that made up the compound and the tall wire fence that surrounded it. Already a klaxon had begun to let out its unnatural wail and, at the same time, brilliant spotlights suddenly sliced through the darkness, huge white circles gliding across the tarmac.

Tad ran on, but with every step he found himself slowing down, realizing the hopelessness of his situation. There was no way out of the Centre. The gate was too heavily guarded. The fence was unclimbable. And everywhere he looked there were more security guards, some on foot, some on motorbikes, making sure every centimetre of the compound was covered.

"Escape alert! Escape alert!" The inhuman voice rang out across the rooftops. Tad stumbled and came to a breathless halt.

On the other side of the fence he could see houses. In the distance there was a pub. He almost wanted to cry. The real world, ordinary people doing ordinary things, were only a few metres away. But he couldn't reach them. He would never see them again. There was no way out.

"There he is!"

It was a man's voice, coming from just behind him. To one side a Jeep suddenly sprang forward, its headlights slanting down. Tad stood where he was. There was nothing more he could do.

And then it happened. At the last minute, just when he thought it was all over, there was the blare of a horn and a London taxi appeared out of nowhere, accelerating towards the fence. Tad watched as it burst through, snapping the wire, and hurtled towards him. Meanwhile the Jeep had also accelerated and suddenly the two vehicles were heading straight for one another in what had to be a head-on collision. It was the driver of the Jeep who lost his nerve. With millimetres to spare, he wrenched the wheel. The Jeep swerved, crashed into a building and disappeared in a pillar of flame. The taxi screeched to a halt in front of Tad and the back door opened.

"Get in!" a voice commanded.

Tad hesitated. But then there was a gunshot and a bullet hammered into the taxi's body-work and, without any further prompting, Tad dived forward. His head and arms passed through the open door and he was full length on the back floor and the voice was yelling "Go! Go! Go!" The taxi leapt forward again, made a complete circle and shot through the hole in the fence. There were more shots. The back window shattered and fell inwards, covering Tad with glass. The driver cursed as the taxi mounted the pavement then rocketed into the road. But they were away! Round one corner and through a set of red traffic lights and they had left the Centre far behind.

Tad lay where he was, stretched out on the floor. He was bruised and exhausted and there was glass in his hair and all over his clothes. But he was safe.

"All right. You can sit up now."

Tad recognized the voice and felt the hairs on his neck prickle. A hand reached down and dragged him into the seat. Tad slumped back, the last of his strength draining out of him.

"Good evening, Bobby-boy," Finn said. "What a turn-up – eh! We been looking all over for you."

GREAT YARMOUTH

"Aren't you pleased to see me?" Finn demanded.

"And me!" The driver peered over his shoulder and grinned. It was Eric Snarby. He had a broken cigarette between his lips. In all the excitement he'd bitten it in half.

"Keep your eye on the road, Snarby," Finn snapped. "And your foot on the axe-hellerator. We got a long way to go!"

Tad turned to Finn. "How did you find me?" he asked.

Finn brushed broken glass off his shoulders. The whole of the window had fallen in but fortunately it was a warm night – and a dry one. "I been looking for you ever since that little business in Nightingale Square," he explained. "In fact I 'ad the 'ole network out. All over London. The barrow-boys and the traffic wardens. The thieves and the beggars.

The cleaners, the cabbies and the couriers. I was worried about you, you see, my boy. I was worried about what might 'appen to you."

"You mean, you were worried I'd be picked up by the police."

"I wanted to find you." They drove past a street lamp and for a moment the skin behind the spider's web glowed a horrible orange. "And you're lucky I did, Bobby-boy. If old Finn hadn't come looking for you, 'oo knows what would 'ave 'appened to you. Shampooed to death, perhaps. Or bubble-bathed 'til you was insane..."

Tad leant forward. "You know about the Centre!" he exclaimed.

Finn smiled. "There's nothing happens in London that Finn don't know about," he replied. "And the nastier it is, the sooner I hear..."

Tad twisted in his seat and looked out of the broken window. The street behind them was empty. "Where are we going?" he asked.

"You might as well lie back and get some kip," Finn replied. "We're going to the country. Life in town's a bit 'ot for old Finn at the moment. We're going to join the fair."

"Great Yarmouth!" Tad remembered the Snarbies talking about the move."

"That's right. Boring, snoring, rain-always-pouring Great Yarmouth. But we can lie low there and work out how to earn a dishonest penny or two."

"Your mum'll be glad to see you!" Eric crooned from the front seat.

"Shut up and keep your eye on the road!" Finn snapped. "And get a move on for Gawd's sake. You're only doing a hundred miles an hour!"

Eric Snarby slammed his foot onto the pedal and the taxi leapt forward, racing into the night.

The Pleasure Beach at Great Yarmouth was a true, permanent, old-fashioned funfair. It was more wood than plastic, more falling apart than thrilling. All in all there were about thirty rides, dominated by a huge roller coaster that stretched out parallel with the sea. There were dodgems, of course, a leaky water flume, a waltzer and a ghost train so old that it could have been haunted by the ghosts of people who had once ridden it. Its most recent attraction was a Mirror Maze, a circular building mounted with speakers so that anyone passing could hear the cries and laughter of the people inside. But the Mirror Maze, like the rest of the funfair, was closed. It was seven-thirty in the morning. And, as Tad gazed up at the highest loop of the roller coaster, he was utterly alone.

Eric Snarby had a caravan just across the road from the Pleasure Beach and he and Finn had gone in to get a few hours' sleep. Doll had not yet woken up. There wouldn't have been

284

enough room for Tad, even if he had been tired. But he'd slept in the taxi. He was glad to be on his own.

He needed to think.

It was still so hard to believe. His parents, Sir Hubert and Lady Geranium Spencer, running a business that used children in experiments? The brains behind a charity that horribly exploited the young people who needed its help? It was impossible, unthinkable. His parents were decent people. His father had been knighted by the Queen! But as hard as he tried to persuade himself that his parents were somehow innocent, that they knew nothing, Tad couldn't make it work.

In the distance, the waves rolled and broke against the beach hidden behind the roller coaster. The sun had risen but the sky was still grey. Tad shivered and walked on.

What made it so difficult was that he wasn't even sure any more who he was. Was he Tad Spencer or was he Bob Snarby? He looked like Bob. He was beginning to talk like him and to think like him. And (it was only now that he realized it) he was even beginning to enjoy some aspects of being Bob. It was crazy but that was the truth. He liked being thin. He liked being fit, able to run without wheezing and to climb without trembling. It was true that he had lost all his wealth, his toys, his comfortable house and servants but in a strange way he felt almost relieved, as if it were a weight off his shoulders.

There wasn't a lot to admire about Bob Snarby or his background but at least he was free. Tad wasn't sure if he was Tad or if he was Bob but for the first time in his life he felt he was himself.

But what was he going to do?

He couldn't stay with Eric and Doll Snarby, not if that meant working for Finn. At the same time, he had nowhere else to go. And then there was the real Bob Snarby to consider. Tad remembered his meeting with the fat boy in Knightsbridge. Could he allow Bob Snarby to remain in his place? It didn't seem fair. It didn't seem right.

He looked up and blinked. Although he hadn't noticed it before, there was one caravan in the fair, an old-fashioned gypsy-style caravan that he would have recognized even without the sign above the door:

*Doctor Aftexcludor —
Your Future In The Stars.*

Tad stared at it. The caravan was parked next to the ghost train and even at this early hour the door was open. Tad thought back to his last meeting with the caravan's peculiar owner. Dr Aftexcludor had known who he was. He had seemed – at least in part – sympathetic. And he had told some crazy story about wishing stars ... how they had caused the switch. False name, false story, Tad thought now. Perhaps this was the right time to find out the truth.

Tad went over to the caravan and looked inside. There was no sign of the doctor or his curious Indian friend, Solo. Tad climbed in.

The thick smell of incense filled his nostrils and he was once again amazed by how the caravan seemed so much bigger inside than out.

"Dr Aftexcludor...?" he called softly.

There was a book, lying open on the table, next to the crystal ball. Tad almost got the feeling that it had been left there for him to find. Moving forward, he turned a page. The paper was old and heavy and really not like paper at all. Tad looked down and began to read.

Two pages were exposed and there was a naked figure drawn on each one, two boys connected by a complicated series of arrows. The figures were surrounded by stars, planets and other astrological devices and some of the arrows pointed up towards these. The book was handwritten, the sentences tumbling into each other and slanting in different directions. Growing ever more uneasy, Tad realized what the book reminded him of. It was like something out of a fairy story. A book of spells.

There were two words written in red but the ink was so old that it had lost most of its colour. Tad ran a finger across them. "The Switch". Underneath, a line of writing twisted in a curve. "Janus. The star of change. Invoking its power. To effect the switch between two personalities..." Tad didn't understand all of it but he understood enough. Anger exploded inside him along with shock and disbelief. He picked up the ancient book and was about to throw it across the room when...

"Master Snarby! How nice to see you again."

Tad whirled round. He hadn't heard anyone come in but now Dr Aftexcludor was standing right behind him, dressed in a dark green velvet jacket and baggy pantaloons. The Indian, Solo, was with him, standing in the doorway, blocking it.

"I'm not Bob Snarby!" Tad snarled. "I'm Tad Spencer. You know that. You're the one who did it!"

"Did what?" Dr Aftexcludor looked the picture of innocence.

"You know!" Tad pointed at the open book. "All that stuff you told me about 'wishing stars' was nonsense and you know it! You're responsible. You're some sort of..."

Magician? Tad stopped himself before he actually uttered the word. It was ridiculous. Real magicians didn't exist, did they? Not real ones. But after what had happened to him, he suddenly realized, anything was possible.

"You did it," he repeated, weakly.

"Why should I have wanted to?" Dr Aftexcludor asked, reasonably.

"I don't know. But..." Tad remembered now. "There was something you were going to tell me. Something about Solo."

"Ah yes." Dr Aftexcludor moved forward and sat down, crosslegged at the table. He may have looked old but his movements were still somehow those of a younger man. "I was going to tell you a story," he said.

"You said I wasn't ready."

"Are you now, Tad? Do you want to hear it?"

"Yes."

Dr Aftexcludor nodded. "Yes. I think so. Draw closer, Tad, Bob, whatever you want to call yourself."

Tad sat opposite the old man. There was a crystal ball on the table and he found himself fixated by it, by the colours that seemed to swirl around inside it. Dr Aftexcludor muttered something in the strange language that he had used before and Solo retired. Tad glanced at him as he disappeared into the next room.

"You said Solo was an Arambayan Indian," Tad said.

"Yes. The last of the tribe."

Arambayan Indians. Moon-fruit. Suddenly Tad knew what this was all about.

His eyes were fixed on the crystal ball and he couldn't have broken away if he had tried to. And now it was as if shapes were forming themselves out of the colours. Maybe it was him. Maybe it was all the smoke in the room that was somehow sending him to sleep but it was as if he were looking through the reflection on a pool and into the world beneath. It was a forest. He had never seen so much green, believed there could be so many different shades. There were flowers, brilliant colours. He could smell them! And now he could hear the rushing of a great river as the images rose and drew him into them.

And all the time he heard the voice of Dr Aftexcludor, coming as from miles away, telling him the terrible story that he was seeing with his own eyes.

"The Amazon basin," he began. "The rainforest west of Manaus. Denser and wilder than anywhere in the world. There are not many places where man has not at some time trodden on this wretched planet, Tad, but not in the rainforests. The rainforests are the last great uncharted territory ... even if the bulldozers are doing their work and the lands are rapidly dwindling.

"There was a tribe of Indians here called the Arambayans. They were not even discovered

290

by white men until 1947, Tad, just after the war. Westerners found them and for a time did them no harm. They were visited by missionaries. And they began to trade – for there was a fruit that grew in the Arambayans' land; a fruit that looked like a crescent moon and tasted of pineapples and lemon."

"The moon-fruit!" Tad exclaimed and saw it, hanging in clusters, brilliant yellow moons against a swathe of dark green leaves.

"The moon-fruit," Dr Aftexcludor repeated. "Now, all would have been well except that the fame of this new and delicious fruit spread across the globe. And a man heard about it. He tasted it. And he decided that he wanted to buy it. All of it."

"Who was this man?" Tad whispered.

"I'll come to that. The trouble is, the Arambayans were a very suspicious people. You see, they'd always been very happy just the way they were. They were peaceful. They just got on with their lives, raising their families and growing their fruit. They sold enough to meet their immediate needs. But their needs, you see, were small.

"They didn't trust this man-from-over-the-seas, and they didn't want anything to do with him. The more money he offered them, the less they trusted him. So when he offered to buy all their moon-fruit, they politely but firmly said no.

"Unfortunately the man wouldn't take no for an answer. He still wanted the moon-fruit. And so he did a terrible thing…"

The crystal ball had gone dark now. It was showing Tad a tropical night sky. But now he saw lights gliding through the darkness. A helicopter. It landed on a rough strip hacked out of the jungle. Tad knew that he was watching something secretive, something wrong. The blades of the helicopter began to slow down and the pilot stepped out. Tad recognized him. It was his father's chauffeur: Spurling.

"I said that the Arambayans didn't like war," Dr Aftexcludor continued, "but they did have enemies. There was a tribe on the edge of the territory who had always been jealous of them and it was to this tribe, the Cruel People, that the man-from-over-the-seas turned. Suppose they were to own the moon-fruit, would they sell it to him? And at a reasonable price? A deal was struck. And one dark night the Cruel People were given what they needed to take what wasn't theirs."

Spurling had heaved three wooden crates out of the helicopter. He was surrounded by black, painted faces now, their expressions ugly and menacing.

"He supplied them with guns. Oh – it's been done before, Tad! The Arambayans had blow-pipes, bows and arrows, spears. But now their enemy, the Cruel People, had joined the twentieth century. They had guns. Automatic rifles. And fuelled by alcohol and greed, they fell on their poor neighbours."

Dr Aftexcludor fell silent but the crystal ball told its own story. He saw the Arambayan village, a circle of straw-covered huts on the edge of a river. He saw the women with their children, the men swimming and laughing in the clear water. Then .there was a shot. It came from the edge of the forest. A young boy, barely older, than Tad, was thrown wounded to the ground and then the Cruel People were on them, swarming over the village as more shots rang out and the flames rose from the first of the houses.

Tad covered his eyes. He couldn't take any more.

"It was my father," he muttered. "It was Sir Hubert Spencer and Beautiful World."

"Solo was one of the very few who escaped alive," Dr Aftexcludor went on. "You might say he's the last of the Arambayans. I've looked after him ever since but he has no real life…" His voice trailed away. "I'm sorry," he said at length. "But you said you wanted to hear. You said you were ready."

"I know." Tad felt an intense sadness, deeper than anything he had experienced in his life. It was as if a river were running through him. "I had to know," he said at last. "And … I suppose … I'm glad I know now."

"Yes."

Tad stood up. Suddenly he knew what he had to do. "Goodbye, Dr Aftexcludor," he said. "Thank you."

"Goodbye, Tad. And good luck."

Tad paused at the door. "There is one thing," he said. "Will I ... will you ever change me back into Tad Spencer?"

Dr Aftexcludor shook his head. "Only you can do that," he said. "You can be what – and who – you want to be."

Tad left. He never saw Dr Aftexcludor again.

When Tad got back to the caravan, Eric and Doll Snarby had finally woken up and were once again tucking into a mountainous breakfast, this time consisting entirely of kippers. Tad had never seen so many kippers slipping and slithering over each other on one plate. Finn was sitting in a corner, smoking a cigarette.

"My Bob!" Doll sobbed by way of greeting. "Back 'ome at last!" She picked up one of the kippers and used it to wipe her nose. "I been so worried about you!"

"It's true," Eric added. "Your mum's been worrying 'erself to death. Some nights she's only managed nine pizzas."

"My little boy!" Doll sniffed.

"And a dozen Mars bars. She 'ad a dozen

Mars bars. But apart from that she couldn't eat a thing!"

"Shut up, the two of you," Finn snapped and the Snarbies fell silent. Finn leaned forward and held something up, a narrow book with a blue cover. His eyes locked into Tad's. "Where did you get this, you thieving vermin?" he demanded.

Tad recognized the cheque-book that he had taken from his own bedroom in Knightsbridge. His hand fell automatically to his back trouser pocket.

"It was in the back of the cab," Finn explained. "Must 'ave slipped out your back pocket."

"It's mine!" Tad said.

"Yours, is it? That's funny. 'cos it 'asn't got your name in it." Finn opened the cheque-book. " 'Thomas Arnold David Spencer,' " he read. He scratched his cheek, his nails rasping against three days' stubble. "So who's he?" he demanded.

"Leave the boy alone, Finn," Doll said.

"You stay out of this, Doll, or by Heaven I'll pull your leg off and kick you with it." Finn turned back to Tad. "Who is he?"

"He's no one. Some rich kid. He's the son of Sir Hubert Spencer. You know…"

"Sir Hubert Spencer, Beautiful World?" Finn weighed the cheque book in his hand. "Pick-pocketed it, did you?"

"Yes."

"What did I tell you about stealing!" Eric Snarby leant forward and slapped Tad hard on the side of his head. "If you're going to steal something, make sure you can sell it. A cheque book's no blooming good! Why didn't you get 'is watch?"

"Wait a minute. Wait a minute..." Finn was thinking. You could almost see the thoughts passing one at a time across his eyes. "The Spencers, they got a place down near Ipswich," he muttered. "Snatchmore Hall or something..."

"What – you going to burgle it?" Doll asked.

"Not burgle it. No." Finn raised the cheque-book to his nostrils and sniffed it. He let out a pleasurable sigh. "A rich kid with his own bank account, that's given old Finn a thought. Maybe burgling ain't the right game for us. Maybe there's an easier way..."

"What you got in mind, Finn?" Eric demanded.

"You wait and see," Finn replied. "Just you wait and see."

PRIME STEAK

Tad clung to the branch of the oak tree, his dangling feet only inches from the razor wire and broken glass below. Using all his strength, he swung one hand in front of another and passed over the garden wall. If he dropped onto the ground now he would break both his legs but, just as he remembered there would be, a great pile of grass clippings had been left, close to the wall. Tad gritted his teeth, then let go with both hands. He fell, hit the pile and sank to his waist in the cut grass. Fortunately, the weather had been dry. The grass was old and soggy, but not the porridge he had feared.

He stood up inside the grounds of Snatchmore Hall, the home that had once been his.

He made his way quickly towards the house, taking care not to be seen. As he drew closer, he ducked behind trees or ran crouching from bush to bush. At last he came to the edge of the lawns with the swimming pool to one side and the side entrance to the house just ahead. As he paused, catching his breath, there was a sudden movement and he ducked back out of sight. A car had started up and was rolling down the drive towards the main gate. Tad caught sight of Spurling behind the wheel. And where was the grim-faced chauffeur off to now, he wondered? Looking for more children to invite to the Centre? Or perhaps selling more weapons to wipe out another unco-operative Indian tribe?

The car passed through the electronic gates which swung smoothly shut behind it. At least that was one less danger to have to worry about. He had already seen Mrs O'Blimey leave the house to go shopping. Mitzy was on holiday. Lady Geranium Spencer would still be in bed.

That just left Bob Snarby. On his own.

Tad had to cross about a hundred metres of open ground to reach the safety of the house and he was once again grateful for this new body of his. He could cover the ground in less than a minute. He tensed himself, then darted forward.

And stopped.

Finn and he had planned all this carefully, taking into account the electronic gates, the wall, the video cameras and the trip-wires concealed in the garden. But they had forgotten the last security measure in the house – and now it was too late.

Vicious had sprung out as if from nowhere. The over-sized Dalmatian stood in front of him, its hackles rising, its lips pulled back to reveal its specially sharpened teeth. There was a savage hunger in its eyes as it padded forward, its paws barely seeming to touch the ground. Tad remembered the last intruder to come across Vicious, the 107 stitches the man had needed. When he had left hospital he had looked like a jigsaw puzzle.

Tad looked around. He was right out in the open with nowhere to run. If he turned and tried to make it back to the trees, the dog would be on him before he had taken three paces. It was about to spring. Every single part of the creature was poised for the attack. Tad closed his eyes and prepared for the worst.

"You can be what – and who – you want to be."

It was as if the words had been whispered in his ear. They were virtually the last words that Dr Aftexcludor had spoken to him and, remembering them now, Tad suddenly had an idea.

He opened his eyes and held out his hand, palm down, showing it to the dog.

"Vicious…" he muttered.

The dog growled again.

"Good old Vicious! Don't you know me, boy? It's Tad! You remember me!"

The dog looked at him blankly. And it didn't stop growling.

"You know it's me!" Tad insisted. He tapped his chest. "I'm in here. I know it's not my body but it's still me. You're not going to hurt me, are you!"

And then the Dalmatian wagged its tail! It recognized him!

Tad let out his breath in a huge sigh of relief. Vicious was drooling now, expecting an éclair. Tad pointed with one finger. "Basket!" he commanded.

"Basket!" Tad said again.

The dog turned and ran into the house. Tad watched it go with a sense of elation. It wasn't just that he had survived the encounter. It was something more. Despite his new face, his new clothes, even his new smell, he now realized that deep down there *was* still a part of him that was Tad Spencer. And always would be.

With more hope and excitement than he had felt in weeks, Tad ran the rest of the way and went in through the kitchen door.

He had known it would be open. Mrs O'Blimey was always forgetting to lock it and, as Tad had suspected, the kitchen was empty. There was a second door on the other side and Tad went through it, passing into a small, bare room filled with television monitors, video recorders and other equipment; the security room of Snatchmore Hall.

Tad sat down in front of a console. Set in the panel opposite him was a colour television screen showing a wobbling image of the main gates. Next to it was a grid with ten numbered buttons and a microphone. Tad punched in a code: 1-10-8.

There was a buzz and the gates swung open.

Tad kept his eyes on the screen. A battered white van had appeared with IPSWICH ABATTOIRS – LOVELY FRESH MEAT painted on the side. Finn had stolen the van the day before and it was of course he who was behind the wheel. As he drove through the gates and onto the drive, he leaned out of the window and gave a thumbs-up sign to the closed-circuit camera. Tad pressed the buttons again and the gates closed.

He was waiting for Finn by the kitchen door when the van arrived. Finn killed the engine and got out. "Any trouble?" he demanded.

"No," Tad replied. "The chauffeur's out. There's no sign of the servants. And Mum … I mean … Lady Geranium must still be in bed."

"Good boy! Good boy!" Finn reached into the van and pulled out a sack. Perhaps it really had been used for carrying meat once, as it was old and stained and smelled horrible. "Right. Let's go," he said.

The two of them set off on tiptoe through the house. Everything felt unreal for Tad – just

301

as it had done when he broke into the mews house in London. To be in his home yet at the same time an intruder, breaking the law … it made him dizzy just to think about it. But he couldn't tell Finn that. In fact, it almost amused him, pretending that he was here for the first time.

"What a place! What a place!" Finn whispered as they crossed the main hall and made for the stairs. There was a little antique table leaning against a wall and Finn stopped beside it. He picked up a silver cigarette box and held it to the light. "Worth a bob or two," he whispered.

"That's not what we're here for," Tad reminded him in a low voice.

"Shame to leave it though." Finn slipped the box into his pocket and crept on. The two of them climbed the stairs and started along a corridor, Finn softly opening each door he came to and peering into the room behind. The door they wanted was the fifth on the right. Tad could have found his way to it blindfolded. But once again, he said nothing. He would let Finn do it his way.

A bathroom. A sauna. An empty bedroom. A dressing-room. Finn reached the fifth door and opened it. The sound of snoring rose and fell in the half-light. Finn whistled softly and hitched up the sack. Tad followed him into what had once been his bedroom.

It was a wreck. The carpet was almost completely hidden by the sweet papers, crisp packets, biscuit boxes, crumpled comics, old socks and smelly underwear that covered it. The neat shelves of books and computer games (his books, his computer games!) had been torn apart and one of the computers had a broken screen and jam all over the keyboard. One wall had been covered by a zig-zagging line of spray paint. The whole room stank of cigarette smoke.

Finn took this all in and smiled. "He treats his room just like you do, Bob," he muttered.

"Sssh!" Tad's eyes had been drawn to the bed, where the room's occupant lay, his stomach in the air, snoring heavily. Once again Tad had the strange sensation of realizing that he was looking at himself but this time he felt only disgust. The boy on the bed resembled nothing so much as a huge jelly-fish. His arms and legs were splayed out and his silk pyjamas had slipped down to reveal a great, swollen belly. Rolls of fat bulged underneath the pyjamas and as the boy breathed they moved – but in different directions. Bob Snarby had fallen asleep with his mouth wide open and there was a bead of saliva caught between his upper and lower lip which quivered each time he snored.

"Is this really me?" Tad muttered. "Was this me?"

"What?" Finn hissed.

"Nothing."

"What a slob!" Finn muttered. "I hope the sack's big enough!"

Tad and Finn crept forward right up to the sleeping boy. They exchanged a glance. "Now!" Finn said.

Together they pounced. Bob Snarby didn't even have time to open his eyes before he found himself grabbed and half-buried in the foul-smelling sack. As Finn hoisted him up, Tad pulled. The sack slid over Bob's head, down his body and over his feet. As the end came clear, Finn produced a length of rope and tied it in a tight knot. "Prime steak," he muttered and grinned at his own joke. "Now let's get him loaded up."

A few minutes later the gates of Snatchmore Hall opened for a second time and the white butcher's van rocketed out and veered off down the lane. Finn was gripping the wheel, staring out with wide, manic eyes. Tad was sitting next to him. The sack was kicking and squirming in the back.

Lady Geranium Spencer woke up at midday exactly, nicely in time for either a late breakfast or an early lunch. She had a slight headache and was feeling depressed after what had been a depressing evening. She and Sir Hubert had taken dear Tad to a performance of Shakespeare's *Comedy of Errors*. Tad should have loved it. It was his favourite play and, as this was a touring production from Athens, it was actually in Greek. But instead of being pleased, Tad had been ghastly. He had complained through Act One, slept through Act Two, eaten too much ice-cream in the interval and then been sick in Act Three. Lady Geranium groaned quietly. The truth was, Tad hadn't been the same since he fell off that horse. Not the same at all.

She got up and went into the bathroom. She paused in front of the mirror and gave a little scream. A hideous brown face stared back at her. Then she remembered. She had gone to bed with a mud pack on her face but she had been so tired she had forgotten to take it off.

Half an hour later, wrapped in a dressing gown, Lady Geranium walked down the corridor on her way to the breakfast room. She passed her son's bedroom and looked in. To her surprise there was no sign of the boy. The room was as horrible as ever ... after twenty-five years' loyal service, Mrs O'Blimey had put in her resignation a few days before and Mitzy still wasn't back following her nervous breakdown.

"Tad?" Lady Geranium called out.

There was no answer but then Lady Geranium noticed an envelope pinned to the door. It was addressed to: SIR HUBERT AND LADY

GERANIUM SPENCER. SNATCHMORE HALL. But the words hadn't been written. They had been torn out of newspapers and magazines.

Puzzled and slightly alarmed, she took the envelope down and opened it. There was a single sheet of white paper inside and on it a message, also set down in words that had been cut out and glued into place.

we have your son. do not call the police or you will never see him again. bring only million pounds in a suitcase to great yarmouth funfair at midnight tonight. leave it at the entrance to the big dipper. no tricks. no police. you have been warned.

Lady Geranium read the note three times. Then she ran to the telephone and rang Sir Hubert.

DARK THOUGHTS

Sir Hubert Spencer held the ransom note in his shaking hands and read it for the twenty-seventh time. His face, never handsome at the best of times, was taut and twisted with anger.

"It's an outrage!" he exclaimed – and not for the first time either. "They won't get away with it!"

"Taking our boy!" Lady Geranium sobbed.

"I'm not talking about the boy!" Sir Hubert exploded. "It's me I'm thinking about! How dare they try to threaten *me*? Don't they know who I am?"

Sir Hubert paced up and down the room like a tiger in a cage. His wife watched him anxiously. "Can you find the money?" she asked. "A million pounds! It seems an awful lot."

"Of course I can find the money," Sir Hubert snapped. "The question is, do I want to?"

Lady Geranium stared at him. "What do you mean?"

"Well, the fact is, my dear ... I wonder if young Tad is actually worth it."

"What?"

"Ever since he fell off that damn horse he hasn't been the same. He's stupid. He's slovenly at the table. He doesn't speak French, German or Greek any more. He's messy. The truth of the matter is, I'm beginning to wonder if this kidnap business mightn't be a blessing in disguise."

Lady Geranium thought for a moment. "It is true," she said in a low voice. "He has changed. Do you think, if we don't pay ... they might just keep him?"

Just then there was a knock at the door.

"Come in!" Sir Hubert called.

The door opened and the chauffeur, Spurling, came in, looking as smart as ever in a freshly pressed uniform. But his eyes were dark and his face was grim. "Forgive me interrupting you, sir," he began.

"Go on, Spurling..."

The chauffeur coughed discreetly, like a doctor about to give bad news. "I've been studying the film, sir. The film taken this afternoon by the security camera at the gate. I think there's something you ought to see..."

The three figures stood, huddled together in

the empty fairground, completely dwarfed by the great bulk of the roller coaster that towered behind them. Somewhere on the other side of it, lost in the darkness, the waves rolled in. They sounded slow and heavy. There was something wrong with the night. The air was too warm. There was no breeze at all. And the sky was tinted an unnatural shade of purple – as if it were in pain.

"There's going to be a storm," Eric Snarby said.

"It's a 'orrible night," his wife agreed.

"Shut up!" Finn hissed and glanced at his two companions, who pursed their lips and looked away.

Finn was holding a radio transmitter and now he pressed a black button on the side. "Testing, testing. One, two, three…"

"I can hear you, Finn. Loud and clear." Tad's voice came back thin and disembodied. He could have been anywhere but in fact he was on the other side of the road in the Snarbies' caravan.

"You all right, Bobby-boy?" Finn held the transmitter only inches from his lips. "'ow's our guest?"

"Trussed up like a Christmas turkey and twice as fat," came the reply. "I'm fine, Finn."

"All right. Robert and out." Finn clicked the transmitter off and grinned. "You know what this is?" he said. "This is the perfect plan!"

"You said that last time," Eric muttered.

"And the time before," Doll added.

"This time I got it all worked out. The Spencer kid is in the caravan with Bob – but nobody knows that. Only us. Now at midnight, I'll be at the roller coaster. His lordship will come with the money. The two of you will be watching from the ghost train…"

"I don't like ghosts," Doll said.

"It's only plastic! It can't 'urt you!"

"Go on, Finn…" Eric rasped. He was looking pale and nervous. Perhaps it was just the heat of the night but there was a film of sweat on his forehead and cheeks and his sty was wet and glistening. His whole head looked like a rotten fruit.

"You'll 'ave a radio transmitter," Finn went on. "When I got the money and I know everything's all right, I'll signal you. That's when I 'op it. You signal Bob and tell 'im to bring the Spencer boy over. Then you leave too."

"What if it's a trick?" Doll asked. "What if it's the police what turn up?"

Finn shook his head. "They won't risk the police," he said. "These rich types – they treat their kids like spun glass. They wouldn't do nothing to hurt little Tad. No. I'll get the money and I'll be gone. You Snarbies'll 'ave plenty of time to get clear. And then we'll all meet in London and we'll be rich!"

"What about Bob?" Eric asked. "If 'e 'ands

310

over the boy, they'll 'ave 'im!"

Finn smiled slowly, his silver fillings glinting in the night. "We don't need Bob any more," he said. "He's not the same any more. 'e 'asn't been the same since that business with the glue. 'e let me down badly in Nightingale Square and I been thinking ... maybe it's time 'e spent a bit of time with 'er Majesty."

"Prison?" Doll muttered.

"They'll only give 'im a few years. It'll do 'im good." Finn was friendly now, simpering at both the Snarbies. "You won't miss 'im," he added. "Another couple of years and 'e'd 'ave left 'ome anyway."

"That's true," Eric Snarby said.

Finn slid his walking-stick through his belt and took the Snarbies' arms in his hands. "A million quid!" he said. "And one less to share it with." He laughed quietly. "Now let's go and get a drink."

Tad put the transmitter down and drew back the curtain. Bob Snarby was lying on Eric and Doll's bed, his hands tied behind him, his ankles taped together and a gag drawn tight across his mouth. As soon as he saw Tad, he began to squirm, rocking his body back and forth and trying to shout out. But the gag cut off virtually any noise and all Bob could do was plead with the other boy with his eyes.

"I'll undo the gag," Tad said. "But if you

shout out, I'll put it right on again. Do you understand?"

"Mmmmm!" Bob jerked his head up and down.

Tad went over to him and untied the gag. It was an old scarf of Doll's and he dreaded to think what it tasted like. As soon as the cloth fell free, Bob opened his mouth and drew in a great breath. Tad was tensed, ready to pounce on him – but Bob didn't shout. To Tad's astonishment, he simply burst into tears.

For the first time, Tad actually felt sorry for the other boy. Lying there with tears streaming down his pudgy cheeks, his smart clothes all wrinkled and disarrayed, he really looked pathetic. Bob Snarby probably hadn't cried since the day he was born. But it seemed that he had changed. It seemed that they both had.

"It's all right," Tad said. "No one's going to 'urt you."

"You already have hurt me!" the other boy replied. His voice was petulant. Tad had often used that voice when he couldn't get what he wanted.

"Do you want a cup of tea, Bob?" There was no reply.

"Would you prefer it if I called you Tad?"

"No…"

Tad gazed at his prisoner. "It seems to me that you *are* Tad now," he said. "And I *am* Bob. We really have switched!"

"Is that why you've done this?" the other boy cried. "You've kidnapped me because you're jealous that I've taken your place."

"No." Tad smiled. "You probably won't believe me, but I don't want to switch back any more." Even Tad was surprised by what he had just said. It was as if he'd only just realized it himself. But now he saw the boy he had been; a great, spoiled ball of flab in an expensive suit. He remembered how his parents had earned the money that had turned him into that. And he knew that it was true. He could never go back. Not to Snatchmore Hall. Not to them. "I don't want to be Tad Spencer any more," he said. "I think I'm happier being you."

Bob tugged at his cords again but Finn had tied them and they stayed firm. "So why *have* you kidnapped me?" he asked.

"It was Finn who kidnapped you," Tad said. "He did it for the money and I didn't have any choice. But I been doing a bit of thinking and I've got a plan of my own."

"What plan?"

"That's my business." Tad smiled. "But you listen to me, Tad Spencer. You do exactly what I say, when I say it. And eveything's going to be all right."

In the security room at Snatchmore Hall, Sir Hubert Spencer sat down in front of the television screen.

The cameras had caught a figure running from the edge of the shrubbery across the lawn. Spurling had frozen the image and now he closed in on it until a boy's face filled the screen. The image was hazy, distorted at the edges but still recognizable.

"I know him!" Lady Geranium exclaimed.

"We all know him!" Sir Hubert snarled. "He's the little brat you found at the mews house. The one you sent over to ACID."

"The one who escaped from the Centre!" Lady Geranium's face had gone white … all of it apart from her nose. After so many operations, the nose seemed to have a life of its own. Sometimes it even blew itself when she wasn't expecting it. "So what was he doing here?" she asked.

"A very good question, my dear."

"Do you think it was a coincidence?"

"No. I don't."

Sir Hubert stared at the image on the screen. With a shaking finger he drew a line across Tad's face. "First the mews. Then the Centre. Now here." There was a long silence. "This boy – Bob Snarby – must know about us. Beautiful World. The experiments. Everything!"

Spurling coughed discreetly. "Would you like me to deal with him, sir?" he asked.

"Yes, Spurling. I would."

The chauffeur reached into his jacket and

drew out a slim, black revolver: a Davis P-380 .38 automatic.

"What are you going to do?" Lady Geranium asked.

"Don't worry yourself, my dear," Sir Hubert said. "This kidnapping may be just what we need. Great Yarmouth funfair at midnight? That's where the boy will be … along with his accomplices."

"If you want me to murder them all, sir, might I suggest the TEC-9 automatic machine gun?" Spurling said.

"No, Spurling." Sir Hubert smiled. "Your job is to get the boy. Just the boy." He reached out and picked up a telephone. "First of all we're going to call the police," he said. "When we go to Great Yarmouth, they'll come too. And of course they'll be armed."

"They'll shoot the boy!" Lady Geranium cried.

"Spurling will fire the first shot. It'll be dark. Nobody will know what's happening. And yes! The police will open fire. With luck everyone will be killed."

"Can you be sure, sir, that the police will oblige?" the chauffeur asked.

"No, Spurling. But you'll be there. And I want you to find the boy." Sir Hubert began to dial. "Whatever happens, you're to put a bullet between his eyes. Do you understand me?"

"Perfectly, sir." Spurling reached out and turned a switch below the television monitor. The screen went black.

ROLLER COASTER

The first drops of rain began to fall at five to twelve. Fat and heavy, they exploded on impact like bursting tennis balls. From somewhere far away came a low, deep rumbling of thunder. It was a horrible night; close and sticky. The sky was streaked with mauve and throbbed as if it were about to burst.

Eric and Doll Snarby were waiting in the shadows of the ghost train, the two of them jammed into a single carriage that had been decorated to resemble a vampire bat. Neither of them looked happy.

"No good will come of it," Eric was saying. "I tell you, my dear. I've got a bad feeling about this."

"Me too," Doll moaned.

"You and me ... we was 'appier before we met Finn," Eric went on. "I mean, we was never in any trouble. A bit of shop-lifting, maybe. There was always the smash-and-grabs, of course. We did thieve a couple of motor cars. A couple of dozen, now I think about it. And then there was the pick-pocketing. But apart from that we was honest people, you and me. Honest, decent people."

"We should never 'ave fallen in with 'im," Doll muttered. "'e's an 'orrible man and no mistake."

The subject of their discussion was pacing up and down with his walking-stick about a hundred metres away in front of the roller coaster. In fact, Finn was staggering as much as pacing. He had drunk half a bottle of gin – and the other half was still in his pocket. Another great ball of rain fell down, hitting him on the shoulder. Finn swore, wiping water away from his nose and chin. Somewhere in Great Yarmouth, a clock struck midnight. Finn peered through the darkness. A car had appeared at the entrance to the Pleasure Beach. A white Rolls Royce.

The car stopped and Sir Hubert Spencer got out, carrying an attaché case with a silver combination lock. The thunder rumbled again.

Sir Hubert closed the door behind him and walked through the funfair, passing between the silent machines. His feet rapped against the concrete, the sound all around him as if he were being followed by a crowd of invisible bodyguards. But he seemed to be on his own.

As he passed in front of the ghost train, Eric and Doll Snarby shrank from sight, then quickly looked back the way he had come. The Rolls Royce was on its own in the street. Nothing was moving. Eric raised a hand with the thumb up. Finn saw the signal and nodded.

Neither Eric nor Finn had seen the figure who had been hiding in the back of the car. Neither of them was watching as the door slowly opened, then clicked shut again. But even as Sir Hubert Spencer walked the last few steps up to the roller coaster, Spurling slipped out of the car and hurried into the shadows. A street lamp glimmered on something metallic that he held in his hand. But a moment later he was gone, swallowed up by the darkness.

Sir Hubert Spencer walked up to Finn and stood, towering over him. Two more different men would have been hard to imagine. Sir Hubert was dressed in an expensive raincoat, his hair immaculate, his face grim and businesslike. Finn was as sly and as shabby as ever, leaning on his walking-stick, one eye blinking over the tattoo. The two of them were worlds apart and yet as they drew close their eyes connected and each seemed to recognize something in each other.

"Good evening, Sir Hubert," Finn began.

"Let's not waste words," Sir Hubert snapped. If he had noticed Finn's peculiar tattoo, he showed no reaction. "You have my son?"

"He's safe, Sir Hubert. And very near. Do you have the particulars?"

"The what?"

"The money!"

"Where's the boy?"

"The money first!"

There was a long pause. Sir Hubert seemed unwilling to open the attaché case and suddenly Finn was suspicious. "You do have the money?" he demanded. "You haven't tried anything fancy, I take it?"

"Of course I haven't," Sir Hubert replied. "What do you think I am?"

Finn's lips stretched in a sly smile, dragging the cobweb. "Oh, I think I know what you are, Sir Hubert," he murmured. "I'd say you're pretty much the same as me, although I dare say there aren't many who'd suspect it. You're wondering how I know? Well, it takes one to know one, as my old mum used to say before she went on the bottle. Oh yes – you got your fancy title. You got a position. But I can see what's what and I can smell it too and you're not going to try and tell me any different, are you!"

Sir Hubert laughed. "All right," he said. "Why not admit it? You're a rogue and so am I, But there is one difference between us, Mr…"

"Finn. Archibald Finn. What is the difference, Sir Hubert?"

"Only this." Sir Hubert's face twisted with contempt. "I am successful. Immensely, stupendously successful. But you're nothing. A petty criminal. That's the difference between us, Mr Finn. I've got away with it. But you've been caught!"

Sir Hubert raised his hand and Finn shrank away, lifting his own walking-stick as if in self-defence. But Sir Hubert wasn't going to hit him. The movement was only a signal. Finn saw it and understood its significance too late.

A shot rang out, astonishingly loud in the wet night air. Finn screamed as a bullet hammered into his shoulder, throwing him forward into Sir Hubert's arms. For a moment the two men stood there, locked together, their faces almost touching.

"You cheated me!" Finn whined.

"Of course I cheated you!" Sir Hubert smiled. "That's what I do!"

Desperately, Finn lunged for the attaché case and managed to rip it away from Sir Hubert's grasp. The case fell open and suddenly Finn was surrounded by hundreds of scraps of paper, tumbling and scattering around his feet. Newspaper. Sir Hubert hadn't brought a million pounds. He hadn't brought any money at all.

"No..." Finn whimpered. His shoulder was on fire, blood trickling round his neck.

Sir Hubert laughed a second time.

And then two searchlights exploded into life and there was the roar and clatter of engines as two police helicopters came in low, flying over the sea. Somewhere a whistle shrieked. There was another roll of thunder and immediately after it an amplified voice that could have come out of the clouds themselves.

"This is the police! Stay where you are! We are armed! Do not attempt to move!"

But Finn was already moving. Cursing and weeping at his bad luck, he had stumbled away from Sir Hubert, dropping the worthless attaché case. He had dropped his walking-stick when the bullet hit him and his empty hand was clamped over the wound. Now he searched for a way out. But it was too late. Two police cars tore in from opposite directions, skidding to a halt outside the main gate. Uniformed police poured out of them whilst more men with dogs suddenly appeared at the edge of the fair and began to spread out in a line. Then the helicopter searchlights swung in on him and Finn froze. He was trapped by the light, blinded and flattened by it like a germ on a laboratory slide.

"Stay where you are!" the voice commanded again. It was coming from the first of the helicopters that now hovered over him, whipping up the dust and sending the blank paper notes flying. "We are armed!"

For a moment Finn was lost in a dust-cloud.

He realized he had one chance and he took it. With a great shout he hurled himself over a low wall and onto the tracks of the roller coaster itself. And then he was away, staggering towards the corner and the first ascent. By the time the police had reached Sir Hubert, Finn had gone.

A thin, grey man in blue and silver uniform had marched up to Sir Hubert. This was the chief inspector in charge of the operation. His name was Jones. He was in his late fifties with the drawn, skeletal face of a man who never slept. "What happened?" he demanded. "Who fired the shot?"

"It was him!" Sir Hubert replied. "He had a gun. When he saw there was no money, he tried to kill me."

"But it looked to me like he was the one who was hit, sir," Jones said.

"Yes," Sir Hubert explained. "I managed to get hold of the gun. He pulled the trigger and he hit himself."

The chief inspector gazed at Sir Hubert. He was obviously puzzled by something. But he didn't speak.

"The man's getting away!" Sir Hubert shouted, pointing at the roller coaster. "Why don't you get after him?"

The chief inspector nodded. Three policemen jumped over the wall and began to run down the track. All of them were armed.

Meanwhile, Finn had reached the highest point of the roller coaster, a length of track that ran flat for just a few feet before plunging down again in what would have been the biggest thrill of the ride. For a few moments he stood there, swaying. The two helicopters buzzed around him, their searchlights sweeping across him without settling on him. Finn batted at them, a miniature King Kong. They were giving him a headache. He wanted them to go away.

Climbing the track had taken all his strength. He had lost blood. There were little pools of it behind him, every few steps. He looked at it, marvelling. A terrible, deafening burst of thunder came rolling in from the sea and he almost lost his balance. As he swayed on the metal track the night exploded, smashed by a massive bolt of lightning. The light danced in Finn's eyes and he sang out drunkenly.

"It's all over for you, Finn," he cried. "This time it's the end, old friend. There's nowhere for you to go now."

He glanced round, alerted by the sound of men climbing. The three policemen were already halfway up the track, using their hands as well as their feet to move forward on the rain-swept surface.

"Go away!" he shouted. "Leave me alone!"

The policemen squatted down, their guns

aimed at Finn. "Throw down your weapon!" the nearest one shouted.

Finn threw back his head and laughed. "One last drink!" he shouted but the wind snatched away the words before they could be heard. "A toast to Sir Hubert lousy Spencer and his rotten, stinking son. And a toast to prison! Back to prison we go! Back to the old cell!"

He reached into his pocket.

The three policemen, believing he was going for his gun, opened fire as one.

For a moment Finn stood there on the track, his arms outstretched, his face twisted in a ghastly smile as if he were welcoming the storm and the night that was rushing in to take him. Then he plummeted forward.

Still hiding in the ghost train, Eric and Doll Snarby watched Finn as he seemed to dive into death. There was a last, high-pitched scream. The two of them covered their eyes. But months later they would still be unable to sleep, remembering the dreadful thud as the body hit the ground.

The ambulance came about twenty minutes later.

With the police still combing the Pleasure Beach, Finn was carried into the ambulance, his body covered by a blanket. Chief Inspector Jones watched the body go. It was half past twelve but the night seemed to have gone on forever. He sighed and shook water from his head as a younger policeman approached.

"Sir?"

"Yes!"

"There's still no sign of the Snarbies, sir. But we found this ... next to the ghost train." The policeman handed Jones a radio transmitter, dripping wet. "Apparently they've got a caravan, sir," the policeman went on. "Across the road."

Jones slid the transmitter into his pocket and nodded. "Then that's where we'll find Tad Spencer," he said.

Three minutes later, the chief inspector and his men had the caravan surrounded. Sir Hubert Spencer had followed them over and was watching with keen, narrowed eyes. The door to the caravan was closed but the lights were on behind the windows. Apart from the raindrops hitting the roof and bouncing off, there was no sign of movement. The rain was falling so hard now that it seemed almost solid, a single mass of water. The chief inspector drew his raincoat around him and shivered.

He gave a signal and about a dozen policemen hurried forward, their feet splashing down in puddles as they closed in on the caravan. But Jones wasn't taking any chances. He had guessed the kidnap victim was in the caravan but he still didn't know who might be with him. He lifted a megaphone and held it to his lips.

"This is the police!" Even amplified, his voice was almost drowned out by the rain. He turned up the volume. "The caravan's surrounded," he called out. "Open the door and come out with your hands up…"

The rain lashed down. The door of the caravan remained closed.

Jones sighed. He put down the megaphone and walked forward. There were just ten metres between him and the caravan. He didn't try to run.

With Sir Hubert and all the other policemen watching, he reached the door. He opened it. A dozen guns were raised. A dozen men waited to run forward.

Jones shook his head. The caravan was empty. There was nobody there.

And it was then that the radio transmitter that he had put in his pocket suddenly crackled into life. The chief inspector pulled it out and stared at it. It was the last thing they had expected.

"This is Bob Snarby," came a voice, and it was Bob Snarby's voice even if it was Tad who really spoke. "I've got the kid and I've got a knife. I'll give 'im up … but only to Sir Hubert Spencer. If 'e wants the kid back, 'e'll find 'im in the Mirror Maze. Back in the fair.

"We're in the Mirror Maze. But Sir Hubert's got to come alone. No tricks. I've got a knife and I'll use it. I want to see Sir Hubert and I want to see him alone."

THE MIRROR MAZE

Tad didn't have a knife.

He had guessed Sir Hubert would double-cross Finn and at ten minutes to twelve he had crept out of the caravan taking Bob Snarby – his hands still tied and his mouth gagged – with him. The two boys had been in the fun-fair when Finn had fallen to his death. After-wards, they had slipped into the nearest attraction to hide.

It was only when he was inside that Tad realized where he was. Flicking on the torch that he had brought from the Snarbies' cara-van, he had been astonished by the sight of about a thousand reflections of himself, leap-ing out of the darkness. He swung the torch left and right and was dazzled by the thousand beams of light that shone back at him. And behind the torchlight, everywhere he looked, line after line of Tad Spencers stared back, an army of scrawny, fair-haired boys, standing there, their faces grim. And Bob Snarby was also there of course. Line after line of him, dripping wet and shivering, his hands securely tied.

He was inside the Mirror Maze.

Tad flicked off the radio transmitter and set it down, wondering how long it would take Sir Hubert to arrive. He had no idea what would happen to him when this was all over but he supposed he would end up in jail. He no longer cared. It seemed to him now that everything had led to this moment, a last meeting with the man who had almost had him killed. Tad knew that he couldn't go to the police. No matter how terrible his crimes, Sir Hubert was still his father. But there was one thing that he could do. Somehow he would make his father recognize him. He would tell him about the switch and everything that had happened since. He would tell him what he knew about ACID and Beautiful World.

And then he would turn his back on him and never see him again.

Outside the Mirror Maze, Sir Hubert had arrived.

He was walking with the chief inspector, shielding under an umbrella as the rain crashed down. The Mirror Maze was partly surrounded by the other police officers, all of them dripping wet. As far as they were concerned, the excitement was over. Finn was dead. There was only some crazy kid to deal with. They just wanted to get home to bed.

Jones paused outside the front entrance to the Mirror Maze. "Are you sure you're going to be all right, Sir Hubert?" he asked.

Sir Hubert shook rain off his umbrella. "Don't worry, Chief Inspector." He sniffed. "I'll talk to this wretched guttersnipe and see what he wants – if he even knows himself. I'll talk him out into the open and then you and your men can deal with him."

"He did say he had a knife, sir," Jones reminded him. "And there's still the matter of the gun."

"What gun?" Sir Hubert asked.

Jones looked at Sir Hubert curiously, as if he were trying to look through him. "The gun that you said Finn had, sir. Somebody fired a shot but we still haven't found the gun…"

Sir Hubert smiled. "I'm not afraid," he said. "If the boy's got a gun, so much the worse for him." He stepped forward eagerly. "Now let's get this over with. I've wasted enough time with this young street urchin already."

As Sir Hubert approached the entrance, another figure flitted out of the shelter of the dodgems and ran the few paces to the back of the Mirror Maze. Nobody saw him. The man worked quickly, using a screwdriver to prise three wooden planks away from the rear wall.

This made a hole large enough to slip through even though this was an unusually large man.

Spurling. Sir Hubert's chauffeur.

He tore his uniform as he squeezed inside and for a moment his arm hung outside in the rain with his sleeve caught on a nail. Water dripped off his hand and the cold metal barrel of the gun it was holding. Then he unhooked himself. He pulled the gun in. And turned to find the boy he had come to kill.

Sir Hubert let the door swing shut behind him and stood in utter darkness. He listened for any sound of movement but the rain beating down on the roof and walls would have muffled it anyway.

"Is there anybody there?" he called out. "Bob Snarby? I understand that's your name. Do you want to speak to me?"

Silence. The darkness unnerved him. But just before the door had closed he had noticed a bank of electric switches set to one side and now he groped for them. He flicked one of them on but there was still no light. Sir Hubert thought he heard something – a faint electronic whine – but against the pattering of the rain it was hard to be sure. He left the switch down and found another. This time a single red bulb came on, high above the mirrors.

It was enough. Sir Hubert found himself facing a corridor of glass that broke off immediately in three different directions. There were panels everywhere. Some were transparent, some were mirrors. If you moved forward too quickly you could easily crash into an invisible barrier – or into a reflection of yourself. The light that Sir Hubert had turned on wasn't strong enough to reach the outer walls of the Mirror Maze. The deep red glow spread out in a wide circle. But the mirrors, the sweeping corridors, seemed to go on for ever.

And everywhere he looked, Sir Hubert saw the faces of the three people who had finally come together.

One thousand Tad Spencers.

One thousand Bob Snarbies.

One thousand Sir Huberts.

Reflections of reflections of reflections.

"Bob Snarby," Sir Hubert said.

"I'm not Bob Snarby. I'm Tad. I'm your son."

Sir Hubert didn't understand. It was the rough-looking boy who had spoken, the one with the studs in his ear. His son couldn't speak. He was gagged.

"You tried to kill me," Tad said.

Sir Hubert said nothing. He would let the boy talk. A few more seconds and Spurling would be ready.

"When I was in the Centre ... I couldn't believe it was you. I didn't want to believe it! My own dad. Doing experiments on kids off the street. It was like I was seeing you for the first

333

time – and what I saw ... it was horrible!"

"I'm not your father!" Sir Hubert snapped. He took a step forward and cried out loud as he banged into a sheet of glass. He spun round. The reflections watched him.

"I know about the Indians too," Tad went on. "The Arambayans." Dragging Bob with him, Tad made his way to the very centre of the maze. He felt safer here, with glass all around. "How could you do that, Dad?" he shouted. "Kill all those people just to make money! Didn't you have enough?"

"There's no such thing as enough!" Sir Hubert shouted back. "And why do you call me your father?"

"Because you are!"

"No. You have my son with you. This whole thing is ridiculous. Let him go and we can sort this all out. Nobody's going to hurt you." He took another step forward. All around, his reflections moved as well.

"Stay where you are!" Tad also moved and once again the patterns shifted, endless lines of men and lines of boys crossing and recrossing each other in the Mirror Maze. "Admit it!" he cried. "I admired you so much but it was all a lie. You're a criminal. Worse than Finn!"

And then Sir Hubert saw it. A fourth image had appeared in the mirrors, on the very edge of the red circle ... a huddled shape reflected round and around. Would the boy have seen him? Of course he would. But there was nothing he could do. Sir Hubert allowed himself a thin, cruel smile. Spurling was here. It was finally over.

"You want me to tell you the truth?" Sir Hubert called out. "It's my pleasure!" He slammed his hand against a mirror. A thousand hands thundered at a thousand reflections of Tad. "Yes – boy – you have learned rather too much about me. My little experiments in the Centre? How else can I be sure that my products are safe? The stupid public gets all upset when it's rabbits or mice or monkeys on the operating table but who cares about delinquent children dragged off the London streets? Homeless, hopeless children like you? So – yes – my charity, ACID, turned you into a laboratory rat as it has done a hundred children before you. It's all you deserve."

"And you kill people!" Tad cried, horrified and sickened by what he was hearing. "The Arambayans..."

"Primitives! Savages! Animals!" Sir Hubert laughed. "They wouldn't sell me what I wanted so of course I had them wiped out. Do you think anybody cares? When people pay seventeen pounds fifty for a bottle of Moonfruit Massage, they're not thinking of a tribe of Indians on the other side of the world! Nobody ever thinks of anybody else. That's what capitalism is all about!"

Once more the pattern changed. A thousand guns took aim.

"Kill him, Spurling!" Sir Hubert snapped. "He knows about me. I want him dead!"

"Kill him, Spurling! I want him dead!"

The words echoed all around the fairground just as every word had echoed ever since Sir Hubert had accidentally turned on the loud-speakers in the Mirror Maze. The police had heard everything. Sir Hubert Spencer had confessed to unspeakable crimes. Experimenting on children! Genocide! And now attempted murder.

The chief inspector was the first to react. While everyone else just stood there, as if in shock, he ran forward, heading for the entrance to the maze.

Inside, Spurling's finger tightened on the trigger. A single bead of sweat drew a careful line down his forehead. His target was only a few metres away from him. But which target? Where should he fire?

"Kill him!" Sir Hubert shouted again.

Tad was utterly surrounded by guns. They were in front of him, behind him, above him and below him. He spun round, trying to find a way out but now he realized that he too was trapped in the Mirror Maze. His fists struck out at the glass walls. They seemed to have closed in on him, boxing him in.

"Mmmm..." Bob Snarby shook his head

from side to side and at last he managed to get his shoulder to the gag, dragging it off. The guns seemed to be pointing at him too and his eyes bulged with fear.

The chief inspector kicked open the door of the Mirror Maze and ran in. He shouted two words. "Sir Hubert!"

Spurling fired.

And everywhere mirrors smashed as, one after another, the bullet tunnelled through them, each tiny hole becoming a thousand tiny holes in the reflections as spidery cracks – millions of them – splintered out in all directions. At the same time there was one last great burst of thunder that smashed through the clouds and shook the entire building.

Tad cried out as the bullet hit him, throwing him off his feet. The pain was like nothing he had ever experienced. He felt every tiny millimetre of the bullet's progress as it passed through his skin, his flesh, his muscle and his bone. His shoulders hit the mirror behind him and he slid down, trailing blood behind him. The thunder pounded at his ears and there was a flash of lightning worse than any that had come before, slicing into his eyes, blinding him.

At the same instant, Bob Snarby screamed too.

Tad reached the ground, one leg bent under him, the other outstretched. And in the last

337

few seconds before darkness came, he saw what had happened.

A uniformed policeman. Spurling with the gun. Sir Hubert, his eyes staring, photographed a thousand times.

Then a gunshot. Two more. Two thousand sparks of flame. Mirrors shattering. Spurling's reflection falling back and disappearing.

Suddenly there was no more pain. Tad closed his eyes. Suddenly there wasn't anything.

The boy with fair hair and two studs in his ear shivered and lay still.

TOGETHER

The Saint Elizabeth Institute for Juvenile Care was a plain, modern building in Sourbridge, on the outskirts of Birmingham. It didn't quite look like a prison – there were no bars on the windows – but it was just about as welcoming. The front was bare brick, the doors solid steel. The Institute had been built on the edge of a busy road but as the traffic thundered past nobody turned to look at it. It was the sort of place that had been designed not to be seen.

Three months after the shoot-out at Great Yarmouth Pleasure Beach, with the last of the summer hanging in the air, a boy stepped out of a door at the back of the Institute and stood in front of the fenced-in square of tarmac that was the football pitch, the exercise yard and the garden for those who lived inside. The boy was fourteen years old with short, black hair. Although he was dressed in the pale blue shirt and denim trousers that was the uniform of the St Elizabeth Institute, there was something about him that suggested he was used to more comfortable clothes.

The boy's name was Thomas Arnold David Spencer. He paused outside the door as if looking for someone. Then he started to walk forward.

There was a second boy sitting on a bench at the far end of the yard, also dressed in blue shirt and denims, his arm in a sling, chewing gum. This boy was much thinner than the other and had long, fair hair.

Hearing the footsteps approach, Bob Snarby turned round. He seemed to take a long time to recognize Tad and when he did finally speak his voice was unfriendly. "What are you doing here?"

"I've been sent here," Tad said.

"What? You're living here too?"

"Yes. I just got here today."

"So what happened to your mum and dad? Sir Hubert and Lady Money-bags. And what about Snatchmore Hall?"

"Snatchmore Hall's up for sale," Tad replied. "My parents are in jail."

And it was true. Tad Spencer was back in his own body. Bob Snarby was back in his. But everything in the lives of both boys had changed.

Tad still didn't know how he had switched

340

places again – whether it was the storm or the shock of the bullet that had hit him. He even wondered if Dr Aftexcludor hadn't played a part in it. After all, with Sir Hubert's confession and subsequent arrest, the Arambayans had been revenged and hadn't that been the whole point?

He hadn't died in the Mirror Maze. What he had experienced was the jolting, terrible power of the switch as it fell on him a second time, sucking him out of Bob's body and sending him back to his own. He had thought he was dying. But seconds later, he had stood up, his arms tied behind him. He was unhurt.

It was Bob Snarby who had been rushed to hospital and emergency surgery and for the next week had remained in a critical condition. But Bob had always been tough. Slowly he had begun to recover and four weeks later the doctors were finished with him. He was allowed out of the hospital. Eric and Doll Snarby weren't there to greet him.

For the Snarbies had both disappeared. Although the police had discovered several cigarette ends and a cold steak and kidney pie in the ghost train, Eric and Doll had simply vanished into thin air. There had since been a few sightings of them in Ireland, a huge, fat woman and a balding little man, working as fish and chip sellers in a mobile van. Apparently there were never any chips, as the woman constantly ate them all. But since then they had moved on again. The police had given up hope of arresting them.

Spurling was dead. He had made the mistake of turning his gun on the police and the chief inspector – who was also armed – had shot him in self-defence. The chauffeur had been buried a few days later in the same cemetery as Finn.

With the arrest of Sir Hubert and Lady Geranium Spencer, Beautiful World had collapsed. NONE OF OUR PRODUCTS ARE TESTED ON ANIMALS. When the truth about the tests had become known, the entire country had recoiled in horror. Several of the shops were actually burned down by furious, shouting crowds. The police had raided the Centre, freeing the children who were still there and making over a dozen arrests. Sir Hubert's knighthood had of course been withdrawn. He was now just plain Hubert Spencer: prisoner 7430909 in Wormwood Scrubs – where he was sentenced to remain for the next ninety years.

It had been one final twist of fate that had thrown the two boys together.

The police had decided to overlook Bob's part in the kidnapping and the break-in at the house of Lord Roven. He had, after all, been under Finn's influence and Finn had now paid for his crimes. It was quickly decided that Bob should be put into care. But Tad, too, had no parents and nowhere to go. His was a more difficult case in that he did have relatives who could look after him but unfortunately they had all disowned him, not wanting to be involved in the scandal. His file had been passed around from committee to committee but eventually he had been taken into care as well.

Both boys had been sent to the St Elizabeth Institute. They had arrived on the same day.

Now Tad waited for Bob to speak. Bob gazed at the other boy. His face was blank, neither hostile nor friendly. "You aren't so fat any more," he said.

Tad shrugged. "I've been doing more exercise. And I don't eat so much now."

"And you've 'ad your ear done."

"Yes." There was a silver stud in Tad's right ear. He rubbed it gently. "I got to like having one." He paused. "There were quite a lot of things I liked about being you, Bob."

"Well, you're not me any more," the other boy snapped. "So why 'ave you come looking for me? Come to 'ave a good laugh?"

"I've got nothing to laugh about," Tad replied. "I'm the same as you now. My parents are gone and it looks like I'm stuck here." He sighed. "Bob, I came to say I'm sorry."

"Sorry?"

"It was me who Spurling came to kill. And

it was me who should have got shot. I suppose I did. But it was you who had all the pain, the hospital, all the rest of it. I didn't know we were going to switch back again…"

"It certainly couldn't 'ave happened at a worse time," Bob agreed. He swung round – but slowly. "So you're stuck here, are you?"

Tad nodded. "I don't care," he said. "I couldn't have gone back home anyway, even if Snatchmore Hall hadn't been sold."

"Didn't you 'ave uncles? Aunts?"

"They didn't want me." Tad looked around him and sighed. "I might as well stay here as anywhere," he said. "It's only for two years. Then I'll be sixteen and they'll have to let me out. And then I can start again."

Tad fell silent. There were a few trees near the yard, their leaves turning gold with the arrival of autumn. Behind them he could see the sun, already beginning to set.

"So what now?" Bob Snarby asked.

"I hoped we could be friends," Tad said.

"What? You 'n' me?"

"Why not?" Tad sat down next to Bob. "Nobody's ever known each other as well as you and I have. I mean, we've actually *been* each other."

"Did you ever tell anyone?" Bob Snarby asked.

"About the switch?" Tad shook his head. "No. I didn't think anyone would believe me."

"Me neither."

"It's only two years," Tad went on. "And then we'll be on our own. No parents. No Finn. Nobody to tell us what to do or turn us into what they want us to be. In some ways, maybe that's the best thing that ever happened to me."

"Yeah? And what then?" Bob wasn't convinced. "What do you think will happen to us then? You say you're the same as me now. Well, what chance do you think people like us ever have?"

"I think we can be anything we want to be," Tad replied. "If we stick together. And if we want it hard enough. With what you know and what I know ... together we can take on the world."

Bob smiled for the first time. "Listen to you!" he said. "I bet you was never like this before you was me."

"I bet you've changed too."

"Yeah. Maybe." Bob shrugged ruefully – the movement made him wince. "You know, in the end I didn't much like being you," he admitted. "It was lovely to start with. Like having Christmas every day. But can you imagine Christmas every day? How bored you'd get? I was beginning to feel like I was drowning. No wonder you were the way you were. You were spoiled rotten."

"Eric and Doll weren't great parents either."

"That's true."

Bob stood up. Tad helped him get to his feet, then held out a hand. "Friends?" he asked.

Bob Snarby took the hand. They shook.

A bell rang inside the Institute and together they began to walk back.

They had been each other and now they were themselves. But best of all they were together and as they slowly crossed the exercise yard, walking side by side, Tad was filled with hope and with happiness, knowing in his heart that the adventure of his life had only now begun.

New pupils are made to sign their names in blood... The assistant headmaster has no reflection... The French teacher disappears whenever there's a full moon... Groosham Grange, David Eliot's new school, is a very weird place indeed!

"One of the funniest books of the year."
Young Telegraph

"Hilarious ... speeds along at full tilt from page to page."
Books for Keeps

A year ago, David Eliot would have been happy to escape from his weird school and its ghoulish teachers. Now he's fighting for its survival. Someone is trying to get their hands on the Unholy Grail, the source of all power, and unless David can stop them, Groosham Grange will be history!

"A first class children's novelist."
The Times Educational Supplement

"Horowitz has become a writer who converts boys to reading."
The Times

London is dirty, distant and dangerous ... but that's where orphan Tom Falconer is heading. And he's got a whole assortment of vicious criminals hot on his heels.

Tom is helpless and alone until he meets Moll Cutpurse, a thirteen-year-old pickpocket. Together the two of them find themselves chased across the city by the murderous Ratsey. But it's only on the first night of a new play – *The Devil and his Boy* – that Tom realizes the fate of the Queen and indeed the entire country rests in his hands.